Snow on the Roof

Another Case of Detective Lyle Odell

Paul John Hausleben

Cover art and design by Getcovers and Paul John Hausleben
The Detective Lyle Odell Logos and all artwork by Paul John Hausleben
Photography by Paul John Hausleben

Published by God Bless the Keg Publishing LLC
Henrico, Virginia, U.S.A.

ISBN: 979-8-9894490-6-4

This is a work of fiction. Names, characters, businesses, places, events, and incidents are either the product of the author's eccentric, strange and unusual imagination or used in a fictitious manner. Any resemblance to actual persons, living or dead or actual events is purely coincidental and it was not the intention of the author.

Dedication

"To Odell, and Grundy, and Christina, and all the others; thank you. It has been a hell-u-va fun ride of words.

Snow on the Roof

Another Case of Detective Lyle Odell

Paul John Hausleben

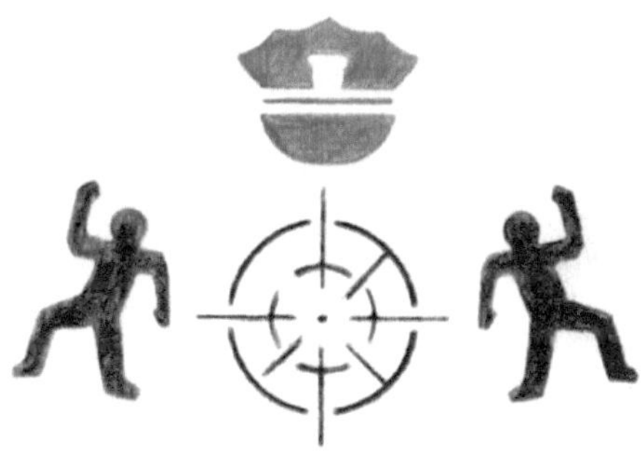

Contents

Acknowledgements

Many thanks to Frankie T for the help on advice for the legal processes and jurisdictions of states, corporate structure and rules, and other pertinent legal information. A few tips of the beer mug to Harry M. Rogers Junior, to Ms. Cali Rose, my beloved Uncle Ed, and to all the readers who enjoy Detective Odell and his cases. He has been a favorite character of mine, too. It has been a fun ride with Lyle and all of his friends. For sure. I will miss him, and Grundy and all the rest of the gang.

"Mrs. Burgess, the reality is that immense sadness and a multitude of tears lie beneath each and every human smile."

Paul John Hausleben

01 August 2025

Another Case of Detective Lyle Odell

Prologue

For late September in Mohawk City in upstate New York, it was not too bad of a day weatherwise. The sun was out. The morning had been a little cold, but now that it approached eleven in the morning, it was warming up rather nicely. It was a pleasant day.

Mohawk City Homicide Detective Lyle Odell carried a newspaper under his arm, while he made his way down the sidewalk on Main Street in downtown Mohawk City, New York.

Technically, his title in the police department was Police Inspector Lyle Odell, having received a promotion to that rank about five years ago. Odell despised the promotion and the title, and he insisted that he was still Homicide Detective Lyle Odell.

Odell made his way down the sidewalk, heading for the corner of Fifth Street and Main Street. He was heading for Grundy's Bar and Grille on that same street corner. The establishment was his best friend and long-time police partner, George Grundy's retirement dream. Odell could have parked off the street, in the parking lot behind the bar and grille; however, he chose to park on the street. Specifically, on the side street at the corner of Fourth Street and Main Street, rather than take up precious parking for the customers. You see, it stated, "Grundy's Bar and Grille" on the sign out in front of the establishment, but along with George Grundy and his wife, Marjorie Grundy, Lyle Odell was also a part owner of the establishment. Odell preferred to remain a silent partner, and he would rather not advertise that fact.

Detective Lyle Odell wore his usual workday attire. His suit jacket was too large, and it hung baggy and drifty all along his body. He wore a wrinkly shirt that looked as if he slept in it and he might have done so, too. In fact, the odds were very good, that was the case. Odell only tucked his shirt in on one side of his waist. Odell's pants were baggy too and slipped a bit at his waist. His necktie hung loosely around his neck; barely tied. And in the gentle breeze of this late day in September, Odell's non-police regulation hair flopped all around and stuck up in many directions. His once jet-black hair now had a few streaks of gray and white mixed in. His eyebrows, too. His back was just a little bent. He looked nothing like a police officer, or a man of his prestigious inspector's rank should look. There was no police badge clipped to his belt, or buttoned to his jacket or on his shirt; and he did not carry his service weapon. Odell seldom did so.

The explanation of why he did not carry his service weapon was a standard Lyle Odell answer. He gave the same reply for as long as anyone could recall.

"Nah . . . seldom carry one these days. Most of the time, when I conclude a case, the bad guys are not in a shooting mood. I usually have the bad guys cornered and dead to rights. No need to resort to shooting."

So goes the legend of Homicide Police Detective Lyle Odell.

Some of the great detective skills of Lyle Odell included his profound and unworldly observation skills. Those who worked with him and knew him well said that he could take snapshots with his eyes.

Odell saw the scene unfolding from about fifteen feet away. He took some snapshots of the scene.

Detective Lyle Odell stopped walking, tapped his suit jacket until he found his tattered pack of cigarettes. He must have sat on them because the pack was all bent and twisted, and it took some effort for Odell to shake one cigarette loose from the pack. He did so as he watched the scene continue to develop in front of him. Odell stuck the cigarette in his mouth, then lit it with the lighter that he found rather easily in his back pants pocket. He watched and took a long drag and then blew the smoke into the air.

Three street thugs were eyeing up the elderly man as he carried his groceries from the corner market. They were all too obvious as they gathered in the doorway of an abandoned and boarded-up office building, plotting, and whispering to each other. Amateur punks. It was going to be an ambush of the elderly man to steal his wallet, the groceries and whatever else they could shake down from him. The city streets of Mohawk City were tough and mean. After a microsecond study of the elderly man, Odell knew that he did not have to intervene. This ambush was not going to end well for the street thugs. No wallet lifting, no free groceries. The elderly man spotted the ambush at the last second. . ..

He reacted.

The punch from the elderly man landed squarely on the chin of the saggy-pants, hooded thug. The young thug staggered backwards. After a slow collapse, the thug landed on the sidewalk with a resounding thud. His thug accomplices turned heel and ran, leaving their leader sprawled out on the sidewalk.

Detective Lyle Odell strolled over, let the cigarette hang on his lower lip as if he glued it there, looked down at the thug and then over to the elderly man, who calmly picked his grocery bag off the sidewalk and began replacing the spilled items into the bag.

Odell bent down to help him, and as he did so, he pointed at the man's military boots and said, "Army lacing, huh? Polished up perfectly. Lemme guess. Vietnam vet?"

The elderly man seemed surprised, then he recovered and said, "Yes. U.S. Army. La Drang Valley."

Odell whistled as he tossed the last wayward orange

into the bag.

"Shit. Sorry. Tough stuff. You made it in, and you made it out. God bless you. Thanks for your service. I am retired Coast Guard. Look, I know that I look like a bum and that I slept in these clothes, which I might have, but I must inform you that I am a Mohawk City Police officer. Homicide Detective Lyle Odell."

"Oh, oh. Geez. Am I under arrest, Detective Odell?"

"For what?"

"Assault. I knocked the punk out with one punch."

The Vietnam War vet glanced over at the still-out-cold thug lying on the sidewalk.

"Nope. I saw the whole thing," Odell said as he waved his right arm at a nearly empty city street. One or two persons crossed the street and steered clear of the fracas.

"So did all these witnesses."

The Vietnam War veteran looked around, and other than the same one or two people crossing the street, he saw no one else around. However, he went along with where Detective Lyle Odell was leading him.

Odell stopped waving at invisible witnesses and said, "Those punks tried to steal your bag and would have tried to grab your wallet, too. And maybe some other things. Self-defense. I knew from your fighting posture that you were ex-military, so I stood and watched the show. Should've sold popcorn and soda. They picked the wrong guy to mess with."

Odell smiled, stuck out his hand, and shook hands with the elderly man.

With a wave, Odell said, "Snow on the roof. But a fire in the furnace. Gonna leave the thug there. Let 'em wake up with a headache from a lesson learned. See ya."

So goes the legend that was, and is, Homicide Police Detective Lyle Odell.

Chapter One

The Newspaper

The restaurant sat on the corner of Fifth Street and Main Street. The establishment had been there in the same location for close to fifty years. For all that time, patrons used to know the establishment as Gulliver's Bar and Grille. Now it had changed hands; George Grundy, his wife, Marjorie, and a silent partner owned the cornerstone of Fifth and Main Street.

New beginnings.

How it came to be Grundy's Bar and Grille was an interesting story. . ..

In the heyday of the police partnership of the two best friends, Patrol Sergeant George Grundy, and then, in the latter few years of his long career, Lieutenant George Grundy, and Homicide Detective Lyle Odell, shared many, many beers and drinks and exposed their souls together at Gulliver's Bar and Grille. Underneath the turmoil and complex fronts and surfaces, they were both very simple men on a mission of justice.

The two law enforcement officers, and best friends, and companions, would often take their assigned barstools while seated at the bar, along with a cast of characters that were in the inner circle of Odell and Grundy over their long careers. There they would lament, touch lives, share stories and emotions, solve cases, and conquer the world and destroy evil together.

Now, life was different. Very different. For sure.

Grundy retired at the rank of lieutenant from the

Mohawk City Police Department, after a long and a storied career of about thirty years in law enforcement, and after about five years and some more time of dealing with Hell on Earth in combat in the United States Army. Yet Grundy knew that he had some more years left to give a second career as a shot. George was only fifty-six years of age, and George and his faithful wife felt as if he had a chance at fulfilling a long-time wish to purchase and operate his own business. The now, civilian George Grundy knew the business that he wanted to target. It was one of his favorite places, and a place near and dear to his heart. A place of shared memories; some painful; some joyous. A place where George Grundy and his best friend celebrated success, where they drowned sorrows, and where the pain and the joy of their combined lives were forever stuck in the walls of the structure and atmosphere of the establishment. A special place in George's heart. His wife knew of his dreams, and she knew of her husband's adventures, and because she was a special wife and companion, Marjorie Grundy knew that she needed to support her husband in fulfilling his dreams.

Shortly after his retirement and the final payment on the parent-student college loans that haunted him for years and years for their children's education, (now that night was a celebration of a magnificent magnitude!) George and Marjorie Grundy approached one of the relatives of the original Mr. Gulliver, who was the current owner, about selling the bar and grille. They were open to selling, and then they tossed a figure out there. George Grundy did not have that kind of money stashed. It would take all that the husband and wife had worked and saved for and be too risky.

Even if it was a thriving business.

When he was about to give up on his dream, George Gurndy was hanging out with Lyle Odell. They were tipping a few beers, and watching the New York Rovers hockey game on television at Odell's house, when George mentioned his dream and his ensuing letdown at the asking price for the business to his best friend, Homicide Detective (Police Inspector) Lyle Odell.

In typical Odell fashion, Lyle casually took a sip of his (newly acquired taste for light beer) beer glass and said, "I will give you the balance of the dough that you need to buy the joint, George. Make me a partner with you and Marjorie and keep me in the shadows. Only you and your glorious wife will know of our partnership. I insist. I have no relatives. No children. No one to love but you and Marjorie and Christina-Fuentes-Colombo as my beloved best friends. I gave Christina a bunch'a dough for the baby and to stash away for a nest egg for her future education. It would be my pleasure to help you fulfill your dream. I saved a ton of dough over the years. Nuthin' and no one to spend it on. Especially since Marlin left. It is not like I spend it on furniture or luxuries."

Lyle Odell waved his hands in the air to reflect upon his modest house and his meager furnishings and belongings. George set his sights on the bare walls. The black and white television set on an upside-down cardboard box, with a pair of rabbit ear antennas for the reception of the hockey game. Grundy sat on a folding chair next to Odell's easy chair. The only other piece of furniture in the living room was the end table next to Odell's chair. An end table that held an ancient brass table lamp with a faded brown lampshade perched upon the top of it as if it was a well-worn top hat for an old vaudeville character.

Grundy nodded his head and said, "True. Can't argue with you on that one, Odell. I have seen crypts with more luxuries. I can't even crash on ya couch after hangin' out with ya and havin' too many beers. Because ya ain't got a couch."

Odell continued to explain.

"Besides, it is only fitting that we own a bar and grille

together. Especially Gulliver's Bar and Grille. Soon to be Grundy's Bar and Grille. We sure shed some tears and enjoyed some joy there, too. I think that I am correct. As Holmes would say in the fictional world and we would say in a non-fictional world, 'It is rather elementary.'"

Odell shifted in his legendary easy chair in his sparsely furnished living room, and the great detective took another sip of his beer.

"Seeing that most of the bad guys that we locked up over the years owe their incarcerations to our mutual tipping there."

Odell jumped out of his chair and pointed at the old television. He was exuberant.

"Hey! George! Lookie there! Big save by Rumblehowser in the goal! We might win this game after all! Nothing better than beating the Boston Bears!"

Grundy jumped up and out of his chair, too.

He spilled his beer and shouted, "Nothing better! Big save. Love Rumblehowser! I can't stand Boston! Anything 'bout them or any of their teams! They talk funny there in Boston, too! Go, Rovers!"

Odell commented, "I might remind you, George, that just last week, you stated that Rumblehowser was the biggest bum in all of hockey."

"Well, he was. That is the life of a goalie. One minute ya a bum, and the next minute, everyone loves ya. It is like being a cop."

Odell smiled at his best friend, and George Grundy smiled back. The two of them shared more than any words could ever describe.

Hockey and otherwise.

Brothers-in-arms. And then some. Horrors and joy.

Pain and happiness.

Two careers and two lifetimes.

Odell settled back in his chair.

Grundy did, too.

"George, just tell me the amount that you need to close the deal. I will write you the check. Right now."

Grundy swallowed hard. Despite the moment, his words came quickly.

"Okay, Odell. Deal."

"Deal. Want sum Irish to toast to it?" George Grundy asked.

"Sure. Nowadays, I reserve the Irish for special occasions. This is special. Top cupboard in the kitchen. Left side. Glasses are in the right cupboard. Above the sink. If you are hungry then, please order a pizza from Frank's West. The number is on the refrigerator magnet. Money is in the same cupboard. In the coffee can. Should be e'nuff for the pie and for a tip for Matty."

"I am always hungry, Odell. Thanks."

"No, George. Thank you for you."

Just like that, the sale of the business was a done deal.

Technically, his rank was Police Inspector Lyle Odell. The rank was on his business cards, cast in deep imprints upon his police badge that displayed the rank, and engraved on the placard outside his office door at the Mohawk City Police Headquarters building. Not that Odell was in his office all that often.

Lyle Odell did not use his official job title. If a person referred to Odell as Inspector Odell, then Odell quickly corrected them and asked them to use his detective title.

"It's just Homicide Detective Odell. I am Homicide Detective Lyle Odell. The inspector stuff is just some official stuff that the change of command pinned on my ass to avoid putting me out to pasture."

Odell remained understated, but incredibly forceful.

It was Monday morning in late September. Just past eleven o'clock. It could be cold in late September in upstate

New York. Today the sun was shining, and while it had been chilly overnight, now, it was rapidly warming up.

Lyle Odell sat and read a newspaper at the bar of Grundy's Bar and Grille in downtown Mohawk City, New York. "Ya want sum Irish in that coffee, Odell? Just checking. I know you mostly stick to the beer-flavored water these days," George Grundy asked as Lyle Odell sat at the bar of their establishment on that Monday morning at just past eleven o'clock. Odell did not, at first, react to the words of his best friend asking the question. Odell remained intensely focused on reading his newspaper, and his attention remained fixed upon what he was reading.

"Ah, Lyle? Come in Odell. Do you hear me? Irish whisky? In your coffee? Just a splash?"

Grundy waited. No answer. George studied what Odell was doing and looked at the newspaper and pointed.

"Is that the Mohawk City Times Union that you are reading? I did not think anyone ever read the newspaper these days."

Odell finally acknowledged his friend's questions. Yet, it was in the typical disjointed Odell manner, within the opaque, yet obscure world of Lyle Odell's world. A world where his profound genius hid in plain sight within a shroud of obscurity.

"Negative on the Irish. Thank you, George. Technically, I am working today. Straight coffee picks me up where I need to be right now. I am happy with the beer-flavored water that I enjoy these days. That light stuff. Seldom dip in the Irish whiskey these days. Oh . . . yes, Christina is very happy."

Police Inspector—Homicide Detective Odell completed his statement; he held the newspaper open to the page that he was reading, but tilted the newspaper to the side.

Despite the new title and rank, he was still the same Lyle Odell. A few more lines in his face now. A few across his brow. His hair hung long, messy and was anything but a police regulation haircut. Odell's hair was still thick with some hints of jet black, with just a few more tinges of gray and white along the edges and on his sideburns than were there a few years ago. Usually, Lyle Odell did not shave high and tight; then his whiskers arrived with gray and white tips mixed into the jet black. Odell still wore his suits and jackets oversized; he could hide his gizmos and crime-fighting gadgets there in the mix. His necktie hung askew, and if there was a knot there, it was not discernible.

Retired Police Lieutenant George Grundy loomed large behind the bar. He moved around behind the bar like an immense iceberg drifting in the South Atlantic Ocean. The Mohawk City Police Department missed George Grundy, his power, his experience, his size, and his fearlessness. Just as Lyle Odell groomed Detective Miles Bradford to fill his void when he moved onto the inspector rank, George Grundy groomed Sergeant Larry Hicks, and now, Lieutenant Larry Hicks, to fill his immense void. Hicks was a large and powerful man, too. Not as large and powerful as the legend known as Grundy was, but he was powerful, courageous, and capable. Grundy and Odell selected their heirs very well.

The two best friends made a formidable team for many years; yet, criminals in the dark streets of gritty Mohawk City in upstate New York did not receive a ticket to ride with the team of Bradford and Hicks.

In his role as Police Inspector Lyle Odell, he did not report to the police chain of command; instead, he reported to the Mohawk City Police Commissioner and the Board of Police Commissioners. Odell was a consultant of sorts, and Detective Bradford, while very capable, tapped into the genius mind of Lyle Odell when needed. Especially on a homicide case. . ..

After the Ivan Petrov case and all the emotions wrapped within that multiple homicide case, Lyle Odell hinted that he felt that he was at the end of his career and that he might retire. Rather than lose Odell to retirement, the hierarchy of the Mohawk City Police Department created and offered this special rank to Odell. So far, in numerous cases, Odell had proved that while older, he was still sharp as a tack. Lyle Odell even consulted on a loan downstate to the New York City Homicide Detective Bureau and solved one of their "unsolvable" homicide cold cases. When Odell took on the case, many thought that it would be the first case in his over thirty-year detective career that would defeat the great detective. It took Police Inspector—Homicide Detective Lyle Odell—three days to crack the case and make the arrest.

The New York City detectives worked on the cases for over two years with no leads.

Odell remained a legend both within police circles and outside of them, too. His eccentric and unorthodox investigation methods were standard practice, and criminal science and justice students studied those same odd investigation methods in coursework at universities.

Lyle Odell looked up at George Grundy, who was standing behind the bar and staring at him, and Odell asked, "What time do you open?"

Grundy stood there behind the bar; polishing glasses, and he did his best to focus on the world of Lyle Odell. As well as he knew his best friend for all of these years, it took some shaking off of the cobwebs to do so. After gathering his thoughts, and realizing that his best friend was very preoccupied in his eccentric world, George Grundy answered.

"We, I must remind you that it is *we,* Odell, since *we* own this bar and grille along with Marjorie, *together,* we open at eleven in the morning. I did not mention Christina. Not sure where that came from, in your Odell-mind. But I am happy to hear that she is doing well."

On the surface, it seemed as if Odell was not paying attention to George Grundy's words. Although with Lyle

Odell, the appearance versus the reality remained very vague.

Lyle Odell carefully folded the newspaper and then he set the newspaper in his lap. Now, he remained preoccupied with plucking a bent cigarette out of the crevices of an inner suit jacket pocket of his suit. After doing so, Lyle Odell studied it and then shook his head in a plain disdain for the condition of the cigarette, but regardless of its condition, Odell stuck it in his mouth and allowed it to hang precariously upon his lower lip as if it was a twisted tribute to cigarette smoking in the golden ages. When the cigarette was in place, Odell perked up and spoke to Grundy.

The unlit cigarette bounced on Odell's lip as he spoke. Some things never change.

"Correct that you did not mention Christina. You were thinking about Christina and how we used to sit here all the time together. How she made us laugh. How she touched our souls. How we were a team. I saw your eyes wander over to her stool next to me when you asked me if I wanted a dash of Irish in my coffee and I declined. A quick lament about the new times versus the old times. A perfectly normal human emotion and reaction, George. Old friends and such. New adventures."

Grundy smiled and sighed, all at the same time. It was an Odell moment. He could do that to your soul. Odell, of course, was correct in his reading of George's mind and emotions. The great detective always remained keen on observing every human emotion and reaction. After all their years together, one might think that Grundy was familiar with his best friend's eccentric ways and mesmerizing detective skills; however, Odell always pulled out another trick from his endless bag of tricks to amaze George Grundy and many, many others.

Odell looked at Grundy for a fleeting second to confirm his observations and statement, and then he continued to speak.

"But yes, anyway the baby is doing well. She's one-year-old already. Geez. How time flies. They are very happy in Albany. Her husband had already received a promotion in the fire department. Some kind of special rank. Halfway between a firefighter and a paramedic. A specialist. Good for him. Smart man. Dedicated. A rare breed these days. They bought a nice house over in Colonie. He will be an officer very soon. Good move for them. Get the hell outta Sin City here."

Grundy smiled and continued to polish glasses in preparation for opening for the day. He would shortly move to slicing limes and lemons and stacking them in the dispensers along the bar. George knew that eventually Lyle Odell would circle back and answer the question that he initially asked.

"That is wonderful. Do you think we will see her and the baby before the holidays? It is already late September."

Odell shrugged his shoulders in a vague response to Grundy's question. In a distraction, to the question, Lyle Odell fiddled with the bent cigarette in his mouth and plucked it out of his mouth, attempted to straighten it, then after deeming that it was hopeless, he stuck it back in his mouth and let it hang upon his lower lip.

"Maybe. I hope so. I miss her. Yuppers. Great mind that gal has. Yes, indeed . . . a great mind."

George felt his best friend's discomfort with the question and the situation. He knew how much Christina meant to Lyle Odell. And Grundy shared his feelings and affection for their mutual friend. The three of them had been through the wringers of life and then some. And Christina loved the two of them back; and she never forgot that Grundy took a bullet for her, saved her life, and almost died on the operating table from the wound.

Almost. But it would take more than one bullet to penetrate the immense armor of George Grundy.

Gratitude has no boundaries, and it is endless.

Although they missed their friend, they wished her only joy in her new life.

Grundy responded and decided to move on in the conversation and subject a bit. To remove some of the pain of retrospection.

"I miss her, too. Miles doing, ok? Ya hear from Cap Moore?"

Odell paused in his words, then he lifted his eyes around and he studied the interior of the bar. Lyle Odell then settled his eyes upon the liquor bottles behind George Grundy. For a few fleeting seconds, Grundy thought that Odell would change his mind and dip into the Irish whiskey once again. Ever since Lyle Odell's crawling back to semi-soberness after falling into the pits of despair at the loss of his beloved lover, Ms. Marlin Santini, Odell remained stalwart in his resistance to falling again into the throes of alcoholism. George Grundy supported his friend in his efforts, yet he remained cognizant of Odell's self-control and his use of substances to clear and to focus his mind. Particularly when Odell was hot on a case and pursuing any person with nefarious intentions. In his heart, George knew that Odell had always remained in control of his desires and his addictions after what they both now called, "The incident."

That was a difficult sequence of events, where Grundy, and Christina Fuentes-Colombo and other friends and close associates of Lyle Odell had to intervene to prevent a disaster in Odell's life.

And the lives of many others, too.

After a careful study of the bottles and the surroundings, Lyle Odell resisted the temptation. It was obvious that he drifted to potential sources to ease the pain, and then he decided otherwise. Grundy sighed in relief. He would never judge, or lecture, or try to impose undue or unwanted influence on his friend, unless required in a desperate moment. Instead, he trusted that Odell knew what his own situation was. After the study, Lyle recovered and spoke.

"Miles is doing great. Top-notch detective. The best. Captain Moore made a good move, too. Yes. I spoke with him last week. Poughkeepsie is a better fit for him than Mohawk City is. As you know all too well . . . this city can eat you up."

Grundy nodded and said, "It sure can, Lyle. It sure can. Cap Moore was a great guy, though. Tough situations for him here. The Petrov case was too much for him to handle. He got stuck between a rock and a hard place."

Detective Lyle Odell peered at retired police lieutenant George Grundy out of the corner of his eyes. Odell replied in agreement that also contained an observation.

"Yeah, he was a great guy, George. I agree. He worked so hard at not being a pain-in-the-ass that he became a pain-in-the-ass. But yeah, he was a great guy."

Grundy nodded and said, "I agree. Very true. How is the new captain? What is his name?"

"I don't know the new captain. His name is Captain McCarver. Never met him. Do not work with him."

Grundy stopped working on the glasses and set the one he had just finished working on aside on the plastic bar tray. George Grundy knew Lyle better than any other person, alive or dead. Except maybe for Marlin Santini. Marlin knew the real Odell in a way that no other human would ever know. Grundy was still probing to see how his best friend was dealing with the new angle in his career. Trying to gauge his mood.

"Gotcha. Is Crump, okay?"

"Lieutenant Crump is fine. Doing his usual C-S-I mystery stuff. What a wonderful team he has."

"Sure does. Great officer. We sure chewed a lot of the same dirt together over the years. You happy, Lyle? I mean, with this new inspector position bullshit? You can always retire and work with me here. You know that. Of course, you do. You own some of this joint. So much has changed in a few years. Do you miss it? All of our friends. Being in the trenches together?"

Odell plucked the unlit cigarette from his mouth and set it on a bar napkin. Odell then picked up the newspaper from his lap, opened it, and once again began to study it. He took a long sip of coffee and set the coffee mug back onto the mug plate. From behind the newspaper, Lyle Odell answered.

"Somewhat. It's okay, but can be boring at times. I know that. Yes, yes, and yes. I miss many things, George. Yes, I still read the Mohawk City Times Union newspaper. It is a funny thing here in the headlines. I just read it. A few minutes ago."

Grundy smiled. After all the years of being with Odell, he followed his systematic answers. He knew that the entire time, Odell, and his genius mind had kept exact track of the questions and queued the answers for the proper time to answer them.

"Please. Can I have a refill on the cup'a Joe? It has been a busy day already, and now I read this article here. Already handled a routine case on the way in here today."

"Sure, Odell. And yes, I gotcha and understand on the Irish." Grundy grabbed the coffee mug from in front of Lyle Odell and added, "then I gotta open the door. Almost eleven. Joey is ready in the kitchen. Annie will be in at four. Time to make dough, pour the cold ones and the not-so-cold-ones, and make those famous grilled cheese sandwiches! With the bubbly melted cheese and burned and crispy edges on it. I am gonna have Joey make me one, too. I am hungry. You handled a routine case on the way over here, huh? What are you, a routine beat cop now, too?"

George Grundy stepped back to the coffeemaker and refilled Lyle Odell's coffee mug, and he set in on the bar counter in front of Odell. Lyle remained lost in the newspaper and he mumbled without looking up, "Nah, on walking the beat. I parked up on Fourth Street. Kept the parking lot spots open for the customers. Yuppers, on the way down the sidewalk, while huffing it here, some street thugs picked on a Vietnam veteran. Tried to mug him and the vet knocked the thug out with one punch. The others took off in terror. I just watched. Knew the vet could handle it. Polished up old guy. Snow on the roof, but a fire in his furnace. Thanks, George."

Grundy waved, grabbed the door keys, and stomped off in typical Grundy fashion to open the front door for business. Parts of the Earth quaked when George Grundy stomped off on a mission. Grundy greeted a few of the regulars as they filtered in. Two retirees that always were openers, a few city sanitation workers off the early morning graveyard shift now looking for beers and chow, and a businessman and his assistant. George knew the drill. In the five or thereabouts years of owning and operating the bar and grille, Grundy proved to be an astute operator of the establishment. His storytelling ability was as immense as he was. After all the adventures of Grundy, Odell, Christina-Fuentes-Colombo and all thc others seemed endless. And big George sure could spin 'em!

The regulars took their usual seats. The businessman and his assistant obviously had a working lunch planned. They took a table so they could spread out their papers and a laptop computer. Grundy took their orders, prepared, and poured their drinks and promptly delivered them. Joey was on the meal requests.

George wandered back to where Odell still studied the newspaper. George knew that behavior from Homicide Detective Lyle Odell. Something now stuck in Odell's genius mind, and George just had to ask. A random newspaper article that thousands of other readers would read and take away nothing from it; however, Lyle Odell captured something from nothing.

"You just watched, huh? Good for the vet. Taught those punks a lesson. I hope. What is the funny thing that you just read in the headlines, Lyle? I am almost afraid to ask."

Lyle Odell did not immediately answer George's questions. Instead, he set the newspaper aside on the unoccupied barstool next to him. He picked up the coffee mug and downed the last of his coffee. He mussed with his already messy hair so it stood up at odd angles and then he carefully folded the newspaper and placed it in his lap.

"Annie is ancient but very effective, George. Do we pay her well?"

"Yes. Very well, Odell. She gets great tips too. She is talking 'bout retirement after Christmas. Been here for over forty-five years."

"This Christmas?"

"Yes. More coffee?"

"Negative. Thanks. I am heading into the office now. Oh, wow. She is irreplaceable. Annie will change her mind. Anyway, the business headline today. In the newspaper. Caught my eye. Let me show ya, George."

Odell once again picked up the newspaper and unfolded the paper, set it on the bar counter in front of Grundy, and pointed at the headline on the business page. George flipped his eyeglasses, which formerly perched upon his head, down over his eyes, just as Joey rang the kitchen bell to signal the food was ready.

"Be right back. Food is up!"

Grundy hustled and delivered the meals, refilled drink orders, served two more walk-in customers, and returned to Odell's position on the bar.

"Gettin' busy." Grundy leaned in and read the headline of the article.

"Ah yes, I see this. Dr. Eleanor Burgess takes over as the CEO of Standard Insurance Company."

Grundy's eyes scanned the words as he continued to

read the article. Homicide Detective Lyle Odell watched his best friend's eyes as they made their way through the very short article. Odell was studying Grundy for his reactions.

Grundy finished reading the rather brief article and said, "Good for her. Taking over a big company like that one is. A powerful and intelligent woman taking over as the big chief. I see here that her older brother croaked a few weeks ago. She was next in line, I guess. Makes sense. She is now in charge of the family business."

Lyle Odell seemed a little disappointed that Grundy did not react more inquisitively to the article.

Grundy flipped the eyeglasses back up to the top of his head and folded the newspaper up, and slid it back to Lyle Odell.

"Exactly, George. In charge of all the satellite and sister companies, too. An empire. All this happened shortly after they moved the corporate headquarters from Westchester County to lowly and gritty Mohawk City. Other than tax breaks and monetary incentives, it is quite strange as to why they did that. Built that fancy facility in the heart of our sins and grit."

"Good for us, Odell. Yup. Tax breaks for sure. Still, it is nice tax income for the city, even with the breaks they gave 'em. They worked a deal. Lot cheaper here than downstate, and they kept the New York State presence. Nice to have new construction and sumthin' fancy here in this old city rather than abandoned garment mills and boarded up factories. Redevelopment. Rebirth. Bringing very good paying jobs. Good for us. For all business. For the city. Why are you dwelling on this? I ain't following ya."

"One point that I would like to bring out is that she took over as CEO from her older half-brother. Randolph Burgess was fourteen years older than his half-sibling sister is. Same father. Different mothers. The first wife of Wesley Burgess died when Randolph was about ten years of age. Wesley then remarried a few years later, and the couple had a daughter together. Dr. Eleanor Burgess is a botanist. A former professor of botany and horticulture at a very prestigious and elite university in California. New York born but now, she is a Cali gal. Quit her teaching position and head of the department to come here to Mohawk City to assist her half-brother when he took ill in running one of the largest independent, and privately owned insurance companies in America. Randolph had ticker issues. She used to travel back and forth to help after his first heart attack. Randolph bounced back pretty well. Then she traveled to New York only when needed. Ya know how it is with these business jet-setters. The rich and famous can rack up the air miles while jetting coast-to-coast. But then he had another heart attack and a bypass operation. She was here more often after that."

Grundy nodded his head in acknowledgement of the outpouring of information from Lyle Odell. He knew better than to ask how Lyle Odell knew all this random information about Dr. Burgess and the Standard Insurance Company. Police Inspector-Homicide Detective Lyle Odell knew almost everything. The more random and obscure the information was; the more Odell knew about it.

Grundy noticed a patron required service for a drink refill.

"Okay. Not sure where ya heading, Odell. Seems honorable. Sister took care of her older brother when he had heart issues and operations, and she helped with the family business. Half-brother or not. Oh, wait. Be right back."

George returned from serving the customer and, after having some time to think, Grundy made the connections. He now knew what bothered Lyle Odell about the article. A lifetime of working together gave Grundy keen insight into the eccentric and complex mind of Lyle Odell.

"I gotcha, Odell. Ya ain't liking the fact that this gal's half-sibling-brother croaked right after building that fancy building here in Mohawk City and moving up here from downstate. Then the fancy-ass professor takes over the empire." Grundy then pointed at the newspaper and added, "She seems fairly young. Maybe fifty-five? She is very beautiful in that picture. For a newspaper photo. The half-brother had major heart issues and was older. Hey, Odell. I need to tell ya this one. You could meet her in person and judge for yaself. Standard Insurance is sponsoring this month's Mohawk City Chamber of Commerce meeting with a tour of the fancy corporate headquarters. On the heels of their grand opening. We have an invitation. This Thursday at five in the afternoon. As a business owner and Chamber of Commerce member, you could attend with Marjorie and me. So, lemme know."

Lyle Odell did not answer Grundy's questions. George lost him.

Odell now went off on an intense preoccupation with attempting to tie his necktie properly. This was after picking up the unlit cigarette from the bar napkin and stuffing the same unlit cigarette into the confines of his right-suit-jacket inside pocket. Grundy knew that he had plenty of time; therefore, off he went, serving patrons, seating new guests, taking orders and tending to tables and refilling drinks.

When Grundy returned, Odell was up and out of the bar stool and ready to leave.

"Dr. Eleanor Burgess is fifty-four years old. Very lovely woman. Stunningly gorgeous, tall. About five feet, eleven inches. Thin, long, and graceful neck. Great figure. Wonderful cascading auburn hair. High cheekbones. A super-genius. She is one of the great academic minds in her teaching fields of expertise of our time. Very well-respected within academic circles and otherwise."

"Well, there you go, Lyle!" Grundy gently tapped the bar counter to emphasize his point. "That makes her half-brother sixty-eight years old. Not old, but a little on the older side. Big executive job. High-stress levels. Lots of pressure. He died a little too early. The article does not say much, but knowing Lyle Odell as well as I do, I know that you already have prior knowledge of his death. I am going to guess that he died of another heart attack. Am I right? Seems as if his ticker was barely ticking."

"Well, yes, you are right on, George. Mr. Randolph Burgess died of a major heart attack while on a cruise sponsored by a worldwide insurance not-for-profit promotional organization. A floating mega-conference, so to speak. The cruise ship crew found him in his locked cabin room on the cruise ship, dead in bed. No autopsy. Out of the country. Floating around on the ocean."

Grundy nodded and waved his hands in the air while scanning the interior tables and the bar area for any patrons requiring service.

Satisfied that all the patrons were good for now, George asked, "How about the old man? This Wesley guy. The father. What did he croak from, Lyle?"

"A heart attack. Might be a weak genetic link there. Heart issues run in the family. Perhaps?"

"Okay, there you go, Lyle. The half-brother and his father both had ticker issues. Genetic stuff. Nothing suspicious going on there. Not everyone has, as you say, nefarious intentions. Stressful job. Long hours. This guy was in rough shape, already had heart operations and procedures, and he keeled over and croaked. An older, sick guy in a locked room on a cruise ship. You and I both know these things happen. We've seen it in our careers too many times to count. Sad but true."

Lyle Odell paused and stood for a second or two next to his barstool, as his eyes wandered around the bar and grille. He was calculating something. Grundy had seen this odd and eccentric behavior from Lyle Odell a few million times before in their lives together.

Odell spoke with his finger in the air while he attempted

to smooth out his hair with his other hand.

"No . . . not all people." Odell failed in his efforts to smooth his hair out, and he seemed to realize it. He paused and then gave up on the effort. After the pause, Lyle Odell continued to speak. It turns out that the pause was just Odell's way of calculating and gathering information.

"To be exact. Forty-three percent of the general population will commit a crime if they think they can get away with it. Ten percent are just evil, and they will commit crimes because they are evil. The rest commit crimes to survive. The remainder are honest. Lots of crime out there. One half of young people, regardless of gender or race, will face arrest and jail time and charges before the age of twenty-three. If all arrested Americans were an independent nation, they would be the eighteenth largest nation in the entire world. Therefore, George, you and I had and have great job security."

Odell paused, thought, and then nodded.

He said, "Yuppers. I want to see that fancy new building. It sure does seem strange to me that a successful company like Standard Insurance is, would abandon an almost-just-as-fancy corporate campus downstate in Westchester for Sin City here. It does bother me. Yuppers. I will take you up on that offer and attend the Chamber of Commerce meeting. As long as no one knows that I have an interest in this business. I am just a friend of Marjorie and George Grundy. I like to remain in the shadows. Especially with this new bullshit police inspector rank tagged on my old ass. Although Doctor Burgess is a genius and if she prepares properly for this meeting, then she will investigate all the attendees and business folks flopping around her new fancy building so she will find out that we I am involved with the bar and grille. Oh well. Others won't know."

Odell tapped the various crevices of his suit and pants to check and make sure he had everything. And then plucked the open newspaper off the bar counter and folded it and tucked it under his arm.

With a gentle wave, Odell said, "See ya later, George. Glad to see we are busy. Good thing that Meredith is here to help work the floor. I just saw her car go around the building. I think she is late. Again. You forgot to mention that Meredith Jameson works the opening shift and in the afternoons. College gal. History major. Very cute. Great last name. Historic. She gets great tips and brings in the good old boys to stare at her backside and large chest. Good hire on your part. Expert marketing. I predict that she will stay on with us after graduating. She can earn a lot more dough here than she will while teaching history. I am off to my office. I have a mission now. Instead of sitting and making hand puppets on the walls. See ya, George. Talk to ya later."

"Later, Lyle. Ya comin' back after work?"

"Dunno. Depends on how much research I do today on this new case."

"Case? This is now a case? A company builds a new corporate campus because of a great deal and tax breaks and, unfortunately, the CEO, with a history of heart issues, croaks shortly after the move, and his already successful half-sister takes over, and it is a case. How the hell did you determine it was a case from reading a newspaper article? The guy died in a locked room! On a cruise ship. Alone. In bed! Seems like unfortunate circumstances, but kind of a natural death."

Odell waved and walked out without answering Grundy's questions.

Grundy shook his head and mumbled, "Of course it is a case. Why the hell would I even ask him about it?"

Grundy knew that he would not see Lyle Odell later. He just knew it. Police inspector or homicide detective or whatever Lyle Odell was these days, was good at his job. As in very, very good.

Chapter Two

Dr. Eleanor Burgess

Some women can wear a string of white pearls around their necks and pair them with diminutive white pearl earrings in their ears, and they can create a wave of male testosterone to erupt that is large enough that it would capsize the Titanic. As Police Inspector Lyle Odell correctly described her, Dr. Burgess was a 'very lovely woman. Stunningly gorgeous, tall. About five feet, eleven inches. Thin neck. Great figure. Wonderful cascading auburn hair. High cheekbones.'

Of course, Lyle Odell was spot on in his description.

She had the type of voice that could make a man leap for joy or cry for a lifetime.

As the hostess for the Mohawk City Chamber of Commerce event, she was the center of attention. She was charismatic, well-spoken, the perfect hostess and all that and more, too.

Dr. Eleanor Burgess wore a form-fitting black dress with a low-cut neckline, which had a tastefully woven thin black lace woven into the cut, to direct attention and hide, to a certain extent, her ample cleavage; yet, just allow a hint of the beauty that lies below it. The dress was open at the back, and it gracefully plunged down her back and stopped about halfway down her elegance. Stopping just short of revealing the beauty that lay beneath the soft folds of the fine fabric. Yet, the dress was so form-fitting that it was easy to determine how glorious her beauty was. And then there were those pearls. They were spotlights beaming down upon her to enhance attention to her beauty. The twinkling stars in the sky, the icing on the cake, and the closing outro to a fantastic piece of music.

Dr. Burgess led a guided tour around the brand-new and stunningly impressive facility for the Standard Insurance Company. Dr. Burgess showed the attendees the glorious main conference room and the plush and elegant board of directors' conference suite, equipped with a high-rise view of the Mohawk River, downtown Mohawk City, and a fully stocked wet bar, stocked with top-shelf liquors, expensive craft beers on tap, and fine wine, along with a fine selection of teas from around the world as well as unique coffee roasts, too. She pointed out the nuances and the unique architecture; particularly proud of the impressive lobby, fully furnished with light oak wood trims and finishes, along with a black and gray marble floor. Then she displayed the vaulted atrium ceilings and the sprawling center of the facility with elegant brass-door-equipped elevators in the center of the building. Next, Doctor Burgess proudly explained about and led a tour of the full restaurant/cafeteria serving three fully cooked and prepared meals each day, and even equipped with a cocktail bar serving wine, beer, and cocktails along with finger food for after-hours enjoyment and entertaining of guests and visitors.

In the facility's expansive auditorium, Dr. Burgess delivered a keynote speech where she detailed plans for her company and for the not-for-profit Burgess Foundation's commitment to the restoration of business in Mohawk City, the role of the Chamber of Commerce, her plans to guide the future together, and she even paid tribute to her late half-brother and his vision and commitment to business and the community. Her speech was full of her intelligence and her mastery of the English language. Dr. Burgess worked the crowd like a great oil painter paints a canvas with beautiful art, fine oils, and a vision. She captivated those in attendance.

Well, most in attendance.

After the keynote speech and the tour and the business concluded, it was time for sampling of finger food, mingling of the guests and attendees and conversations, all while sipping and enjoying cocktails, wines, and beers. Standard Insurance Company spared no expense for this gathering. It was the finest food, the finest craft beers, and fine wines with top-shelf cocktails.

"Well, my, my!" The elegant voice of Dr. Eleanor Burgess echoed across the small area outside the main auditorium and just off the lobby. She continued to speak and asked, "What do I owe the pleasure of running into the famous Police Inspector Lyle Odell at this Mohawk City Chamber of Commerce meeting? Until now, I did not know you had a business interest or interests in our city. Or am I wrong and making assumptions?"

Detective Lyle Odell had been intensely examining a light fixture and how the rays of light cast shadows on a catering table set up in the side wing of the lobby. A catering table, staffed by a waitstaff member from the catering crew. The crew member was a young man dressed in an impeccable black suit. The young man stood rather awkwardly behind the table watching as Odell, with his oversized suit and mussed hair and his askew necktie carefully moved and studied the angle of the light shining upon the finger food displayed in the silver serving trays, chafing dishes, and various bowls. Detective Lyle Odell poked around in the various pockets and folds of his suit and mumbled repeatedly with words that the young man could not hear or understand, until finally, Lyle Odell produced a small foldable magnifying glass from the inner confines of his suit, unfolded it, and peered into the tablecloth to study some unknown particle. The young man stood mesmerized by what this odd man was doing. The catering server thought that perhaps this strange man had one too many cocktails. He breathed a sigh of relief when he heard the words of Dr. Burgess and realized that Lyle Odell was a police officer. Although, given Odell's ragtag and messy appearance, the young server was not quite sure that it was true.

Detective Lyle Odell stood up and pulled away from his studies and looked over in the direction of the elegant voice. He nodded and then went back to studying the tablecloth through his magnifying glass.

Dr. Burgess moved closer to where Odell stood. She moved elegantly and silently despite her footwear and the polished stone floors underneath her feet. Her shoes hardly made a sound as she gracefully glided across the stone. Her beauty allowed her to float. In her hand, she held a martini glass with a long, polished, gold stem. She held it at an angle to her body and with a bent elbow, and she held it rather high in the air; almost shoulder-height. Dr. Burgess held the martini glass as if it were a beacon of light to broadcast her beauty forth.

Odell spoke as he studied the tablecloth.

"Please, Dr. Burgess. It is Homicide Detective Odell, or just Odell. I'd rather not go by that inspector stuff. The police inspector rank is just some bullshit tag they hung on my old ass to prevent me from retiring. They think that I am too old now. A lick of gray hair, some white hairs here and there. My eyebrows and my beard stubble are mostly all gray or white. My knees creak a little. My lower back is sore and bent. The big brass, they want to put me out to pasture, but are afraid that something will come up that they need me for. So, for now, I guess they thought that I was worth keeping around. It's all bullshit."

Dr. Eleanor Burgess threw her head back a bit, and she laughed with some exuberance, and she did so without spilling a precious drop of her martini and without moving the glass from its position of display.

After her laugh, Dr. Burgess said, "I love that word. Bullshit. It is all bullshit. I agree. You are correct. Okay then. Homicide Detective Odell, it is. You still look awfully good to me. I am sure your legendary skills are still more than valuable, Detective Odell. After all, you are famous not only here in Mohawk City but throughout the land. However, I must ask you . . . what it is that you are studying? Surely, there have been no crimes or homicides in and around my catering tables and chafing dishes. And the young man there appears rather innocent of any crimes."

Odell continued to study the subject matter, and he spoke while he did so.

"Appearances, Dr. Burgess, are like costumes at Halloween. The person dressed as an axe murderer is really a good person pretending to be evil for attention. However, the person dressed as a cute little kitty-cat is the one that you need to dig a little deeper into."

After hearing the reply from Homicide Detective Lyle Odell, the young server stepped back from the table. Then he walked over to one of the chafing dishes and lifted the lid and stirred the food contents in the dish to mix the heat evenly throughout the contents. Odell did not move, but he continued to speak.

Odell's eccentric ways were on full display. It seemed as if he had eyes in the top of his head because Odell never looked at the server working the table.

"The young man is uncomfortable with my inferences. He moved away from me in nervousness. Must think I am a nutcase. I don't blame him. In the air here, I detect some heavier applications of a strong men's cologne. Slight pine scent. One of those fancy Italian brands. Fairly effective at masking odors, but not completely effective. It smells as if he smoked some weed before reporting to work and stole a nip or two of the top-shelf hooch, but he is innocent of any homicides. No homicide crimes here. Not at this location. Other locations are open for investigation possibilities. I call it job security. To answer your questions. I am actually studying these food crumbs for future clues and experiences. I always try to remember, no matter what the circumstances are and despite any bombs dropping all around you . . . that exact facts and details are very important in investigations. And in our lives, too."

Odell then floated his nose over the tablecloth to detect an odor. As he did so, he held his small magnifying glass in his right hand out at an angle while using his left hand to brace his body with a grip on the table. It was as if Detective Odell required a particular angle to detect what it was that he was smelling.

Dr. Burgess smiled at the eccentricity of Odell. It was a smile in appreciation of his genius and intelligence, and not of his oddness. She now stood right next to where Odell stood at the end of the table, and she took a gentle sip of her cocktail, and her perfect lips left just a gentle imprint of lipstick on the edge of the glass.

"Fascinating, Detective Odell. I do agree with you about the exact details. In my studies, I always stick to exact details. Botany and horticulture are rather beautiful but exact. Are there bombs dropping here? And you did say that you would answer my questions. As in plural. However, you only answered a single question and skipped answering my initial questions."

Suddenly, Lyle Odell stood up rather abruptly at the words of Dr. Burgess.

He nodded and then handed the magnifying glass to her and said, "Here, take a look for yourself."

Dr. Burgess nodded. She went to set her martini glass on the table and then stopped, and she smiled. Instead, she turned and handed the glass to Detective Odell.

Dr. Burgess said, "Placing the glass there would be a

serious procedural error, Detective Odell. If it spilled on the table, then it would contaminate the evidence."

"Excellent call!" Odell was excited at her intelligence and her proper approach to examining the scene. There was instant magnetism between the two of them. Instant attraction and admiration. Odell explained as he held her martini glass in the air and watched Dr. Burgess carefully.

"It certainly would destroy this evidence and make your observations tainted by the gin, and vermouth, and the dirty part. I can also detect olive juice. I will hold your drink while you investigate."

Dr. Burgess spoke as she circled the table.

"Correct. A dirty martini. Now you are not going to sneak a peek at my breasts as I lean in here. Will you, Detective Odell? My dress is very low-cut and revealing. I was not counting on being part of an unofficial police investigation. Still, here we are, and I want to concentrate on the investigation and not my breasts falling out of this dress. My brassiere is fairly flimsy, and my breasts are rather large and full."

"Negative, Doc. No peeks required. The evidence is very clear. Even without full exposure, it is easy to detect that you have lovely breasts."

Odell paused, mussed his hair with his free hand, and failed in his attempts to smooth his hair out on his head.

He added with a low growl while maintaining his usual deadpan facial expression.

"Ya ain't gotta be a detective to determine those facts."

Dr. Burgess smiled widely and said, "Thank you, Lyle, for the compliment. Please. Can I call you Lyle? You may call me Eleanor."

"Nah on the Lyle stuff, Eleanor. I prefer Detective Odell. Or just Odell."

"Okay, Odell."

She took the magnifying glass and leaned over the table to study the locations that Lyle Odell had studied. As she did so, Detective Odell went into a long diatribe as he explained his studies and observations. And the exact details, too.

"The food crumbs are not from the food offered at this table. They are a mixture of cheese and crackers. Whole wheat crackers. I would guess that the server brushed away most of the spill but left these remnants. And you can see a splash spill of whiskey in and around the food remnants. The lights above allowed me to detect that, and then a close examination of the spill brought the identity of the details into focus. A smell test tells me that it is Scotch. Most likely, the person who spilled these food crumbs and splashed the Scotch is drinking the whiskey neat. I firmly believe that since I did not see any ice particles or remnants thereof. And since the splash hits first at a location near the cracker and cheese crumbs and then jumps over a few inches away to continue the spill, I would classify the spill as rather extensive and the spiller is a little tipsy. The person required a refill after spilling this drink. Since the splash is large, I would say that the person is tall. The whiskey fell from a height. Most likely, the person piles his food high and is a big eater. I think it is a man. And he leaned in over the table while chomping down on the cheese and crackers, spilling some from his mouth or from a tilt of the plate and then spilled the whiskey. He did not like the look of the seafood nibblers offered here, or does not eat seafood, so he moved on for a refill of the whiskey and to pluck some more food from other tables."

Dr. Eleanor Burgess stood up. She carefully folded the magnifying glass into a compact fold and then motioned with her eyes and a nod of her head for Odell to hold out his free hand. Detective Odell did so, and Eleanor carefully dropped the tool into his open hand and then gently wrapped his fingers over it with a seductive clasp after the glass was firmly in his grip. Warmth and attractiveness and an instant sexual tension exuded from their interaction.

After the handoff, Dr. Burgess locked eyes with Odell. Her height allowed her easily to do so; Lyle Odell was a large man. He stood about six foot two, or thereabouts, and while his baggy clothes and messy appearance hid his body beneath the folds, a careful study would reveal a muscular frame and a man who remained very physically fit.

"Here, Odell. I agree one-hundred percent with all your observations. I have studied many plants under glass and microscopes and studied and dissected many seeds, too. I am very comfortable with scientific observations, so there is a direct connection. Remarkable detection on your part."

After speaking, she smiled and blinked a few times. It was obvious that Detective Lyle Odell's intelligence and investigation exercise fascinated Dr. Burgess. It was also obvious that she found him to be very attractive, too.

"May I have my martini?"

"Sure. Here ya go."

She took a long sip and peered at Odell over the rim of the glass. After the sip, Dr. Burgess took the investigation to the next level with her next words. "So, can we go a little further in this fascinating experiment and display of investigation genius?"

Odell tilted his head at the question. Yet, he understood where the question led next.

First, he mumbled, "Sure."

Then he turned and pointed at a stocky, portly, and very tall man standing about fifteen feet away from where they stood. A man with very little hair, huge jowls that worked in unison with multiple chins.

"That guy over there is the guy who spilled the drink and the food crumbs. He is tall. Has a big belly and a huge ass, so he eats a lot. He piled his plate high with food, because finger food is not enough to satisfy a big guy like he is, and if you look closely . . . there are some food crumbs and spills on the front of his suit. Sloppiness from being tipsy and being an unfit man. Seems as if he cannot bend very well because he is a tubby pile of lard. The bartender filled his whiskey glass high. It remains high, indicating a recent refill, and it is a neat pour. That is my suspect."

Dr. Burgess immediately turned to the young server working the table and asked, "Young man? Please. Just a moment."

The young man hustled right over to where Detective Odell and Dr. Burgess stood. Obviously, he knew who the hostess was!

"Yes, Doctor Burgess. I hope that I am not in trouble and gonna end up in the clink for smoking a little weed before this shift. And yes, the bartender accidentally poured an extra drink and handed it off to me. I am very nervous working at a high-class event like this one is, but I need this job. Geez, that detective guy is like a Sherlock Holmes guy or sumthin' else. I took only one glass of whiskey and a few puffs on a joint. My apologies."

"He is rather . . . sharp. You are fine . . . no worries . . ." she leaned in to look at the nametag on his lapel and said, "Timothy. Confession is very good for the soul. The tall, heavy-set man over there," Dr. Burgess tilted her head with a nod and then continued with her questions, "did he come over to your table, stand on that side there and check out your food?"

Timothy looked at Odell's "suspect" and then he answered right away. "Sure did. I think he is a little drunk. He spilled some of the food that was on his plate and some of his drink. Then, after checking out what we have for food at this table, he walked away saying he does not like seafood. I cleaned it all up to the best that I could. Then about fifteen minutes later, the weird police guy came along and started checking it out where I cleaned. My goodness! Am I in trouble? Is he in trouble with the law for sumthin'?"

"No, no. It is all fine. Thank you."

For just a fleeting moment or two, Dr. Burgess seemed slightly uneasy at the confirmation of the exact details of the scenario; just as Detective Lyle Odell dictated how it would be. She quickly downed the remainder of her drink and then asked the young server another question.

"Dear Timothy. Can you please fetch me another martini? The bartender at the lead table will know how to mix it for me. Lyla is her name. Please. Let me see if Detective Odell wants a drink. Hang on."

"Odell. Would you like a drink?" Homicide Detective-Police Inspector Lyle Odell did not answer right away because trying to find the correct pocket to replace his magnifying glass in preoccupied him for the moment.

Dr. Burgess asked again. This time, she increased the volume of her voice. "Odell! Would you like a drink? A cocktail? A whiskey? Wine? Beer? Water?"

Lyle Odell finally looked up and said, "Water is fine. Thank you." Timothy was off, and Dr. Burgess returned to Odell's side.

"Well, suspect confirmed. Thank you for the eye-opening exercise in police detective work. I hold a high admiration for your skills and intelligence, Detective Odell."

"Oh, yeah, thanks, Eleanor. It is all very simple observations to make and very logical deductions to conclude. To answer your questions from before our investigation began, I am here with my best friend, the now retired Police Lieutenant George Grundy, and his lovely wife, Marjorie. They own a bar and grille downtown and are chamber of commerce members. And since you already investigated all the members in attendance, then you know that I am a silent partner with them in the establishment. When you asked me the questions, you worded it very carefully to frame it as a possible wrong assumption. You also, worded it so carefully that I knew you were just seeking confirmation of my relationship to the business. Since George and Lyle Odell worked together in the Mohawk City Police Department for over thirty years and are well known around the city, and the business lists an official third owner without a name, you assumed that Odell was the silent owner. Which was correct." Odell's eyes darted around the spacious interior of the glorious facility. It was as if he suddenly recalled that George and Marjorie were part of this adventure. Odell lost track.

"I am not exactly sure where George and his wife went off to. He is a major foodie, so I am sure he is drifting and sampling food somewhere. They knew this was not my bag, so they might figure that I took a taxi and booked out of here. Might have until I stumbled upon this investigation."

Timothy arrived with the drinks, handed them off, thanked them, and promptly returned to his table.

"No alcohol consumption, Odell?" Dr. Burgess asked and then added a tidbit of conversation. "Without being too forward, I have heard that you do like to partake in the tastes of your heritage. Irish whiskey. Maybe?"

Odell took a long sip of the water and swallowed.

"Used to drown in it. Yuppers. Ya heard right, Doc. I am a lush that hangs close to the edge. Been good for a few years now. Just dabble in light beer, or as I call it, beer-flavored water. Once in a while, I have a few glasses of the Irish. For special occasions. A celebration. Came too close to ruin a few years back. I am certainly not a teetotaler, but try to keep it between the lines now."

"I respect that and understand. If you prefer, I can have the caterers bring you a light beer. The craft beers might not be what you want."

"Nah. The water is fine. Ya seem to know a lot 'bout me? Why is that?"

Dr. Eleanor Burgess took a seductive sip of her martini as she peaked over the rim of the glass at Odell. She had an elegant way of sipping a martini that could melt a man. . ..

"Oh my. That is strong. I might lose myself. Relax Detective Odell. I am not stalking you. I have. . .."

Odell interrupted. Now it was his turn in a play of seduction.

"Lemme tell ya sumthin.' Lose away. I will keep my eyes on ya. I would not mind it in the least if a beautiful, super-intelligent dish like ya were actively stalking me, Eleanor. Sure, as hell beats most of the stalking in my past."

"I cannot even imagine what your career is like. As far as the stalking goes, I will keep that in mind, Odell. Rather easy explanation . . . when my academic friends and associates heard of my semi-permanent move to Mohawk City and our company's relocation, and the construction of this marvelous new facility, some of them shared stories about you. As I said, you are a legend, and I have many friends and associates who teach criminal justice and law and such. Your methods and career cases are the subject of many lectures and taught at many universities. It was then that I read up on you. I enjoy reading."

Odell replied, "Gotcha. Not exactly sure about the legend stuff, but thanks."

While holding his water glass in one hand, Odell, with his free hand, began to pat his suit pockets and venture into a frantic search amongst his oversized maze of pockets and nooks. Dr. Burgess watched as, once more; his eccentric ways surfaced.

"Say, Doc. I would love a smoke of a cancer stick. If I can find 'em. Is there someplace that I can smoke in this fancy joint of yours?"

Dr. Eleanor Burgess turned and pointed to the rear of the open atrium area and said, "Yes. This way. On the patio. We can smoke out there. I will show you and join you."

Odell seemed surprised at the statement and the fact that Dr. Burgess would enjoy a smoke with him.

He plucked the wayward cigarette pack from a hidden lair, shook his head at the fact that his actions had bent the cigarette pack as well as slightly squished them and said, "Oh. Okay. I was not expecting that you would smoke too. Sorry that these cigarettes are not going to be in the best of condition. I must'a sat on 'em."

Dr. Eleanor Burgess wandered ahead of Homicide Detective Lyle Odell, and as she cut in front of him to lead the way to the designated smoking area, she quickly downed the remainder of her martini and then handed off the empty glass to Odell.

"I would expect nothing more than disheveled cigarettes from the outwardly disheveled Homicide Detective Lyle Odell. Here, Odell. A refill. Please. The lead cocktail table staffed by Lyla. We just walked past it. A few steps back on your left. She knows how to mix them for me. Cut in line, Odell. Once you mention my name, they will forgive you. It is a lovely September evening tonight. It was a cold morning and will be cold tomorrow morning, but right now, it is still warm outside. Meet me on the patio. Be there. Don't be square."

Lyle Odell took the glass and watched along with what seemed like ten thousand other men, as Doctor Eleanor Burgess swung her hips and swayed and made her way to the patio. Her breasts bounced in time with her steps, and her form-fitting dress hugged her glorious figure as she made her way and dropped a few jaws along the way. The pearl necklace caught the light and danced within her beauty. Her pearl earrings enhanced her long, thin neck, and she made her way to the patio while breaking hearts along the way.

Unbeknownst to Detective Lyle Odell, George Grundy and Marjorie stood off to the side while watching the scene unfold.

Between bites of an exquisite chicken lettuce wrap and swigs of a craft beer, George asked his wife, "Should I see if

Odell is ready to leave?"

Marjorie looked at her husband with a rather puzzled look, and she shook her head, smiled a bit, and took her husband by the hand and led him off to the next table to sample some more food.

Marjorie Grundy knew the way to her husband's heart.

"Ah, no, my dear George. I mean, look at that woman. She is stopping hearts and popping eyeballs as she walks around here, and with a woman's observation on another woman, there is little doubt that she has Odell in her sights. Something tells me that Lyle is going to be just fine. Leave him be. He will find his way home. I am quite sure of it."

"Yeah, she is a gorgeous knockout. But Odell is actually not interested in this meeting or in mingling with common humans who do not understand his eccentric ways. He is sniffing around on a new case."

Marjorie Grundy's eyes opened wide, and her mouth hung open a bit. Then, after recalling the many years of adventures of her beloved husband and his best friend and partner on the police force, and knowing the eccentricity but brilliance of Lyle Odell, Marjorie recovered.

"Yes, of course he is. George, I don't want to know."

"Nah, honey. Ya don't wanna know, babe. It is Odell-stuff. Good luck, Odell. I hope you come up for air and survive. Hey, lookie there, honey!" Grundy exclaimed, and then he nodded, and he was off to the next table. "Seafood! Baby, I think these are crab cakes. Or something like crab cakes! Geez, I am hungry!"

Doctor Eleanor Burgess proudly announced, as she stared at her martini glass and proceeded to take a gentle sip, "On my way out here, I instructed a server to dedicate her focus to us but to give us privacy. She will bring refills. If you chose to upgrade your water to your beloved Irish whiskey, or some of that . . . how and what did you label it?"

"Beer-flavored water, Eleanor."

"Yes, exactly. Please let her know."

"Yuppers. Sure thing. Thank you."

The looming night sky was purple with tiny perforated puffy white clouds and the last remaining rays of sun peeking through while the sun dipped low over the horizon. Dr. Eleanor Burgess took a long drag on her cigarette and then she blew the smoke high up into the air. It seemed as if her martini consumption within the evening had finally captured Dr. Burgess. Lyle Odell stood and observed and admired her beauty in the fading sunlight of the day.

When twilight looms, there is beauty all around. In many ways.

There was no question that she was a remarkable beauty. Homicide Detective Lyle Odell was keen on observation. As in very, very keen.

Odell matched her drags of the cigarette. His sips of water matched her sips of her martini. For some reason, and Odell sensed it with his uncanny perception, it seemed as if Detective Lyle Odell had arrived at just the right time in Dr. Eleanor Burgess's life. As if she needed his presence and his intelligence, his power, and his eccentric ways. Something clicked. Something changed. The ever-in-tune with human emotions, Detective Lyle Odell, detected pain and suffering, and raw emotional churning within this gorgeous woman standing in front of him. She was drowning her pain in a bath of martinis. That was a feeling and behavior that Lyle Odell could relate to.

This situation and the details of this possible case were something more than what he initially thought. His instincts were not incorrect whether there was a serious crime afoot, just slightly off kilter in the direction thereof, and perhaps, in Odell's focus of the original subject that he targeted.

Odell could correct this. It was imperative that he do so.

Although Detective Lyle Odell might not have planned this evening to end as it was shaping out; no, no, no. Initially, there was little question that he might have had other intentions and a specific purpose in mind. . ..

Dr. Eleanor Burgess was feeling loose, and the workings of the multiple martinis allowed her to no longer maintain the upright and professional appearance that her hosting of the meeting required. She lost some inhibitions as she walked to the edge of the patio and leaned her body against the low stone wall separating the patio from the spacious turf areas of the property. In the growing darkness, she studied Homicide Detective Lyle Odell. It was obvious that, martinis or not, she enjoyed what she saw.

"Could you tell me why you don't seem as if you ever smile, Detective Odell? You should smile. Often. You are ruggedly handsome, and I feel that a smile on your face would only enhance your handsomeness."

Doctor Eleanor Burgess asked and commented, and after doing so, she posed with her martini glass in her hand, while dripping with elegance. The white pearl necklace around her neck shone elegantly in the decorative lights, whose main purpose was in enhancing the stone walls surrounding the patio. In this case, their other purpose was enhancing the beauty of Doctor Eleanor Burgess.

"Dr. Burgess, I only smile when it is worthy to do so. I reserve smiles for special and precious moments in time. When you have seen the underbelly of evil, as I have for over thirty years, smiling becomes quite difficult."

"I imagine so," Dr. Burgess answered as she seductively peered over the edge of her martini glass, and then added, "I thought we agreed to call me Eleanor . . . Odell."

"We did. Your question and comments seemed rather intense, so I chose to answer with your formal title. To hide underneath the words."

Eleanor took another sip of her martini and then carefully set the glass on top of the stone wall. She leaned back and flexed her back, and her breasts lifted as she took a deep breath. Odell studied her every move; both as a detective and as a man.

"They were intense. Honestly, I find you remarkably attractive. Both in appearance and in your genius. You must have seen and dealt with so much over your long career. Blood. Murders, homicides, grisly scenes. Pain, suffering, horribleness. Grieving families. I cannot fathom such a career. Seeking justice in a world full of injustice and evil. Still, there is much to smile about in life."

She waved her free hand in the air to capture the setting.

"I mean, look at this wonderful evening and gathering. Look at us standing here sharing drinks and conversation and enjoying meeting each other. Perhaps it is the beginning of something very special."

Odell lifted his eyes and looked around the patio and up at the sprawling facility and the remarkable architecture. Wealth surrounded them. It was so unlike the majority of gritty Mohawk City. The beginning of a transformation. A phoenix rising from the ashes.

"Eleanor, the reality is that immense sadness and a multitude of tears lie beneath each and every human smile."

"True, Odell. Very profound and true words. You see, there is a remarkable chasm that exists between persons such as you and I and other persons in this magical world. The chasm. It has endless depth and goes on forever. The separation between the commonplace and the extraordinary. Not to belittle others, but you understand. There is no peace in possessing a higher intellect. It is a curse because we never find peace. Our minds never rest. We are always searching for clues and angles and the meanings of life and the mystery of things that exist within life and this world. Hidden or obvious. You search for clues in cobwebs and dust, and I peered into the magical world of plants and trees, and flowers and beauty. This gift is slow torture. I know that you understand. You feel it too. Don't you?"

In typical Odell fashion, Odell did not immediately answer. He stored the statement of Doctor Burgess away for attention later. Instead of commenting, he mussed his hair, took a last sip of the water, and emptied it. Then attempted to smooth his hair out. His effort proved fruitless. Odell finished his cigarette and ground it out on the sole of his boot. Doctor Burgess studied Odell from her position on the wall. She finished her cigarette and her martini. She ground it out on the stone wall and left the spent butt there alongside the empty martini glass. Odell walked over, picked up the butt and its remnants of the cigarette and tossed it in a nearby trash can along with the empty water bottle. As promised, a young woman, the previously instructed and diligent server, magically appeared, with a refill of the water for Odell and a fresh martini for Doctor Burgess.

"No upgrades, Odell?" Doctor Burgess asked.

"Nope. The water is fine. Thank you."

The server delivered the drinks, took the empty martini glass, and with a quick nod, and an exchange of thank you, she disappeared into the building.

"Please. Ask away, Detective Odell. Please do ask any of the questions that are floating around in that intense mind of yours there. I know the last thing you wanted to do tonight was to attend a Chamber of Commerce meeting. Ha! Your mind was so bored that you found clues in food crumbs. Hence, the aforementioned chasm."

Doctor Burgess took a sip of the newly delivered martini, and she once again seductively stared at Homicide Detective Lyle Odell over the rim of the glass. Her intelligence matched Odell's. Perhaps, exceeded it. This remarkable and gorgeous woman was a step ahead of the great detective.

And then she added the shin-kicker.

Off Doctor Burgess went in a martini-influenced explanation, all while locking eyes with Odell and doing her best to read his mind and his soul.

"I loved my half-brother. He was much older than I am, and after my mother and our father both passed, he was really my only living relative. Half-sibling or not . . . my only sibling. We have some distant second cousins, but we were and are a small family. From what I know, I was a surprise baby for my parents. Randy and I were not exceptionally close, mostly because of our age difference, and having different mothers, but I respected and loved Randy. Often, it was difficult to connect with Randy because of our age difference. When I was only a youngster, he was already a man, and our father was grooming Randy to inherit this company. Even when I was older and a teenager, we did not connect on many levels or interests because he wanted everything to do with this business, and I wanted zero to do with it. He did not have hobbies, or love music, or enjoy movies, or anything that I enjoyed. Certainly not plants! He was not a doting older brother. It was all about business. Worked himself to death. Literally. Even when he had his first heart attack and issues, he refused to slow down. I came out here to help him as best that I could when he first took ill, but really, I was ineffective due to my disinterest in the business."

Doctor Burgess paused in her words, and she swallowed hard. The loss of her half-brother hurt her. She did care for him deeply, and there was no question that she loved him. Absolutely no question. Odell focused on her every action; her body language, and her words. Detective Odell had read and interpreted countless testimonies over his career. He was listening and studying but also testing her sincerity. Because everyone is a suspect. . ..

Odell's focus was intense. But a person did not need to be Detective Lyle Odell to feel Doctor Eleanor Burgesses' pain at the loss of her half-sibling. Love transcends.

Doctor Burgess could feel Odell's eyes studying her. Right through to her soul. She steadied and continued to speak.

"Randy never married. Seldom even had woman friends. He certainly was a very good-looking man, but this business was his love. I did my thing, and he did his. I was very happy with my career and my studies. From a very young age, I always loved plants, and I knew what I wanted to do for a career. I had a garden when I was six years old. Drove our father crazy with my seeds and plantings. I think the dumbest wish we all have as children is to grow up someday. Lost innocence is like losing part of your soul. I grew up, but I never left my plants. Their leaves crave the sun and love. Just as we do. Their roots are just like we are. Digging deep in the world for stability. My half-brother was highly intelligent, as was, and is, most of our family. What I have left of them, that is. He was a remarkable man. I did not kill my half-sibling to gain control of this insurance empire." Doctor Burgess took another sip of the martini and paused in her words for the hard swallow of the mixture before she spoke once more.

"This is not a fairy tale of the evil half-sister and her mother out to get the half-brother and take over the company after daddy dies sort of situation. You don't believe in fairy tales, Odell? Do you?"

Odell immediately. "I only believe in the Big, Bad Wolf. I ran into him far too many times in my career. He has quite a huff and a puff, too."

Doctor Burgess understood the deep meaning of Odell's words. She nodded and almost smiled before continuing with her thoughts.

"My half-brother died of natural causes. He had a terrible heart and numerous heart attacks. Bypass operations. High stress. An awful lifestyle. Drank way too much for how poor his health was and it was a bad choice mixing it with the medication that he took for his heart. His heart was very weak. Wretched heart disease. Same as our father did. He took after him in so many ways. Our father loved his cocktails, and he had heart disease, too. What a high price the glory of owning this wretched company turned out to be." Doctor Burgess stopped speaking and with a sly smile, she pointed her cocktail glass in the direction of Odell, who stood there studying her. He was admiring her, too. Doctor Burgess was a little wobbly, but still in charge of her actions and words. The martinis were slowly taking over now. Her face gave away the fact that she wanted to ask a question but she wanted to word it correctly. She did.

"How did you even learn of this situation and gain these feelings that there are crimes here?"

Odell answered without pause.

"I read an article in the newspaper a few days ago."

"That is amazing. You read an article in a newspaper and feel as if you should investigate crimes. Anyway, Odell. Come on now. I think you are incorrect on this one. There is no homicide. I know you are the genius detective, but my goodness, he was alone in his cabin on a cruise ship. The yearly floating convention of insurance boredom. I know that is why you originally came here tonight. To sniff around in the corners and in the layers of wealth and opulence for homicides and for crimes. Honestly, I would be disappointed if you did not arrive here in my world tonight. The new facility. A beautiful corporate campus. An evil insurance corporation that tries very hard at never paying out a fair claim! Ha! The CEO dies on a cruise ship floating around in the ocean off the Caribbean islands. The much younger and suspicious half-sibling-sister takes over the company. Her mother is dead. Their father, too. The company is all hers to take over. All too lustful for the great mind and the great Detective Odell to ignore."

Doctor Burgess took a deep breath. She was becoming very emotional. She choked up and it was obvious that the words were a struggle to find.

She shook her head emphatically and loudly proclaimed, "No! No! No! I was perfectly happy in my world. Studying plants, teaching. Sharing love and intellect with my plants, my career, and with my students. I made my own career. My own money. There was no need for all of this."

Doctor Burgess set her martini glass on top of the stone wall and then she waved her arms in the air to encompass the facility, the property, and the world of Standard Insurance Company.

"My condolences on the loss of your half-brother. I get it. One question, Eleanor," Homicide Detective Lyle Odell finally spoke, "why Mohawk City? Why build this palace here in this gritty, old, horrible city? A city of sin. Of crime. Of horribleness and an old city beleaguered beyond comprehension. Urban renewal my ass. No hope here. No renewal. The building and property are gorgeous, as you are, but it is a fish outta water."

Doctor Eleanor Burgess contemplated the question for a few long seconds.

She took a sip of the cocktail and then looked over at Lyle Odell and said, "I honestly do not know. I never asked Randy. I did not care enough about this bullshit company to ask and steered clear of the business. And now it is too late. To ask him. I must play the part for now. Until I can find a way out of this and someone else to take it over. Or just sell it all."

"Do you know who was on the cruise with Randolph? It was all business-related. I presume. Business mixed with cocktails, and cruise ships, and fun in the sun."

"Sure. Herbert O'Leary, who is our general legal counsel and head of the legal department. And Randy's administrative assistant, Ms. Lily Livingston."

"What do you know 'bout them?"

"Well, not much," Doctor Burgess took another sip of her cocktail and continued, "I mean. They both seem nice enough. Herbert has been with Standard Insurance for over thirty years. No red flags with Herb. He does his job, works long hours, and goes home to his family. Has a ton of grandchildren. He has pictures of them all over his office walls. Pride and joy sort of thing. He does tend to talk a lot. Rambles on and on and I lose interest in what he is saying. Lily left shortly after Randy died. The executive assistant position is now open. Young. Going back to school for a master's degree. Very well spoken. Beautiful. Professional. They both were very upset at the death of my half-brother. Especially Lily. I guess they became very close over the years."

Odell grimaced as little as he stated, "Interesting. Old Herbie is trustworthy. Okay. Pictures of the family. Sounds happy. Talks a lot. I never trust yappers. The more a person goes on rambling about bullshit and explaining a situation, the more I think they are guilty and are hiding something. And I bet Lily has a knockout figure and is not married."

Eleanor paused a bit with her drink in her hand. Then she shook her head and took a gentle sip.

Recovering from Odell's testimony, Doctor Burgess said, "Odell, even though we just met, I can tell that your knowledge and intuition are uncanny. You more than live up to your reputation. Your insight is endless. It is boundless across the chasm. Yes. She is a stunner. Perfect figure. Gorgeous breasts and curves in all the right places. Yes."

Odell took a sip of his water and said, "Gotcha. And very friendly. Vivacious. Intelligent. Personable. Lots of magnetism. What is she studying?"

"Exactly. Perfect description. Studying? Chemistry. I think. She wants to do some type of research on something.

Honestly, I am not exactly sure because I am guilty of not really paying much attention to her after she announced that she was leaving our employment. Odell, I might need to finish this cocktail and order another. I need to become numb. I fear where this supposition and probing of yours are leading."

Odell waved and provided some advice and a statement of his experience.

"You might not want to get too numb. Take it from me. It really does not last long enough. Herbert O'Leary. ESQ. The kind, old, dedicated, and trusted attorney. Family pictures are on his office walls. The stunning young assistant. An attorney with power. Attorneys. I never have much good luck with them. They all seem to have crazy looks in their eyes, and they have angry eyebrows and hidden agendas. When they look my way, they have immediate disdain. Well, don't cheat, lie, murder, connive, break the law and you will never have to deal with me. And now we add to the mixture the gorgeous, intelligent, young chickie-poo with great breasts and a wiggling tookus. Studying chemistry. Seventy percent of all crimes are committed by people under the age of thirty-five. They don't give a rat's ass because they have not earned anything and don't have a rat's ass to give to this weary world. The older folks, such as Herbie, have it all, but it ain't ever enough. My goodness. I fear that this situation is very deep and very dark and the circumstances of this mess are very complex. Yet, I know you did not kill your half-brother. I think that I've gotta tell you though, he did not die entirely of natural causes. He certainly had a bum ticker and worked too much, drank too much, and had all of that stress, but my gut feeling is that something else happened here. He did not just keel over 'cuz of a stopped ticker issue. Nope. And, Eleanor, in ya heart you know that something is off here. This complex is just too much. Too large. Too wonderful. Too extravagant for an immensely successful, but still a private family business. The same questions that bothered me, bother you, too. You're a genius. The chasm thingy. Until now, you did not know who to turn to for advice. For some guidance and direction. Now you do. Despite the complexity of this case, I can help you."

It seemed as if, for a fleeting moment, her inhibitions left and allowed a crack in her confidence and emotions. Perhaps just a hint of some tears formed in her eyes. Then a recovery and some words.

"Can you, Odell? I am not sure that you can. Even with all of your genius."

"Yes, and yes."

Doctor Burgess paused in mid-sip of her martini, and she smiled widely.

"I knew that eventually you would answer my statement. One yes. Okay. I hope you can help me. Second, yes . . . you understand and feel the torture of the chasm."

"Correct."

Doctor Burgess downed the rest of the martini in one shot. She made her decision; alcohol influenced or not; and she made her move.

However, before speaking, she held her hand up in the air to the young server watching in the darkness from afar. She needed no witnesses to her next words.

"Have you ever been married, Odell?"

"I generally do not answer personal questions. It is my experience in life that the less people know about you, the better. However, I will for you. Negative. No woman could put up with my eccentric ways, the booze, the pain. The phantoms that constantly haunt me. Past and present. The lifestyle. I had a very beautiful relationship once. It was glorious. Beyond description. Just a few years ago. She was much younger than I am. I never intended to get this old this quickly. It just kind of happened. Yet, she loved me because of my age and our shared interests and experiences. Ultimately, it would not have worked. She needed to be free and find someone of her own age and a better fit. She is a genius. Much smarter than I am."

"My guess. Is she a police officer?"

"Yuppers. A detective."

"Yes, good guess on my part. Makes sense. Confession. Since I asked you, I will give it up. I was married once. We were both very young. Too young. Only lasted two years. I loved plants too much. He loved himself more than he loved me. Not a great fit. Ironically, it was Randy who told me not to marry him. I did not listen and should have. I understand about careers."

Her words and breath hitched for a few seconds, but she remarkably caught both.

"Odell, I do know how you can help me. I have not been in a man's arms for a very long time. Odell, I find you immensely attractive. Above this office space in this sprawling complex is an exclusive penthouse apartment for me. That space is the only part of this mess that I enjoy. I much prefer this apartment here. It has every amenity. Including a fully stocked wet-bar."

Doctor Burgess took another deep breath; she focused her eyes on Odell, and a slight smile fell upon her lips.

"Odell, please ditch that water. I will have the server bring you a top-shelf Irish whiskey, come to my penthouse, and spend some time with me."

Doctor Burgess finished speaking, and she did not wait for his reply. Instead, she waved off in the direction of the server, who once again magically appeared. Lyle Odell stood in silence.

"Please, dear, another martini for me, and for Detective Odell, I will allow him to make his choice and order on his own."

The server nodded. The young woman turned with her pad and pen in her hand to Homicide Detective Lyle Odell and waited for his answer.

Odell did not hesitate in his answer.

"Unfortunately, the double lure is very tempting, but I need to stick with water. Water for now. Thank you."

Another nod. She scribbled on the pad. Off she went.

Lyle Odell turned to Doctor Eleanor Burgess, and he smiled and said, "For sure. Another day, or night, Eleanor. In the future. Maybe after this mess is over. Right now, we can be friends. I hope you understand. I must keep conflicts of interest down. Absolutely, I enjoy your company. Let's do dinner tomorrow night. I will pick you up here. Seven o'clock."

She took a deep breath. Her shoulders relaxed with the exhale as the mountains of immense tension left her body. Odell arrived just in time. He could help her in many ways. No one else could.

Doctor Burgess smiled back and said, "Dinner it is. For sure. That will be wonderful. I am deeply disappointed about this evening but encouraged by the dinner date and you leaving our future open. Friends sounds wonderful. For now. Your presence here in my life encourages me. Besides, it was not a complete rejection. A smile reserved for special and precious moments in time. Nowadays, you have left parts of your past behind, and you reserve Irish whiskey only for special occasions and celebrations. You humble and honor me. In that order. My goodness, your face did not crack with your smiling. How sexy was that smile? I just melted into a puddle of lust."

Odell mussed his hair and almost smiled once more. Instead, he spoke out of the side of his mouth and said, "Doc, I assure you that someday, as I said in the future, once we figure this all out, the lust part I can handle. Let's keep the melting stuff on the side and postpone that for now. I am gonna need ya intact. This is gonna be a hell-u-va ride."

Chapter Three

Odell Digs In

It was Friday morning at eight o'clock. The Friday after the Chamber of Commerce event and the morning after Lyle Odell first met Doctor Eleanor Burgess. A night to remember.

"I ain't gonna ask ya if you want a splash of Irish in that coffee, Odell. Getting tired of asking ya."

George Grundy poured a steaming hot cup of coffee into the mug sitting in front of Police Inspector Lyle Odell. Odell had an unlit bent cigarette stuck on his lower lip, and he was studying a pad with sprawling handwriting in a scribble pattern on the pages. Lyle was using a pen to guide his way through the words. He did not even look up from the pad, but he flipped through the pages, lingering only a few seconds on some of them before flipping to the next page. Grundy leaned over and peered in at the page. He recognized the scrawl as Lyle Odell's own handwriting.

After studying the pad and pouring the coffee, Grundy walked over to the coffeemaker behind the bar and replaced the glass carafe onto the warming plate. After doing so, George tested the "speaking" waters with his best friend. Knowing full well that since Lyle Odell remained embedded in his notes, an answer may or may not come.

"And I am dying to ask ya how last night went. But it is really none of my business. Man, Doctor Burgess is a knockout, Odell. Beautiful. That food there was amazing. I had some kind of seafood lumps in a beer batter. I think they were crabcakes. Marjorie got angry with me when I stuffed a few extra of those guys in her purse to take home. I told her to calm down. I wrapped them in napkins. Had them as a snack this morning when I got up. At six."

Odell still did not say a single word, but he continued to flip through the pages of the pad. Grundy pulled out a cutting board and four bags of lemons and limes and took a knife from the knife rack to begin slicing the garnishes for the day. Odell suddenly stopped studying his pad. He closed it up and set the pen down on top of the pad. Odell ran his hand through his hair, and his hair stuck out in all directions.

The unlit cigarette bounced on his lip as he suddenly spoke.

"Negative and outstanding. But there was no intimate romance between us. At least, not yet. Attraction, yuppers. Romance, negative. As you know, that at this point in the case, it would not be proper police procedure. But we are becoming friends. Nothing wrong with that, and after this case is over, we can see where we end up."

George continued to slice the limes and lemons, and he smiled as he did so.

"Gotcha, Odell. I understand. My goodness. So, I guess there were no nefarious intentions there with Doctor Burgess or any evil, dark, shadowy figures lurking around the hallways of that beautiful facility. She did not kill her half-brother. Otherwise, Odell would not have spent any time with her or considered it for the future. Can't fraternize with potential suspects."

"Doctor Burgess is not guilty of any crimes. No, she did not kill him, nor does she have any knowledge of who did so. In fact, she thinks that I am completely wrong-o, and she has doubts that her half-brother is even a murder victim. Thinks his bad ticker just quit on him. Who knows? She might be right and I am wrong. Time will tell! I checked into his death a little. Have to spend more time on it that just last night. No autopsy on the half-brother's body. Doc Burgess is his closest next of kin. Half-kin, but it counts to inherit everything, 'cuz the rest of the family, except for some distant cousins, is history. He died out of the country, which is always a hassle. She got a little choked up last night talkin' 'bout it, so I did not want to make it messy for her. Plus, I was tinkering with the romance thingy, too. She is a totally gorgeous woman. Yet, she knows and senses that there is potential danger afoot and that there has been some less than scrupulous business conducted. But yes, plenty of nefarious intentions and, unfortunately, plenty of evil, dark, shadowy figures there. Somewhere and everywhere. I am going to do my best for her, George. My best. She is very special. Highly intelligent. A genius."

Grundy continued with his work.

He said, "I understand. What-cha got on the pad? Odell notes and stuff?"

"Yuppers. Notes. Been doing hours of research on many subjects. George, do we know a Vance Livingston? Didn't we run into him a few years back on a case? Wasn't he working as an attorney intern for the D-A? On the Hepburn investigation. They tried to keep me away from digging in too deep on that flunky college kid related to the acting attorney general in Massachusetts. The case where the punk was drunk and driving and ran over the innocent guy on the bicycle?"

Odell paused, looked up, and added, "Oh yeah. I don't blame Marjorie for getting after ya ass. Could have leaked grease all over the inside of her purse."

Grundy set his knife aside and gathered up the slices and began to stack them in the garnishment trays alongside the bar counter.

"I wrapped them in napkins, Odell. Whose side ya on here? Don't answer that. Anyway. Yuppers. You're right on, Odell. Livingston. A punk protecting a punk. They were college buddies. He never made the cut for the D-A office, nor did he stick around after his buddy went to the clinker for the manslaughter. Slimy bunch of bananas. You solved that case in two days. Sumthin' 'bout matching tire tread patterns or sum other kind of Odell stuff that Crump and his team confirmed in the labs. That stuff was always above me. Ole Grundy was more the muscle on those cases than I was the brains. I never liked that Livingston punk. Another Boston rich boy. His old man was some kind of blue-blood rich-bum real estate magnate in Boston."

Grundy clenched his fists at the mere mention of Boston.

"Can't stand anything Boston. Especially those Boston Bears! Bums, and they all talk funny. Like marbles in their mouths. Bums."

Odell stared off into the space behind the bar. He closed his eyes for a few seconds, and Grundy, knowing all too well his best friend and crime-fighting partner for all of these years . . . Grundy returned to his garnishment mission. Grundy knew that eventually Odell would return.

Police Inspector—Homicide Detective Lyle Odell opened his eyes. He took the unlit cigarette out of his mouth and set it on the pad next to the pen. Grundy looked up from his work and waved the knife in the direction of Odell's notepad as he asked a question.

"Is Livingston there on your pad? In your notes?"

"He is, George. He is now an attorney working for his old man's commercial real estate firm. They operate in Massachusetts, Connecticut, New York, Rhode Island, New Jersey, and New Hampshire. Boston based. Downtown. In the high-rent district. Livingston's old man brokered the deal on the new corporate headquarters for the Standard Insurance Company. Vance Livingston was the attorney working on the deal and the legal papers. He worked with Standard's corporate general counsel on the deal. An attorney guy named Herbert O'Leary. Doc Burgess says he is a nice old man, dedicated, been around forever, always smiling, with pictures of his wife, his family, Christmas trees, grand kiddies on the walls of his office and the family dog."

"Ah, man. That alerted your Odell senses to a high alarm! For sure. I know that drill! Attorneys never smile unless they are counting money or they win a case, and generally, family pictures are always a bullshit prop and a sham."

Odell did not hesitate in his response.

"Yuppers. And happy old Herbie was on the cruise with Randolph Burgess when he croaked. As was his beautiful, young, dynamic, big-chested, and curvy tookus executive administrative assistant. Yuppers. I am sticking with my gut, George. My first feelings. Why they built that corporate campus here in Mohawk City is the key to the entire case. It just does not make any sense."

George Grundy finished his work.

He looked up and said, "A curvy tookus hotty for an assistant, huh? Lemme guess? She somehow has ties to one of the players in the mix. Old Herbie?"

"Nope. Lily Livingston. Old man Livington's niece. The young punk Vance Livington's cousin."

Grundy set his knife aside and as he did so, he whistled another low whistle. His eyes went from the garnishes that required stacking to his best friend; Odell returned to his pad, his bent cigarette, and the pen.

"Ah, shit, Odell. It is a case. Damn. I gotcha. I know you all too well, Odell. Your ways. Too much intertwined and overlapping. Big buck deals. Dead CEO guy. No autopsy. Died out of the country. On a cruise ship. Convenient. Connected and wealthy players in the mix. A pattern. Livingston already proved to be untrustworthy and that he had nefarious intentions in the Odell-Grundy book. And why they built the Land of Oz building here in the grit of Mohawk City bothered you right from the git-go."

Grundy paused for a few seconds in his thoughts, and he gauged his next questions. He needed to make sure that he was reading his best friend correctly. Confident in his feelings and observations, George Grundy asked, "Ya gonna call in Miles? Gonna tap Christina's mind for a woman's point of view?"

Odell immediately looked up and answered.

"Negative. Nothing to go on yet. This one is mine. I would not waste their time. I am driving to Boston right after I finish my cup'a Joe here. Got a few questions for those slimy Livingston guys. Gonna rattle some cages. I called ahead and spoke with an old contact there in Boston. An old Coast Guard buddy. Retired Detective Warren Haskell. Haskell did his twenty-five and got out and is happy as a lark now. Fishes every day that he can. Haskell made some calls for me and worked the deal. He is gonna have an officer meet and tag along with me. Not planning any arrests, just questions. Unless they act up."

George smiled at Odell's answer. It was obvious that Grundy was enthusiastic for his best friend's renewal at an overwhelming challenge on this new investigation.

"Good. Ya needed this, Odell. Ya needed one last hurrah capturing and running down evil, and with a gorgeous woman like Doc Burgess in the mix, well, I can only hope that ya find what ya deserve and what ya need. Odell driving. Wow! That is 'bout a two-and a two-and-a-half-hour drive to Boston. Annie is coming in early today. Ya need me to drive? You usually don't drive on these cases. I know how to like to sulk in the passenger seat, and sit and think while tasting unlit cigarette butts. Gotta give ya time to think."

"I am good, George. I appreciate the offer. Got an unmarked cruiser signed out for today. It is a new world for Odell. You are retired now. In this case, I need to fly solo for now."

"I gotcha, Odell. How can I help?"

Odell smiled a rare smile. He removed the bent cigarette from his lower lip and twirled it in his fingers as he thought and he spoke.

"Just be my best friend. Just be Grundy. Yet, do not doubt, George. There is a terrible danger here. Dicey bullshit. I think we have layers of corruption here and a tag-team match of bad guys and gals."

"For sure. Always. I don't know who else to be, Odell. As you know, Grundy specializes in dicey bullshit. Lemme know." Grundy pointed at the shoulder harness, barely exposed underneath Odell's baggy suit jacket. "You are wearing ya service weapon. I hope you are not expecting much pushback today."

"I am going to wear it from now on. I am not quite sure what is happening and where and who the bad guys and gals are, George. Gonna put major ripples in some ponds today."

"Be safe, Lyle."

Odell nodded, and he gathered up his items, downed the coffee in a few sips, and waved to Grundy.

"Yuppers. Be back in Mohawk City tonight. I will see you in the morning. Tomorrow. I am havin' dinner with Eleanor tonight. Will Marjorie join us for our usual Saturday breakfast?"

"She will. Ya should bring Doc Burgess."

"Maybe, George. We will see how tonight goes. Ya comin' over to my house for the Rovers hockey game tomorrow night, or are we watchin' from here?"

"Your house. Best for me to get away from here occasionally. Light beer only! We can order pizza from Frank's West. I want sum pepperoni pizza. Two of 'em. Extra-large. Like me."

"Beer-flavored water, George. Okay. I will pick up a case. Pepperoni gives ya heartburn. We will get extra cheese. Ya will thank me, and Marjorie will kiss me. And, George, it is the Grundy-Odell book. You first. Always."

Grundy smiled and stacked the remainder of his garnishes as he watched Homicide Detective Lyle Odell as he walked out of the front door of their establishment. George Gurndy whispered a prayer while he stood and watched Odell disappear. Grundy, above everyone else, knew that Odell was walking headfirst and fearlessly into danger. He just knew.

Odell disappeared into the daylight. Into the thick of a case. Into Odell stuff. Detective Lyle Odell was good at his job.

As in exceptional.

It was a mid-rise office building stuck in the Financial District of Boston; near the Atlantic Avenue side. It was an impressive facility. Blue-tinted windows reflected the busy street activities and a bright sunrise. A lovely day in late September in Boston, Massachusetts.

Police Inspector-Homicide Detective Lyle Odell met the uniformed Boston police officer outside the front entrance to the office building. They shook hands and introduced themselves to each other. The officer was young; maybe in his mid-thirties. He was tall, slightly muscular, but not overly so; and projected confidence. He had large hands, a rugged face, with a few more lines than a young man's face should have. Police work will add lines to a face. The officer's voice was deep and powerful. He was articulate and professional. Odell immediately liked the young police officer. Odell provided him with a quick rundown of his intentions, just to ask a few key questions, and sniff around a bit for reactions to those questions. After the briefing, together, they walked into the lobby of the facility.

The revolving door was polished brass, and the floor a white marble with a black pattern. A lobby receptionist sat behind a large red oak desk with a smaller station next to the desk for a private security officer to sit. In front of the security officer was an array of monitors with the screens constantly flipping through scenes broadcast from cameras throughout the interior and the exterior of the facility. Hundreds of eyes. There was a nameplate sitting on the security desk with bold printed words stamped into the face. "On Duty: Security Officer Blackburn."

The lobby receptionist was a heavy-set young woman, with short blonde hair, trimmed neatly, wearing large eyeglasses and fashionable earrings and a necklace with some stone pendants hanging along the chain. She wore a stylish dark red blouse and a plain black skirt. Professional appearance and attire.

The nameplate on the front desk announced, "All visitors and guests, please check in here." A sliding card in another nameplate stated, "Ms. Walker."

"Can I help you, sir?" The receptionist asked as the security officer leaned over to listen and observe.

Odell dressed in typical Odell-like attire. Baggy, oversized suit, his hair was on the longish side, and parts and pieces of his hair stuck up and out in a few less-than-determined directions, his necktie was barely in a knot at all; it was more of a loosely tied loop. For those persons who knew Lyle Odell, they would dismiss his rather unkempt appearance as being just normal Odell. To those who did not know him, they would never guess his profession. The Boston police officer stood off to the side of the desk as he studied Odell and listened in on his conversation.

"Yes. Thanks. Ms. Walker." Odell's distinctive growl rolled out the words. A distinctive growl with an upstate New York accent. A stark contrast to the Boston accents surrounding him. "I am Homicide Detective Lyle Odell from the Mohawk City, New York Police Department." Odell turned and waved in the direction of the young police officer standing alongside him and said, "And this is . . . ah . . . go ahead, officer. Sorry. I forgot ya name already."

The officer smiled and nodded and said, "Officer Benjamin Crane. Boston Police Department, District A1."

Officer Crane pointed at his badge on his uniform and then turned to Odell for his continued introductions.

Odell nodded, mumbled, "Thanks," and then he began to pat, tap, and poke around on the outside of his suit jacket and then he moved to checking the inside pockets of his suit jacket. "Looking for my badge and identification," Odell explained as the security officer, the receptionist and Officer Crane all watched. After removing a disheveled pack of cigarettes and a small folding magnifying glass from his left inside suit jacket pocket, and dropping them on the floor, then gathering them all up in a pile and stuffing them haphazardly back into the pack, Odell finally pulled out a gold police badge and his identification billfold. He replaced the cigarette pack in the same pocket and mumbled, "Left inside suit jacket pocket."

The search process had been quite an ordeal.

Then, Odell held the identification billfold open and the badge in his hand for the receptionist to stand up a little from her chair, lean in, and study Odell's credentials. The security officer did the same.

Ms. Walker pointed at the badge and the identification and said, "This says you are Police Inspector Lyle Odell. Not Homicide Detective Lyle Odell. Which is it?"

Odell nodded, replaced the identification billfold in his left inside suit jacket pocket while mumbling the location aloud, and then, with some great effort, he clipped the badge to his belt.

"Good observation skills. Valuable investigation skills. Exact facts and details are very important in investigations. Here in this lobby, along with your partner, keen observation skills are very important. Ya never know what kind of whacko wanders in here from the streets. Technically, it is Police Inspector Lyle Odell. But that is some bullshit title they gave me, because I am, and always will be, Homicide Detective Lyle Odell."

Never comes the day when these things happen to lobby receptionists and security officers. But today was the day.

The receptionist sat back in her chair and swallowed hard as she studied, Odell. She looked at Officer Crane and then over to the security officer, who was an older gentleman, with perfect white hair and experience written all over his face; she then took a deep breath before asking the next question.

"Okay. Thank you. I have to say that for a police inspector, or a homicide detective, or whatever you choose to identify as, you aren't very organized. You seem to be a mess. Regardless, I am glad we got through that. How can I help you, Homicide Detective Odell, and Officer Crane?"

"Yeah, I have my moments. Some are good. Most are bad. I appreciate the Boston honesty. I am not much for sugar-coating things, either. It is Detective Odell or just plain Odell. No need for the homicide stuff. Here to see, Vance Livingston and Reid Livingston of the Back Bay Real Estate Group."

When the security officer heard the names that Odell announced, he picked up a clipboard from his desk and began to study it.

Detective Lyle Odell spoke before the security officer could and pointed at the clipboard.

"Ain't on the list for today. I don't have an appointment, Security Officer Blackburn. But they are here. I already checked the executive parking garage. They parked their fancy sedan there. Space Alpha Twenty-Six, third level. Officer Blackburn, you did not see me on your camera there because it is not working. As is the camera on level four on the east side. The west side works, but the pan and tilt mounts are frozen. I think you saw parts of me walking in and around the parked cars, but when you moved the joystick controller, the motor froze in place. Need to get those serviced."

Security Officer Blackburn tried to force a smile. The smile did not arrive.

He blinked a few times and then said, "Okay, thanks. I will put in a work order."

"Now, please, can you let the two Livingston guys know that we are here to see them? If you issue us temporary passes for the elevator key cards, buzz up to Josie, the receptionist slash office coordinator up there and let her know we are coming up, then I think we can find our way. Third floor. Their offices are the two east corner offices."

"Have you been here before, Detective Odell? How do you know that Josie is also the office coordinator?" Ms. Walker asked.

"Nah, never been here before in my life. Try to stay away from anything Boston-related. But the directory over there says the offices for the Back Bay Real Estate Group are on the third and fourth floors of this facility."

Security Officer Blackburn seemed puzzled.

He looked over at his lobby partner and then said, "But Detective Odell, you never looked at the directory. I watched Officer Crane and you walk in together, and you walked directly over to this desk."

"Correct. Great observation skills. Very important in your job. Observe and report. Duty of a solid security officer. I did not have to look at the directory. Since the management assigns the parking spaces and parking garage levels according to the floors leased and Livingston's rig is on the third level, it is easy to figure out they are on the third floor. Since they have over five-hundred employees, and the square footage of the floor plates here match up to occupancy levels of about three-hundred employees per floor, based up the maximum occupancy plaque on the east wall of the lobby here, I figured they lease the fourth floor, too. Besides, when I walked around the fourth level of the parking garage, there were Back Bay employee parking stickers, various vanity-type realtor license plates, and some decals and advertising materials for Back Bay on and inside the vehicles parked there. I know that Josie McDermott is the receptionist slash office coordinator because I observed her car on the third level. Her business cards are sitting on the front passenger seat of the car along with some other rather curious items."

Odell's eyes drifted around the lobby a little. He mussed his hair and then tried to smooth it up as the three observers keenly watched this awkward, but still powerful display of a mix of the eccentricity and genius of Lyle Odell.

The good detective continued to explain.

"You can gather an awful lot of factual and valuable information through keen and detailed observations. If you stand outside the facility and study the structure, you can count the window sections and line them up with the steel mullions. It is easy to see that the two corner offices on the east side and on the west side of the third floor are executive offices. The big shots would take the east side of the facility because the sun comes up there in the morning and the tall buildings on that side block the sun's glare for the offices. The west side is open, so the afternoon sun glare is wicked. As you would say here. They would heat up, too. Wicked bad. These big shots with the big egos would give those crappy offices to the bums of the company. The fourth floor spacings seem to be different as far as I can see through the windows. Maybe some I.T. departments on that floor, mailroom and package delivery, facilities maintenance, and office support . . . more wide-open floor spaces."

Odell took a breath. His eyes darted around the lobby, and then he spoke once more.

"So, can we go up now? The Livingston guys and Odell, we are . . . old friends. They know me. They won't be happy to see me, but they know me."

The receptionist sat stunned for a few seconds, and she

did not say a word.

Officer Crane swallowed.

Security Officer Blackburn shook his head, whistled low, and mumbled, "Damn sure fooled me. So much for being disorganized." He sighed and went back to his joysticks and monitors.

The lobby receptionist finally gathered her words. It became rather matter-of-fact from here on in.

Ms. Walker said, "Please sign the logbook. Here are two temporary badges for the elevator, and I will ring Josie on the third floor and let her know you are on the way up."

"Thanks."

After signing in and receiving the temporary passes, Odell and Officer Crane made their way to the lobby elevators.

When they were out of earshot, Ms. Walker leaned over to her partner on duty and whispered, "Charlie, what was it that Detective Odell said? Something about whackos that wander in off the streets?"

Officer Blackburn did not comment. He watched them disappear into the elevator, and then he nodded.

Josie, the third-floor receptionist and office coordinator, was tall, beautiful, very shapely, but lean, and more than just slightly mean. She was the angry bulldog guarding the executive wing from intruders, and from salespeople, and right now, from Homicide Detective Lyle Odell and Boston Police Officer Ben Crane.

"You don't have an appointment," Josie McDermott said as she shook her head back and forth, cracked some chewing gum in her mouth, and glanced at an appointment book. She then looked up at Odell and Officer Crane, and she blinked, then she waved her hand in the air and motioned toward the elevator. "So, go away. I don't know why the lobby receptionist and the security officer even allowed you up here. It is their job to screen people, and if they do not have an appointment, then they should send them away. I am lodging a complaint with the building management over their poor choices in admitting you two and reporting their rotten job performances."

Odell raised his voice just a bit and quickly jumped into the conversation. It was obvious that Josie waving at the elevator did not go over too well with Odell.

"And I will call them, flash my badge, and make a big deal. I will tell them that we are police officers on an important investigation and void your complaint. They did their jobs perfectly. I am a homicide detective investigating a homicide in Mohawk City, New York. Officer Crane is a Boston police officer. That is why they allowed us up here and why we are here. To see Vance Livingston and Reid Livingston. I need to ask them five questions."

Josie continued to crack her gum. She stood up behind the desk and folded her arms across her chest.

"Exactly. In Mohawk City, New York. Not here in Boston. You ain't got no jurisdiction here. So, once more, go away. This is not my problem, and I am not bothering the Livingstons to interrupt their time and business. The Fourth Amendment says no unreasonable searches and seizures. Go get a warrant if ya wanna check shit."

Police Inspector-Homicide Detective Lyle Odell turned to Officer Ben Crane, and then he pointed to Josie.

"Can you believe this gum-cracking chick, Crane? She is an expert in police procedures and the constitution. What piss-poor attitudes ya got here in Boston. No wonder everyone roots against ya sports teams."

Officer Crane nodded and said, "I understand, Detective Odell. I root for the New York Rovers myself."

"I knew that I liked you, Crane," Odell said as he then mussed his hair, walked close to the desk, and put his hands on the desk in front of Josie.

"Ya have a New York accent, and ya car has New York license plates on it. Ya, not from Beantown. I suspect you are from Troy or Albany."

Josie stared Odell down with the gum cracking and chewing and out of the side of her mouth, she spit out some words.

"Wrong-o, smart-ass. I am originally from Cohoes, New York. How do you know about my car?"

"I will get to the car in a second. Smart-ass. First . . . your hometown. Cohoes. Oh my, right next to Troy. Okay, I was off by a mile or two, or three. Lookie here, honey. I could go to Boise, Idaho, and ask police-related questions. Massachusetts and New York have some official legal agreements between them, but Crane is here by my special request of his chain of command. I am here simply for voluntary questioning. Investigatory questioning that the Livingstons do not have to answer. No warrant required. Officer Crane is here to make an arrest if someone acts up, and I need to stop them from acting up to solve the crimes. Now, let's negotiate. Your car is a small red sedan with New York-issued vanity license plates. T-S-E-X-Y-J is the plate. Stands for tall, sexy, and the first initial of your name. . .."

Josie cut off Inspector Lyle Odell in mid-speech. She stuck her ample chest out and batted her eyes in a faux manner.

Josie asked, "So, Mr. Famous Police Odell Guy. Do ya think that I am tall and sexy, too? I get all the guys I want. Young, old, and in-between."

Odell jumped right back into the fray.

"Yuppers. I bet ya do, and they get heartache for their pain of ever gettin' involved with you. I think ya a gum-cracking pain in my-ass. Ya act like ya are hot stuff. And ya really gettin' on my nerves. So, let's cut to the chase. Your car has an expired inspection sticker and expired license plate tags. On your front passenger seat are packs of your business cards, but there also is what appears to be a pipe, some rolling papers, and there is a half-smoked blunt in the ashtray, and a little exposed bag of what might be a controlled substance sitting there in plain sight through the car's window. The sprinkles on the ice cream cone are the pack of condoms sitting there like a beacon of sex. Those custom license plates are an advertisement, for sure. Looks as if Josie might . . . how shall I say? Entertain a certain recreational lifestyle? Ya might have been late to work and not put stuff away that spilled outta of ya purse and along came a'wanderin' Odell. Now, since you are a law and constitutional expert, ya already know that rules for private property are tricky."

Odell stopped and waved in the air with both of his hands. He tugged at his sagging pants and pulled them up to his waistline, only to have them sag down once more.

Odell's eyes studied Josie, and then he replaced his hands on her desk and continued to explain his position and negotiation.

"Oh yeah. Technically, the same building manager you want to complain to about his employees would have to agree with Security Officer Blackburn, who seems to like us, and would listen when we told him 'bout your car combined with your suspicious behavior here. He would ask his boss to invite Officer Crane to check out your vehicle. Crane here could go and check it out and bring along Security Officer Blackburn. I am sure they have rules about controlled substances on their private property, as does your own company here. They might consider the vehicle abandoned since the plates and inspection are currently not valid. Expired. Hello, tow truck. Impound yard fees. Cash only deals. Big bucks. And tsk, tsk, illegal stuff inside. When you do iffy things, then iffy things tend to catch up to you, and it is not always a fun time in the old town. I dunno. Odell might be wrong, but I might be right, too. Just negotiating. . .."

Odell stood up, tried to smooth out his hair, and waited for a response from Josie. Officer Crane coughed. Josie stopped chewing gum.

Odell added, "I need ten minutes. Five questions. No more. No less."

Josie reached for the telephone on her desk, and as she did so, she said, "You are something else, Odell."

"Interesting description of Odell. People generally have a lot worse opinion of me. So, I will thank you for that description."

"You are not welcome. I wanted to use the worst description possible, but figured you would dig up something else to pin on me. Have a seat. I will let them know you are here. I will make the call."

Odell turned and pointed to the camera mounted on the wall directly opposite from where they stood.

"Thanks. But they already know we are here. Been watching us the entire time. Ever since you called them when the lobby receptionist sent us up."

Odell peered in closely at the camera and narrowed his eyes.

There was no question that Vance Livingston was Reid Livington's son. They both looked as if some marketing magnates had plucked them out of a men's magazine full of movie stars. Tall, perfectly styled hair, muscular builds and powerful frames, fine watches, fancy rings on their fingers and perfect teeth. Vance's hair was blonde, and his father's hair had now turned white. Otherwise, they seemed to be interchangeable. Even their voices matched.

"Nice to see you again, Inspector Odell. You are looking well. How are you?"

Mr. Reid Livingston met Officer Crane and Lyle Odell as they walked into an exquisite conference room. He held his hand outstretched to shake hands with the police duo.

The conference room had a large white glass table, with high-back black leather chairs lining the perimeter of the table. Spacious windows afforded fabulous and lofty views of the city below; there were walls full of video and sound equipment and large presentation boards. The room boasted an expensive blue and black looped pile carpet, a wet bar, and a snack nook equipped with snacks and bottles of water. As was the case in the main lobby reception area, and the main corridors of the offices for The Back Bay Real Estate Group, there were numerous professional quality displays of artwork displayed on the walls and photography of various properties, facilities, land, and other projects that the company built, developed, or was otherwise involved in. It was an impressive display and testimony of a successful company.

Mr. Vance Livingston rose from his chair at the head of the conference table and nodded and smiled as he watched the scene unfold.

Odell said, "I am fine, except for dead bodies that always seem to pop up in my city. Well, Mr. Livingston, those statements are not true. It is never nice to see me. Especially again. And I am not looking well. I am actually a mess. I need a haircut. My pants won't stay up, and I did not tie my necktie properly. Always remember that exact details and facts are very important in investigations." Detective Lyle Odell waved his hand in the air before accepting the handshake invitation of Mr. Reid Livingston. As they shook hands, Odell said, "Nice joint ya boys have here. Business must be good. By the way, it is Homicide Detective Lyle Odell. Or just plain Odell. That inspector title is some bullshit the city and police brass came up with to keep my old ass around for a few more years. I will leave my business card here on the table. You will note that it still states, I am Homicide Detective Lyle Odell." Odell plucked a business card from the confines of his suit and placed it on the conference room table. He then turned and pointed at Officer Ben Crane and introduced him to the father and son team. "This is Officer Ben Crane of the

Boston Police Department. He is here as a courtesy and just in case something unusual happens."

Now, Vance Livingston joined the group and first he shook Odell's hand and then Officer Crane's hand.

Vance still smiled widely, and when they finished with the greetings, Vance Livingston asked, "So, despite your reluctance to use the title, I must say, Detective Odell, congratulations on your exclusive title. We know of your outstanding career and reputation. I am sure it is well-deserved. How can we help you and Office Crane today? You did not have an appointment. We are quite busy, but out of respect for law enforcement, we carved out some time to meet you both."

Vance smiled widely as he stood next to his father, who also smiled widely, and they both waited for Odell's response.

Detective Lyle Odell became distracted.

He began to pat his suit jacket pockets, and then his pants pockets, then he mussed his hair, tugged at his pants, and finally turned to Office Crane and said, "Crane, I am very bad at taking notes. I used to have help with that aspect of these investigations. Can you help me out with that? I need meticulous notes. It is very important to me."

"Sure thing, Detective Odell," Officer Crane answered. He unbuttoned his uniform chest pockets and pulled out a notepad and a pen.

Odell mumbled, "Thanks," and then pointed at the Livingstons and said, "I must get the contact information for your dentists. The gleam off ya choppers is blinding." Odell clicked his teeth together, then shook his head and added, "Nah. Hopeless for 'em."

Officer Crane chuckled a little at the words and actions of Detective Lyle Odell, but he composed himself rather quickly, realizing that Odell's methods were rather unusual.

"Anyway, yeah, thanks for the compliment, but it is just

bullshit. The world is full of it. We know about the no-appointment thingy. Josie reminded us of it quite a bit. We had to use some awkward but effective negotiating to see ya guys. Thanks for making the time for us. I am investigating a homicide related to the Standard Insurance Company, which now has a fancy headquarters facility and campus in good old Mohawk City. I would like to ask you five questions, and then we will be on our way. No more. No less. Five. Officer Crane, ya wanna give them the legal mumbo-jumbo since this is your home turf?"

Officer Ben Crane held his pen and notepad in his hand, and he waved them a bit while he spoke the legal information to the Livingstons. He was young, but quite competent.

"Sure, Detective Odell. Gentlemen, this is simply a voluntary interrogation. You have the right not to answer any of the questions and the right to only answer with legal representation present. You can remain silent, expand upon your answers, or simply decline to answer them. You are under no obligation. I am here representing the city of Boston, a city within the Commonwealth of Massachusetts. There are reciprocity agreements between New York and Massachusetts law enforcement agencies, and Detective Odell has the power and the right to ask questions. However, any actual arrests or law enforcement would be under my auspices. Do you have any questions?"

Vance Livingston postured his hips and stood up taller as he explained, "I understand. I am an attorney, Officer Crane. We have nothing to hide over an obscure homicide in Mohawk City, New York. Please ask away. I am very familiar with law-enforcement procedures. I worked for the district attorney in the county where Mohawk City is located."

Detective Lyle Odell shook his head and said, "Negative, Livingston. You interned at the D-A. You tried your best to get your best buddy from college off the hook on a manslaughter charge when he was half-in-the-bag and mowed over and killed an innocent bicyclist on a rural road. You did your best by interfering with my official investigation, and the D-A dismissed you from your internship because of your actions. You did not work in law enforcement. You then came to work at your daddy's real estate company. Here. Always remember that exact details and facts are very important in investigations."

Odell's words clearly upset Vance Livingston. As he faced the great detective, his smile vanished, his jaw tightened, and he balled his fists. Reid Livingston's mood also changed, and he jumped into the conversation.

"Okay, that is enough, Detective Odell, with your negative comments about my son. That all happened a long time ago. Let's move on now. How can we help you? I am losing patience with your antics. We are trying to accommodate you, but we are very busy businessmen. We are working on a massive deal today. What homicide are you investigating? It cannot be the untimely and sad passing of Randolph Burgess. Can it? Mr. Burgess had been in ill health for many years and lived an awkward lifestyle. It was even on the news here in Boston."

"Negative on you asking me questions, there, Livingston. And assumptions are what those folks that possess nefarious intentions always count on us to make, and they can be costly diversions. Question number one. Did your real estate group, Back Bay Real Estate Group LLC, sell the land and broker the deal for the Standard Insurance Company to build their new corporate headquarters on at 460 Reservoir Road in Mohawk City, New York?"

Vance held his hand up to his father; his father nodded and waved in the direction of his son and afforded him the floor to answer the questions.

"Yes. Why even ask that question? It is public record, Odell."

Odell turned to Office Crane, who was jotting notes in his notepad, and Odell said, "These guys don't listen very well. I do not answer your questions." He then turned back to face the Livingstons and asked the second question. "Do you know why Mr. Burgess, and the executive management team of Standard Insurance Company would leave a perfectly fine facility and comparable property, and an only seven-year-old complex in Westchester County, New York to relocate and build a new facility in Mohawk City, New York?"

Reid Livingston took this question. His white teeth reappeared.

"We gave them a wonderful deal! The city provided tax breaks and deferred property tax. We removed an old eyesore of an abandoned factory, and brought jobs to the struggling economy of Mohawk City. An urban renewal. We are very proud of this transaction, the improvement, and the redevelopment of the land into a stunning facility."

Odell nodded and said, "I bet ya are. And a whole lot richer, too. Third question. Do you have any close relatives, friends, or associates who currently work for Standard Insurance Company or worked there in the past? If so, their name or names, please."

Mr. Reid Livingston looked over at his son. Reid swallowed hard, and his swallow was visible as it glided down his throat. Odell studied every move of the Livingstons with his intense gray eyes. Vance nodded to his father to indicate that he would answer the question.

"Yes. My cousin, my father's niece, worked as an executive assistant to the CEO. Lily Livingston. She worked for Mr. Burgess. She has since left the position to return to higher education to pursue a new direction in her career."

Detective Lyle Odell dug right into the next question.

"Gotcha. Thanks. The fourth question."

Officer Crane glanced over at Odell and continued to take notes.

"Were you two bananas present on the cruise for the ocean-bound journey of insurance lust, the same cruise on which Mr. Burgess was found dead in his locked cabin on the cruise ship?"

Once again, Vance answered after a nod from his father. Their interaction was silent, but carefully calculated, and both Odell and Officer Crane studied their movements and made note of their moves.

"Yes. Once more, this is all on record. The ship's logbook can confirm this. Why waste our time with these questions? It was a very sad and unfortunate situation to hear of the death of Mr. Burgess. We do a large amount of business with insurance companies. That cruise is an annual business event for us."

Detective Lyle Odell stood silent for a few minutes. He closed his eyes for a few seconds, messed with his hair, and then smoothed it out and asked the final question.

"For an attorney, ya don't pay close attention to words and conversation. I don't answer questions. Stop askin' 'em. I bet you do a lot of business with insurance companies. All kinds of business. Shady or otherwise. One last question. Then you can go back to working on your big deal. I bet it is a good deal, and a good deal more. Are you aware of your already acknowledged cousin and niece, Ms. Lily Livingston, having some intimate knowledge or inside information of a deep, dark secret or secrets of or about Mr. Randolph Burgess, the former, and now, deceased, CEO for the Standard Insurance Company? Secrets that she was privy to in her former position as the CEO's executive assistant and could be useful in a . . . sugar daddy leverage type of situation?"

Upon hearing the final question, Mr. Reid Livingston blew his cork and spouted out his answer.

"No! That is insulting, demeaning, and ludicrous! Ridiculous! That's it, Odell. You are done here. We are done here! We tried to be cordial and cooperative, but now, you have overstepped your boundaries! My goodness, my niece is an outstanding young woman. She is only thirty-three years old and is now in school to pursue a master's degree! To attack a young woman's credibility and integrity is deplorable!"

Vance added as he waved in the air to usher the two police officers out of the conference room, "Yes, done. Out! There is no homicide and no crime here! This is another product of your whiskey-soaked mind! Out!"

Detective Lyle Odell looked down at the hand of Vance Livingston that Vance placed upon Odell's lower forearm to steer Odell out of the conference room. Odell did not speak, but instead, he stared the grip down with his steely gray eyes. Vance realized his error and dropped his grip, but continued to wave in the air to escort them out of the conference room.

"Good choice, Vance. Broken wrists and fingers take a long time to heal. Funny thing, Livingston. I am now sober. Came up with those questions without the intake of any whiskey. Scary stuff. Can you imagine the stuff I can conjure up when I am half-in-the-bag? Please don't answer that question. That would be six questions, and I am a man of my word. Mr. Vance Livingston. Doctor. Lawyer. Detective. Real estate mogul. He is a multi-talented guy. Another funny thing . . . those were some of the words that you told me years ago during your internship. No crime. No homicide. There is no reason to suspect any nefarious intentions. Yet, your buddy is still in jail to this very day. Good day gentlemen. We can find our way out. I am sure Josie will glare and sneer at us, properly. She is a big fan of mine. You can watch us leave all the way to the parking lot on those monitors over there. The same ones you watched our every move on since we arrived. No crimes, no homicides, no nefarious intentions, no intimate or inside information, then no worries. Remember, if ya hang with iffy people, iffy things tend to happen to you. See ya now."

Odell was correct; of course, Josie McDermott gave them both the evil eye on the way out of the offices.

Outside the complex, Officer Ben Crane tore a few pages out of his notepad and handed off his notes to Homicide Detective Lyle Odell.

"Here you go, Odell. Thanks for letting me tag along. Geez, I learned a ton from you. No wonder you are a legend. I am not a detective, but you sure did put those creepers on their heels. Something serious is going on there. The body language. Not to mention the Josie gal and her defense systems. Good luck."

"Thanks, Crane. Yuppers. Something going on. I am quite sure Vance and Josie are an item. Vance is married with some little kiddies, but Josie is the sideline gal. All these big-shot-Blue-Blood-guys have these side wiggles. It is their nature. Thanks for tagging along. You are a good one. I will call your chain of command to thank them for your assistance and to commend your abilities. Gonna request your services and assistance next time. I will see ya when I return for the arrests."

Officer Crane said, "Thank you, Detective Odell! I would love to see these crumbs go down. I appreciate the good word. Especially from a legend like you are. I am bucking for a promotion."

Lyle Odell had turned and began to make his way down the busy city street. Odell heard Officer Crane's words, but he did not turn around when he answered.

"We will get 'em. I promise. Kind of cornered 'em already. Just a matter of time. As far as buckin' for a promotion goes. Be careful of what ya wish for, Crane. Just be careful. It ain't all that it is cracked up to be."

Officer Ben Crane stood and watched Homicide Detective Lyle Odell as he walked away. He rewound through his mind all that occurred during about a one-hour meeting and within the total time spent with Detective Lyle Odell. All he learned in such a short amount of time. It was miraculous.

Officer Crane took a deep breath, and he knew what many others already knew.

Odell was exceptional in his job. He was a legend.

Chapter Four

Flow Charts and Clues

It was Friday evening at 8:00 PM.

The restaurant was on a side street just off the main drag. Downtown Mohawk City, in upstate New York. Tucked in and around the corner, a few storefronts down from the main intersection of First Street and Second Street. This was a restaurant that Odell frequented. He felt comfortable here. The owners and staff of the establishment passed the Odell test. No nefarious intentions or connections.

Lyle Odell was set to enjoy this dinner and this evening and perhaps relax a little, too. He felt the day and the progress on the case went quite well. His visit to Boston achieved the desired results.

Not that he ever fully let his guard down. Never was that the case. Odell was always on the job. Observing. Noticing. Every detail of life and daily comings and goings. It was what he did. The only way that he knew.

So did the owners, because they knew who Odell was and all that he stood for and represented. The owners took good care of Homicide Detective Lyle Odell. Since a dinner engagement many years ago, which was in the same dark corner of this same restaurant and was also with a gorgeous, but a different woman, Odell had become a semi-regular. The owners called their establishment a gastro-pub. Odell asked a few times what that actually meant, and even the owners could not provide an accurate definition. Yet, the food was excellent, and the menu was diverse; it was pricey, but not over the top, and the wine and craft beer lists were extensive and the cocktails top-notch.

Lyle Odell looked over at Doctor Eleanor Burgess when she asked him the question. "Are you going to order an Irish whiskey or just sip that water?"

"Just the water. For now. It is water with a lemon. Exact details. . .."

Doctor Burgess cut Odell off with a smile, a wave of her hands, and as she sipped her martini, she mumbled over the rim of the glass. "Yes, of course. It has only been two days since we met. I know about those! I have had the perfect teacher."

After a long sip, she lowered the glass and leaned in over the table, and smiled at Odell. Of course, she was stunning tonight in appearance as she was the previous evening. Tonight, it was a red dress. Elegant. A delicate gold necklace with a small line of gemstones wandering along the chain that sparkled even beneath the low lights of the restaurant. Diamond earrings. Her layers of cascading auburn hair. The entire package of elegant beauty.

Odell nodded and pointed at her martini and commented. "Speaking of exact details and such. As the detective around here. I should have deduced that you drank Perfect Martinis. Vodka, not gin. When we met at the event, you had the bartender, Lyla, prepare the drinks for you. Your statement was, 'She knows how to mix them for me.' When you ordered the drink tonight was when I first learned that it was a Perfect Martini."

Doctor Burgess leaned in even more over the table. Odell could smell her perfume drifting in his direction.

"Odell. You are fascinating. You really never stop observing and analyzing everything. Why should you have known that I enjoyed Perfect Martinis?"

"Very easy, Eleanor. Simple observations. We can learn much in life simply by keeping our mouths shut and observing things. Last night at the event, when we walked out to the patio to enjoy a smoke, we passed by the lead bartending table with Lyla working the mixes. She glanced at me, then at you, then at your near-empty glass, and then she reached for the bottles. First a vodka bottle, then she searched a bit and plucked out the sweet vermouth and then lined up the dry vermouth right next to it. A great bartender. An observer. She was gathering the ingredients for mixing your next martini. A Perfect Martini. Plus, I must say that my observations are that you are perfect, too. It fits you."

Doctor Eleanor Burgess leaned back in her chair. She almost blushed at the compliment. Suddenly, she turned and waved to their server, who was standing off in the sidelines, trying not to eavesdrop and intrude, but to remain attentive. Odell and Doctor Burgess were still studying the menus and each other and enjoying their first drinks. The server hustled over to the table.

"Yes, Doctor Burgess. How can I help?"

"Please, Lionel. Bring Detective Odell an Irish whiskey. Double pour of Sexton. The bottle cap is distinctive. It has a skeleton wearing a fancy top hat on the cork bottle cap. Please. Pour it neat. And I will have another Perfect Martini. Thank you."

"Right away, Doctor Burgess. Thank you."

Doctor Eleanor Burgess was highly observant and just as sharp as Lyle Odell was. His equal, or maybe even smarter. They made an interesting pair. She could recall his words in exact detail just as Odell could recite her words, too. After all, exact details are very important, and such. . ..

Doctor Eleanor Burgess turned back to Odell. She smiled, folded her hands seductively, and tilted her head as she spoke.

"You just melted my heart, Odell. Your gray eyes in these lights and that messy dark Irish hair are melting my lady parts. No more fooling around with water and lemons. Done. Over. Tonight is our second night together. It means to be a celebration, and damn straight it is going to be one. What are you eating?"

"Lamb chops and the mixed greens with the potato cake. House salad with balsamic dressing. You?"

"The same."

Lionel delivered their drinks and took their orders, and he hustled off to leave them alone once again. Their table was in a little nook in the floor plan, in a far corner of the dining room. Tucked against some dark oak walls, a fireplace was in the center of the room, about eight feet from the edge of the table, and the other tables were not nearby their nook. Not far; but not too close. The setting was private and conducive to romance. Low music played gently on overhead speakers; a selection of nondescript strings within innocuous melodies. Even Inspector Lyle Odell's encyclopedic knowledge of music could not identify any of the songs.

"Odell, please, just ask me the questions that you need to ask," Doctor Burgess stated as she wrapped her fingers around the stem of the martini glass. "Since we arrived and sat here, you have been speaking in halting sentences, your eyes dart all around, you are drumming your fingers on your glass, and you alternate your eyes from my face, to my breasts, to my cocktail. Just ask. You will not ruin the evening by talking business. However, . . . it comes with a price." Doctor Burgess finished speaking. She raised her glass, tilted it over and took a very gentle sip of the mixture. She peered at Odell over the rim of the glass.

Lyle Odell studied her in his mind and thought, 'I find it hard to believe that the light blubs are not exploding in this restaurant from the sparks she emits.'

Lyle Odell piped up, "Yuppers, ya are right. My apologies, but it has been my experience over these many years that the bad guys and gals don't raise their hands and wave in the air and say, here we are! We are criminals! I have questions eating away at me . . . but did not want to spoil our evening together. You are right on, Eleanor. Gonna have to ask them to get them outta my mind or I will continue with the distractive behaviors. Have to ask them, so the price doesn't mean much. Tell me the damages after I ask the questions. Deal?"

"Deal. Down the rest of that whiskey. Lionel is hovering, and he will promptly bring you a fresh drink. I will keep you under wraps. No fear of wandering off into the inebriated wilderness. Which I am working my way to. Regardless of my situation, I will rescue you, and we can always leave your car here, and I can call for the company limousine to drive us back to the loft penthouse. We can have a nightcap there. So, no fear of any law-breaking, Detective Odell."

Odell downed the remainder of his Irish whiskey and, as predicted; Lionel swooped in for the replacement after a nod from Lyle Odell.

"Gotcha. Let's run through them quickly before our meals arrive. Question one, about Ms. Lily Livingston. Please, other than leaving Standard Insurance to pursue her master's degree, did she give any other reason or reasons for leaving?"

Eleanor sipped her new cocktail, then set it back down and pursed her lips a little at the question. Odell noted her behavior. Rather carefully.

"Just that it was terribly upsetting about Randy's passing. She seemed sincerely upset. Lily was very emotional at the funeral. Heartbroken. I appreciated that she gave three weeks of notice. She left copious notes and files for her successor to follow. One thing that I found very ironic was that Lily was originally from Mohawk City, New York. Especially so, once all the moving of the Standard Insurance Company from Westchester in downstate New York to upstate came to fruition. Lily began working for Standard in Westchester and, of course, returned to her home city when the company moved here. Although she now returned to a university in Westchester, which seems a bit odd. Anyway, I had limited dealings with her, but I can tell that she is quite brilliant and is a person who has bridged the chasm. Super-intelligent, charismatic. Well-spoken and dynamic. And of course, as I mentioned last night, she is very beautiful. Shapely. Perfect figure, perfect breasts, perfect smile. Long blonde hair . . . a stunner who I imagine has her pick of the men."

Odell mussed his hair and then attempted to straighten it out.

He took a long sip of the whiskey and then, as Odell set the glass back in place, he said, "Interesting. Thank you. Fantastic information. Question two. Have you ever heard of Mr. Vance Livingston and Reid Livingston of the Back Bay Real Estate Group?"

Eleanor Burgess nodded her head and answered immediately. "Yes. They were the realtors who brokered the deal for the new building and property. Apparently, their family originally owned the land where we constructed the complex. Previously, it was some kind of old abandoned factory that they leveled to build the complex. An improvement for sure. The business might not be my cup of tea, but it sure is a beautiful facility and property. I assisted with the landscape design. Some special plants there. Of course, some of my favorites."

Odell seemed very pleased with Eleanor's answers and testimony. He almost smiled, but almost does not count with Detective Lyle Odell. Only in horseshoes, hand grenades, and atomic bombs.

"Great. This is extremely valuable information, Eleanor. Question three. How about the Emerald Construction Group? Do you know them?"

"Of course, they built the new complex. I worked with them on the landscape designs and plantings."

"Yuppers. Easy one, but I am gonna combine questions

four and five for a two in one. Were you aware that the primary owners of the Emerald Construction Group are Mr. Vance Livingston and Reid Livingston of the Back Bay Real Estate Group? And did you know that Lily Livingston is Reid's niece and Vance's first cousin?"

Eleanor seemed visibly concerned. She took a sip of her cocktail and then set the glass back down on the elegant tablecloth.

"No. I did not know those facts. I should have picked up on the last names. I feel a bit foolish for missing the connection of Lily to the realtors. And she was originally from Mohawk City. The Livingstons owned the land and such. I bet they all are originally from Mohawk City. It sure is becoming a bit entangled. Isn't it?"

Odell nodded and took a gentle sip of his Irish whiskey and, with the glass still in his hand, Odell said, "Please. Don't feel foolish. You said yaself that the business was not high on your happy list. Yuppers. It is getting a bit overlapping and crowded in the potential suspect's room. For sure. Question six. One last question. For now. Old Herbie. Did he run point on the construction projects along with Randolph and anyone else?"

"He did. Along with our CFO, Gerald Palmer, and our facility manager, Lawrence Rinehardt. And of course, Lily handled a ton of paperwork."

Odell sat motionless for a few seconds. He closed his eyes and then, with his right hand, he twirled the whiskey glass around and around and the whiskey swirled in the glass. He opened his eyes, stopped spinning the glass, and set it in place on the tablecloth.

Odell opened his eyes and said, "It just got a lot more crowded in that suspect's room. You should know that today, early this morning, I left Mohawk City, and I drove to Boston and met with the two Livingston clowns. There, I set the table for a little uneasiness. I also went to my chain of command and briefed them on the case and the fact that

I feel this is a tricky one, but that your brother is potentially a murder victim. Died in United States waters, but technically it is outside of my jurisdiction, but your company is located here. And I think there are plenty of nefarious dealings within your company that led to the homicide. Once I get to a certain point, then I will contact the proper jurisdiction for the final murder summation, but that is a few days away yet. That is e'nuff for now. Done. Are you ready to eat?"

Doctor Burgess seemed even more impressed with Detective Lyle Odell and his relentless pursuit of justice.

"I am ready to eat. I am hungry. Yes. My goodness. Those were intriguing questions. But it is obvious from the amount of research that you do. When do you sleep? You seem to have endless energy, Odell. I am becoming accustomed to your ways. I originally did not share your view that there was something evil here, but now I am beginning to see why you are probing so deeply. It is becoming quite complex. I do admit that the one aspect of this that did bother me was the building of the new complex here in Mohawk City. I agree with your gut feelings, too. It all happened so quickly too. The deal, I mean. Why move from a newer and amazing campus in Westchester to Mohawk City? No offense, but aside from a very select few parts of this old city, it is largely a crime-infested dump. Simple as that. It makes little to no sense. Oh! Look! Here comes our food."

Lionel appeared with an assistant, and he delivered the food with elegance and made sure of the settings and presentations. He recognized the importance of his guests tonight and was working hard to earn a maximum gratuity.

Doctor Burgess continued to alternate between thanking Lionel and his assistant and speaking with Homicide Detective Lyle Odell.

"It looks lovely. Perfect. Thank you, Lionel. I can't wait

to try the food."

Once Lionel and his assistant left the area of the table, Doctor Burgess poised with her fork in her hand and leaned in toward Odell and asked, "So, do you want to hear what you owe me for asking those six questions?"

"Sure. Give me the damage. I made a deal."

Doctor Burgess lingered. She took a sip of her cocktail and stared Odell down. "Well, you are going to owe me six more dinner dates. Or three dinner dates and three lunch dates with my new friend. This place is wonderful, so it works for me, and it works for you. If not here, then anywhere. As long as it is you and me together."

Odell nodded, picked up his fork, and just before he dug into his dinner, he added, "Seven questions. I actually asked you seven questions. Usually, about three hours a night. On average. I still adhere to the old military ways. Sleep when you can. Eat when you can. I sleep while sitting in my chair listening to the local classical music station on my old table radio."

Detective Lyle Odell then dove into his meal by trying the potato cake first. He stuck a slice in his mouth and nodded his head, all while Doctor Burgess carefully watched him and backtracked the questions in her mind. She smiled as Odell swallowed. It was obvious that he was enjoying it.

Odell announced, "That sucker is superb. That potato cake is amazing."

Eleanor rewound the questions in her mind. She smiled as recalled them. She made the connection.

"Yes, seven questions. Classical music. I never would have imagined that you are a classical music fan, but I am not overly surprised by that fact. Three hours of sleep on average. Sleeping in your easy chair. I am a little surprised at your serving in the military. Mostly because you don't look and act stuffy and military. What branch did you serve in? What was your duty or job or whatever they call it? M-O-S? A billet?"

"The Coast Guard. Yes, a billet works. I did investigations. I don't look like it. I did once. Not now. The booze, the blood, the crime and the lifestyle, and the cigarettes made me messy."

"I understand. Investigations. That makes sense, Odell. So yes, back to the seven questions. There were seven questions. You asked me if I was ready to eat. That was the seventh question. Therefore, I get to add one more payback duty."

Odell waved his fork in her direction as he now dug into the lamb chops.

"I am sorry for digging in here. This food is wonderful. I am kind of hungry. No lunch. Long drive to Boston and back. Only had a cup of Joe with George early this morning."

"It is fine, Odell. You should not go all day without eating, but I must say that I am happy to see you enjoying yourself."

"Oh good, Eleanor. Yeah. Sure. Go ahead, Doc, and give me my final marching order."

Doctor Burgess answered right away, and her tone was serious. She was too brilliant not to sense the same things that Detective Lyle Odell sensed.

"Please protect me from whatever it is that is happening, Odell. I am unsure and unsteady and just want this to be over."

In reciprocation, Odell responded immediately.

"Yuppers. I gotcha. I am going to have to escort you home and hang around with you for a bit. I am uncomfortable right now with leaving you alone. I need time to think and digest some of what I know, and it is not worth risking leaving you alone until I have a better handle on what is happening. It might be getting dicey and dangerous. I am getting a feeling now, and I do not like it one bit. I will sleep on the sofa or in a chair or in the spare bedroom. If there is one. Don't need much in the way of fancy accommodations."

Eleanor stared long and hard at Detective Lyle Odell as his words and the situation sank in. She knew that she was in good hands. She did not want to dwell too long within the seriousness of a mood; therefore, she lightened the mood once more. It was worth testing the waters, even if she knew beforehand what Odell's answer would be. Odell was worth testing the waters for. Doctor Burgess took a bite of her potato cake, and she chewed and enjoyed it. After a swallow of the food and a sip of her drink. Eleanor jumped into those same waters.

"Odell, you do not have to sleep on the sofa, or in a chair, or in the spare bedroom. About that lust you mentioned last night. The lust part that you assured me you could handle. . .."

Odell intently studied her as her voice trailed off.

Eleanor continued to swim in the waters with her words.

"I have a nice warm bed that we could share and explore and enjoy. I can only dream of how glorious that would be."

Odell downed the remainder of his Irish whiskey. Temptations stared him in the face. Doctor Eleanor Burgess was stunning, and brilliant, and what every man could ever dream of in a woman. And she was offering up something that took fortitude and effort and commitment to honor in order to refuse.

"As much as that does sound glorious, the sofa will work out fine. I am on a mission. Friends for now?"

"Sure. Friends for now. What else do you need?" She asked as her voice grew husky and Odell's pulse pounded. And a few other parts and pieces pounded, too.

"Another whiskey. A double, to wash out the words that I just spoke from out of my mind. . .."

Doctor Eleanor Burgess woke up. Her arm reached over to the other side of the bed, and smiling while recalling the glory of the entire evening. In her half-sleep and half-awake state, she felt for the presence of Homicide Detective Lyle Odell. Her smile quickly faded. Odell was not there. That was all just a dream. Odell took the chair in the living room. True to his word. To his honor. He had to protect her. But he did want to be friends, and that was a start. Friends to lovers was the theme in her dream. What a dream it was! Suddenly, the bed grew cold. She glanced at the clock next to the bed. Two-twenty-five in the morning.

"Where is he?"

She asked in her sleepy stupor. Remotely, in a far off-land-of-scents, and in her senses, she could smell the whiff of coffee in the air. And faintly in the distance, she could hear soft music.

While she swung her legs over the edge of the bed, stood up, picked her robe off the post of the bed, and dressed in the robe, Doctor Burgess mumbled aloud, "What is Odell up to? There is no question that his mind is at a genius-level. But my goodness, what kind of man have I fallen in love with here?"

Eleanor Burgess softly padded down the winding steps and staircase from the loft to the main living area of the penthouse apartment she lived in. The lights were set in a dim setting; however, through the low lights, she could make out the figure of Detective Lyle Odell, sitting at the dining table in the dining room, a cup of piping hot coffee sitting on the table in front of him; while he was conducting in perfect time to the music playing on the music system overhead in the apartment.

In his peripheral vision, Odell knew that Doctor Eleanor Burgess was there; she was present; yet Lyle Odell did not even look up at her as his arms and hands and his fingers waved in perfect time. Odell was wearing a Mohawk City

Polcie Department tee shirt with the logo of his badge emblazoned on the front of it. He slung his shoulder holster over his right shoulder with his service weapon neatly tucked inside of it. Odell was barefooted, but he wore a pair of Mohawk City Police Department sweatpants. A bent, unlit cigarette hung from his lower lip. It pointed in three directions. While he conducted with his air baton, Odell spoke. The bent cigarette clung to his lower lip, and it danced with his words.

"Modest Mussorgsky. Wonderful. Piano piece. Ten movements. Pictures at an Exhibition. Promenade. Recurring theme. I played the music very softly. I hope it did not wake you."

Eleanor nodded, and she pulled out a chair from the table and sat and watched Odell.

Doctor Burgess replied, "No, no. The music is fine. Usually, I wake up around this time of the morning anyway. Then drift back to sleep. I know the entire work," Eleanor said. "This piece is one of my favorites. Catacombs. The Roman Tomb."

Lyle Odell stopped conducting. He plucked the unlit cigarette out of his mouth and carefully set it aside on a napkin next to his coffee cup and said, "Yuppers. Catacombae. Sepulcrum romanum. Do you want a cup of coffee? I will go and pour it for you."

"Sure, Odell. I have a feeling you are not going back to sleep. Even if you slept at all. I prefer tea, but after last night and not sleeping very much—coffee will work. You never cease to amaze me, Odell. I knew when you mentioned it at dinner that you enjoyed classical music, but I must say that I pictured you as more of a classic rock kind of guy. Second, that you speak Latin, too."

Odell nodded and stood up to make his way to the kitchen to pour the coffee. "Tea, huh? Yes, we will get to the subject of music. Black coffee?"

"Yes. Black is fine. Thank you."

Detective Lyle Odell was off to the kitchen. Eleanor sat half-asleep at the table. Now that Lyle Odell was off working on fetching her a cup of coffee, she noticed that in front of where Odell sat, on the table's surface, were various pages of paper. On some of the papers, Lyle Odell had written copious notes, and the other papers had block diagrams with interconnecting lines drawn on them. All in pencil. Next to the papers were his coffee mug and a small notepad with a special cover and binding. It was not unlike the pads that Doctor Burgess used in the field during her student's field trips to growing and proving gardens and plant trials for horticulture and botany studies. Heavy-duty papers and covers and water and weatherproof.

Odell returned and set the mug of coffee in front of Doctor Burgess and said, "Here you go. I do like classic rock. At times. Dance to classic rock. Relax to classical music. I enjoy classical concerts and selections at night. As I mentioned, I enjoy listening to my old table radio next to my chair. The Saturday night concerts are my favorite. Had that radio forever. It was my father's radio. Still uses vacuum tubes. It doubles as a heater. Works like a charm. Just because something is newer doesn't mean it's better."

"I see. An old table radio with vacuum tubes. A family heirloom and a memory, too. That is so Odell-like. There are more layers to Detective Lyle Odell than there are to an onion. Thank you for the coffee." Doctor Burgess took a sip of the coffee, then she pointed at the notes on the papers and the pad there on the table. "What are you doing here? Aside from conducting Mussorgsky. That is a very neat pad there. I like it. Used a pad like that in the field for my botany notes."

Odell picked the pad up and ran his hand over the cover. Doctor Burgess used a remote-control hand unit to lower the volume on the music system to hear Odell better. It now was just some soft background music. Barely discernible.

He explained, "It is a tactical pad. For years and years, I had assistance in making notes on my investigations and cases. Now, I am on my own. So be it. I am making notes and flow charts and such of the complexities of this case. Then, I will transfer the notes from my papers to this tactical pad so I can quickly reference them in the field. Too many suspects and people involved in this case. I had to make it analog to sort it all out. Slide ya beautiful mind and the rest of ya over here and let me show you. I need your input. Have to see if this all makes sense here."

Doctor Burgess picked her coffee up and walked around the table. She slid into a chair next to Odell, so close that their bodies were touching. She leaned in as the great detective began to dissect his notes. Suddenly, Doctor Eleanor Burgess was wide awake. It was a combination of the coffee intake as well as the invitation to jump into the fascinating world of Homicide Detective Lyle Odell.

"It is quite a cast of characters we have here. First, we have the owners of the Back Bay Real Estate Group. You know of them. We have Reid Livingston and his son Vance. Vance is a little no-good punk. Smart-ass attorney. Not a good man. We have run into each other before. He is evil and untrustworthy. His father, Reid, is evil, but not as evil as his punk son is. But still has nefarious intentions. Reid is a widower. Vance is married with two little kiddies, but he has a sideline chick. I had the unpleasant experience of meeting her. She is a gem. Honestly, the move to the new facility bothered me as did your half-sibling's death, but when I first dug in and found out that the Livingston's had brokered the sale and then the construction company is their company, I really felt as if there were some nefarious intentions going on here."

Odell looked over at Eleanor, and he took a sip of his coffee while he was observing her reactions.

Eleanor said, "I do know the names, but might not be able to place all the faces exactly with the names. We had a grand opening dinner and celebration for the headquarters. Since they were all involved in the sale, the transactions, and the construction, then I am quite sure that most of these folks were there. I think. I tried not to pay much attention. Fled the dinner as soon as I could to come up here and hide in this penthouse."

Odell nodded and continued to point at his chart. "Gotcha." Odell picked up the bent cigarette from the napkin and stuck it back in his mouth and mumbled, "Just have to taste it." He then took his pencil and pointed at his flowchart. Eleanor continued to sip her coffee and study along with Odell. "Then follow this line here. We have Art Livingston. Reid's brother. He is a muckety-muck executive at Emerald Construction Group. Some kind of big shot, but he is actually a little pistol. Hides behind his brother and becomes a money bully. Art is Lily's father. He is evil. We put him on the evil list."

"Really? How do you know that, Odell?"

"I can feel it. Because these Livingston guys are all evil bums. I should have color-coded all the evil bastards with colors to make them easier to spot. Then, we follow this line down to the former executive assistant to your half-brother. We will return to Lily Livingston."

"Okay, but why?"

Odell twirled the bent cigarette in his mouth and leaned into Eleanor and studied her eyes. She studied them back. Lyle Odell replaced the cigarette on his lower lip and continued to go over his charts and notes.

"Because I have to ask you some difficult questions. Could be kinda painful for ya. For now, let's go back up to here on the flowchart. We have Mr. Gerald Palmer. The chief financial officer for Standard Insurance Company. I need to dig into him some more. I have not had the time yet. I am very interested in Palmer because he was a key player in the construction project. Money man. Potential string puller. Potential for cooking books. Access to money taints people. Then we have the facility manager for Standard Insurance Company, Mr. Lawrence Rinehardt. I am only interested in what he might know about the construction project and the two big chiefs. Herbie and Palmer. I doubt he is evil. Then, the cream of the crop is Old Herbie. Ditto for not having time to dig in on him, but my attorney's radar is way up. I want to reserve the proper moment to interview him. Need just a little more background on him before I do that. From your testimony of how nicey-kins and loyal he is and the pictures of the family on the walls and the happiness and such, well, I know he is a key to this case. Maybe the brains, or certainly one of the managers of the evil plans. Of course, I also want to speak to him because he was on the cruise. As I want to speak with Lily, too."

Eleanor put her arm around Odell as she carefully studied the lines, names, and the chart.

She commented, "Odell, this is all very fascinating. How did you find out all this information? My goodness. It is very intense."

"Research, baby. Research. You know about research. Plants don't talk to you about themselves."

"Ha! You do have a glorious way of expressing yourself and being direct, Detective Odell. In fact, you have many glorious ways."

After speaking, Eleanor leaned in and gently pulled him closer to her with her arm. His warmth felt wonderful. Odell continued to explain. Yet, he was not going to comment on the duality of her statement, or reciprocate the romantic move; he was obsessed with sorting this out, and bouncing ideas and thoughts off Doctor Burgess. Not only to bring her up to speed on the complexity of the case, but to help sort it out in his mind, too.

"Then over here on the chart, we have the muscles and the connivers. The evil soul suckers. Jack McDermott. Retired. United States Army Ranger. Sniper. Made Master

Sergeant in rank. Combat time. He works for Emerald Construction as a construction foreman, but he actually is the strong man, the enforcer, and the weapons man. Roughs up the contractors and others who do not pay up and play nicey-nice. Hot-headed bum. Arrested multiple times for drunken barroom brawls, drug possession, and roughing people up both on and off the job. He is evil. Divorced. One daughter. She stayed with Daddy because she is evil, too. Josie. Beautiful gal. Tall, sexy, loose as a goose. Big breasts, big attitude. Various drug habits. Vance got her off with a hand slap for some driving under the influence and a bunch of other charges in Massachusetts. That is the chick that I mentioned who is shacking up with Vance Livingston."

"My goodness," Eleanor said, as she leaned back in her chair and downed the remainder of her coffee. "Quite a bunch. I know of that Jack McDermott character's antics. At least, I think that I do. At the aforementioned grand opening celebration, he introduced himself to me as an executive with the construction company. I could tell from his face and hands that he was hardly an executive. Now, I realize that he was a construction foreman on the project. He was an awful mess. Drunk off his heels and out of his mind. An incorrigible man. Large man. Slimy. Made many very inappropriate sexual advances to me right in front of our guests. Commented on my body and what he wanted to do to me. In fact, now that I recall, I am quite sure that I met most of these characters."

Odell perked up at the report of McDermott's actions and antics.

"Great observations. Exact details are so important in investigations. I might have said that a few times already. Your keen mind from your work provides you with fantastic observation skills. So important. By chance, was Old Herbie there? Or any of these other characters? If so, what did he or they do when bum came onto you?" Odell asked.

Doctor Eleanor Burgess waved in the air and shook her head in a display of some disgust at the recollection of the incident.

"Herbert was there. As was Gerald Palmer. They did nothing. Did not say a word. They just laughed it off. But do know who did reprimand him and force an apology? Drunken apology as it might have been?"

Odell's eyes went to his list and then back to Eleanor's face as she waited for Odell's guess or his answer. Knowing Lyle Odell, it would be an answer. Guessing was not in his repertoire.

Odell's answer arrived within seconds of pondering.

"Lawrence Rinehardt. The facility manager. He most likely worked closely with McDermott during the construction project and knows what a jerk he is. Okay, Lawrence is a good guy, and he gets a good-guy label. He can provide valuable insights. I just jumped him up a few notches on my interview list."

Eleanor's face lit up, and she beamed at Odell's answer and the testimony of his genius.

"Exactly. He might be one of the few good guys on your list, Odell. Lawrence is a large man. Rather imposing, too. He set the drunken fool on his ass with his words and presence. Jack apologized, but it was an awful apology. Simple, mindless, and drunken ramblings. Shortly after that, I left the party. Came here and relaxed and listened to music. My goodness, Odell. This *is* complex. Unreal how you dug all this up. Countless hours. No wonder you are such a driven man. I need a refill of coffee. Do you want to smoke that facsimile of a cigarette? I will take one too. Hopefully, one that you have not sat on, mutilated, or otherwise destroyed in some manner. We can go out on the balcony and smoke with refills of coffee to drown the smoke down."

"Sure. We have poor odds of finding a quality cigarette,

though. It is chilly out there. Let me get my hoodie sweatshirt. Do you want something heavier to go on over that robe?"

"No. I was actually thinking of romance and the two of us kissing in the moonlight on the balcony."

"Yeah, well, down the road with those thoughts. Hold 'em for later. Right now, it is more like smoking in the cool morning air and me asking ya a few more questions related to this case."

"And here, I thought you were a covert romantic, Odell."

"I am. That is romantic. For me, at least. But since exact details are very important in investigations, ya outta luck. There is no moonlight tonight."

Doctor Burgess smiled and laughed a bit at the preciseness of Lyle Odell.

She then added, "I enjoy the balcony. I do not smoke much these days, but I do enjoy a smoke out there and a cup of coffee early. To start my day. Most every morning around nine-thirty. I like to sleep in late. After all, I am the CEO."

Lyle Odell's face and demeanor changed, and he narrowed his eyes as Eleanor studied his reactions.

Eleanor asked, "Is that an issue? You seemed to react adversely to that fact."

"Every day? I mean, you go out there as part of your normal everyday routine?"

Now, even though they had shared many things over a short few days; friendship, perhaps budding love and potential romance, stress, fear, words, and intellect, Doctor Burgess was still learning the nuances of Lyle Odell and how he dwelled upon every word that a person said, digested it, and either tossed it aside or retained it. This statement he retained. It bothered him; his narrowed eyes displayed his concern over such a simple thing that Eleanor did as part of her early morning routine.

"Yes. I guess. Pretty much. Why, Odell? Should I not do that? I mean, I don't smoke much these days. But it is an enjoyable way to start the day."

"I gotcha. Smoking is something that I have greatly reduced myself. Have ya ever mentioned that routine to anyone? Daily patterns are something that we investigators track. The bad guys and gals track, too."

Doctor Burgess nodded and thought about the questions for a few seconds before answering.

"I might have mentioned it in small talk to co-workers. Not sure."

"To who? Legal team? Old Herbie? The CFO guy? The head lawyer guy? The mailroom attendant? Head of security?"

Homicide Detective Lyle Odell drilled down into the small details, and now, he was intensely grilling Doctor Burgess.

"Honestly, Odell, I cannot recall. I know you say how important exact details are and such in any investigation. I am sorry not to provide an exact answer. It seemed like such a trivial item. Small talk. Yes, I might have mentioned it to many people."

Odell nodded, and he perked up a bit. He shifted gears quickly.

"Okay. No, sorry. Ever. It is trivial information but very valuable, too. Time for a smoke. Be right back. Lemme grab my hoodie."

The early-morning air was magnificent.

Eleanor leaned into the cigarette as Odell used his lighter, and she took a long drag, and blew the smoke up into the air. Then she plucked the cigarette out of her mouth, held it in the air, and studied it in the low lights of the balcony and against the darkened sky.

"What do you do to these cigarettes to make them point in three directions at once? They make me cross-eyed as I study the tip?"

"Not sure," Odell answered as he held his own cigarette with invisible "Odell-glue," onto his lower lip. "I think I sit on them because I lose track of where they are on my body. I am going to make a temporary upgrade to my attire for this case. Shortly."

Detective Odell was studying his tactical notepad that he had transcribed his notes to. Obviously, Odell was preparing to bring his notes into the field. Now that he was flying solo, his usual companions, who always took notes for him, were a thing of the past. Inspector Lyle Odell had shifted gears and reinvented his methodology and his operations.

As Doctor Burgess studied Odell, she said, "Go ahead and ask away, Odell. I will not charge you any more demands and dates."

Odell mussed his hand, took a long drag on the cigarette, and then he placed his coffee mug on a table on the balcony so he could flip through the pages of his notepad. The balcony, as was the rest of the living space, both indoors and outdoors, dominated by plants of all types. As a person would expect of any living quarters occupied by Doctor Eleanor Burgess. Detective Odell noticed a plant sitting on the table, then he pointed at the plants and studied a few of them arranged accordingly on the balcony.

He mumbled a bit and said, "All hardy plants. Frost is not an issue."

Doctor Burgess nodded and smiled at his statement. She was not at all surprised by Odell's knowledge of plants and his correct identification of them.

"Okay, Doc. Yuppers. Here we go. Please. Tell me more 'bout your half-brother's death. The circumstances and what you experienced."

Doctor Burgess took a deep breath and began to relay her experiences. Stress lined her beautiful face.

"Well, Odell. I did bounce back and forth between New

York and California, assisting where I could when Randy had health issues. As of the date for the cruise, he seemed improved as far as heath-wise went. I had recently returned to California when I received an early morning phone call that he had passed. The doctor on board the cruise ship called me first. Then the chaplain onboard called me with a heart-felt condolence. Then, of course, I heard from Lily and Herbert. Not too much to tell. I'll do my best to recall everything. Randy did not report to the breakfast table. There was no response to knocks at the cabin door, nor via his phone in the room, or his cellphone. The head of security and the captain of the ship authorized maintenance to use the master key and unlock the door. They found him in the bed there . . . alone. The doctor checked Randy and declared him dead. The head of security checked, but it seemed cut and dry; especially after Lily and Herbert mentioned the multiple heart attacks, and the doctor saw the medications that Randy took for his heart conditions. There were many pills. . .."

Doctor Burgess stopped speaking. She blinked a few times, looked at Odell, who intently studied her and with his eyes, he begged her to finish the painful experience. Eleanor was intuitive of his coaching. Despite how painful the conversation was for her to get through, Doctor Burgess knew that every piece of information was vital to Lyle Odell as he pieced together the facts in his mind.

Eleanor continued to speak.

"Apparently, from the medical examination, the doctor could easily conclude it was a heart attack as the cause of death . . . the body was blue and the fingertips and such."

Eleanor swallowed hard and said, "It was readily apparent. And since the head of security on the cruise ship saw no reason to factor in any foul play, they declared Randy dead of a massive heart attack. I caught the first plane to New York City. The cruise was almost ending anyway, and the ship was heading back to home port in lower Manhattan. I met the ship there when it made port and escorted the body with the funeral director and his staff. Even before I left California, I made all the arrangements for a funeral. We buried my half-brother in the family plot in a cemetery in Westchester County."

"How many days out-of-home port were they when he passed? I recognize the decision to get back into home port. Dying overseas and bringing a body back is hell on paperwork wheels."

"About three days."

"Gotcha. Most, if not all, cruise ships and ocean-going vessels must have provisions for body preservation and body bags and such. Just the way it is. Sorry to say it this way, but they put him on ice. Rather crude of me, but that might be a vital factor down the road here. Sorry, Eleanor. . . ."

Doctor Eleanor Burgess nodded and fought back tears, but she managed to say, "No sorry needed, Odell. I understand the facts are the facts. Human biology and plant biology have many cohesive similarities. I understand the biology very keenly. It is not crude. It is factual, and simply stated in a very blunt Lyle Odell manner. You tend not to sugarcoat anything."

Odell nodded and said, "Thank you. No autopsy. Understandable. Nothing to suspect. Direct burial or cremation?"

"Direct burial. No cremation, Odell."

"Let's shift gears, Eleanor. I know all this bullshit, and the array of questions is painful. I assure ya that it is vital information. You told me when we first met that you really wanted nothing to do with being the owner and the CEO of Standard Insurance Company. What is your plan then? I mean, for a CEO, if you do not want the position."

"Technically, I have made it very clear behind the scenes to those in power that I am the acting CEO due to the death of my half-brother. He was the owner, president, and CEO.

I guess that makes me the same. I am planning to work with Herbert and the rest of the legal team. We would hire one of those expensive executive search companies out of New York City to find a new CEO. I would bring the candidates to the newly reorganized board of directors, but with the majority shares of the corporation, and me being the current CEO, owner, and president and such, I would have to say that I would have the most influence over who receives the position. I plan to pay her or him an extraordinary amount of money and write a multi-year contract and then go back to teaching and forget all about this mess. I would keep my stock and my owner title. As I mentioned to you, Odell, I do not need or even care about money. It means very little to me. My career and life are teaching and research. It made me very happy and earned me a wonderful salary and a solid retirement. The only thing that I will miss is this penthouse apartment. Now, it has even better memories associated with it. Since you arrived."

Eleanor gave Odell a little seductive wink after the statement.

"Gotcha. Ya still would be the big cheese in a roundabout way."

Lyle Odell picked up his coffee, took a sip, and then set it back on the table. The burning cigarette continued its precarious dangle on the cliff known as Odell's lower lip. After a brief pause, a drag on the cigarette and then blowing smoke up in the morning air, Odell then spoke once again.

"I understand your plan. I am a little puzzled, though. Why would your half-brother leave the company to you? What is the status of the company? An S corporation? He knew that you had zero interest in the company. It seems as if he would have planned for a succession. Especially so knowing that his health was not too swift. Maybe involving you monetarily but not dragging you into something that you did not enjoy. I know you said most of your family is deceased and you only have some distant cousins. You certainly are the next of kin in that case. You are blood-relatives. I don't get it, unless for one reason. I fired off too many questions there, Eleanor. I apologize. Please, just answer as ya want to."

Doctor Burgess took a deep breath. She shook her head a little and then answered.

"I lost track of some of those questions. Let me answer the status question first. It is an S-corporation. Technically, the full name is the Standard Insurance Company—a Burgess Corporation. Then we have the subsidiaries and the foundation. We are not a huge mega-corporation. Just the little mouse that roars sort of thing. I own the majority of the shares at fifty-five percent. Which is what Randy left to me. Herbert has some, and so does Mr. Palmer. The rest of the shareholders, I do not know. Let me think about the other questions."

Lyle Odell took the remainder of the cigarette out of his mouth, waved it in the direction of Doctor Burgess, and then, in two long drags, he finished the smoke. Odell ground out the cigarette in an ashtray that sat on the end table.

He then picked up his coffee mug and added, "As I said, I fired off a ton of questions at you. That was an abrupt way of asking 'em. Let me be a little gentler. I feel as if I am beating, ya up. Please take your time, Eleanor."

Eleanor smiled and winked. The pressure on her eased. She said with some allure in her voice before shifting gears to a more serious tone. She finished the cigarette and ground it out in the ashtray.

"You can beat me up anytime or any way that you want, Odell. I don't know why Randy did what he did and did not have a succession plan in place. We never discussed it. I guess because of my lack of interest. I just assumed that my half-brother would have a plan. Our father did. He knew of my lack of interest, so Randy was the successor. Our grandfather on our father's side started the business. He grew it into an empire. After some investors realized the potential and our grandfather's business genius, they pumped some major money in and took it all the way to the success that it is today. It is still a small company in structure and size, almost family-owned in a way, but very successful. It is sitting on piles of cash. Incredible amounts. What began as a small insurance brokerage downstate in Westchester for mostly renter and homeowner's insurance grew into this present-day company. All types of insurance now, but mostly commercial property and liability insurance."

Odell nodded and waved with his coffee mug in the direction of Eleanor. She was familiar with his pre-questions actions by now.

"Need to interrupt ya for a question. When you say a pile of dough. How much dough ya guys sitting on in the vaults?"

"About seven-hundred-million dollars or so. The salaries for the executives are all very high. Above four-hundred-thousand per year. Plus, bonus opportunities. It is all extremely lucrative. Randy was a business genius. As were our father and grandfather."

Odell seemed shocked. He placed his coffee mug on the table and mussed his hair a little and then looked at Doctor Burgess and said, "Holy bananas. Ya guys don't pay out many claims, huh? No wonder the evil bastards are circling like buzzards over roadkill and wiping out the hierarchy and figuring out how to take over the joint. Okay, great information. Please pick up where ya left off. Sorry for the sideline."

Eleanor studied Odell and asked, "Please. Can I have another destroyed and bent cigarette?"

"Sure, Doc. I will pick out the best one of the worst ones for ya."

Odell poked around, found a cigarette, and handed it off, lit it for Eleanor, and after the first drag, Doctor Burgess continued to explain where she previously left off in her explanations.

"So. Where was I? Yes, structure and shares. Relatives. Family. After Randy passed, those cousins received some small shares and some money. We were not close to them. No one other than them left as far as family goes."

"Gotcha. How 'bout you? Relatives on your mother's side?"

"None to speak of. Second and third cousins. My mother's family is very small."

Odell nodded and asked, "Tell me more 'bout the will and ya taking over this joint."

"Odell, as I said, I do not know why Randy did what he did. He did know that I was not interested in the business. He changed his will about two weeks before he passed. He never said a word to me about the change or why he did it. Not a word. The will stated that I must be the CEO, the owner, and the president. I nearly fell on the floor at the reading of his will by his personal attorney."

Odell downed the coffee, and he did so quickly and somewhat violently. Eleanor finished her cigarette, and she, too, ground it out in the same ashtray. She now held her coffee mug with two hands but did not drink any of the coffee. Instead, she fingered the handle of the mug and studied Inspector Lyle Odell. She sensed that his reaction to her testimony had struck a nerve with Odell.

"Let me guess. Everyone thought that the content of the original will and testament had Old Herbie originally receiving some additional shares of the company and then receiving a promotion to the CEO position. You were to be the silent owner, but have the majority of the shares. Not involved in day-to-day operations. So, you can control what you need to control. Or even sell it all off."

"Correct, Odell. Of course, you are correct. That was the

thought. In retrospect, I am not sure many of them knew that I even existed until Randy took ill. Even after I showed up to help my brother, not too many people even knew who I was. I did not mingle."

"This is a vital key, Eleanor. A huge key factor in this case. Thank you so much for sharing. It is imperative that I drill down into this. I think this is another key factor in why you feel so uneasy about this situation. A turning point." Odell grew intense and excited, and Doctor Burgess stood on her heels a bit while absorbing his emotions. Suddenly, Homicide Detective Lyle Odell seemed concerned about this, as he called it, "key factor." His eyes darted around, and then they went from Eleanor to checking the property below the balcony. He narrowed his eyes and stared off into the pitch-black darkness.

"Yuppers. Evil bullshit. It is all here. Ability, opportunity, and intent. The three deadly sins for detective's investigations. These clowns have the ability with gobs of money in their bank accounts, and evil business maneuvering and positioning. They have the opportunity with the inside scoop and insiders within your company, and I suspect some serious blackmail and leverage on your half-brother because of his perceived missteps. They have intent. Takeover the company, pocket the mountains of dough and then sell it all off and ride into the sunset even wealthier than they are now. Obviously, your late half-brother knew something ominous was happening. Sitting on piles of cash. Something happened to him and the evil plan and mayhem caught him up in a mess with no way out. He feared for you, the company, the future, and for his own safety. And this is what makes you so uneasy. This strange and sudden change by your late half-sibling has your senses on alert. You are too utterly brilliant to not be aware that something horrible happened. Now ya need help in understanding why this happened and why it did so."

Doctor Eleanor Burgess swallowed hard. So hard that even in the dim light on the balcony, Lyle Odell could watch and trace the swallow along the length of her elegant neck. She looked down at the coffee mug, decided she did not want the rest of the drink, and set it on the end table.

"Odell, for so many reasons, I am so glad you are here. In my life. Invading my soul."

Odell nodded, and he, too, felt her emotions. He wanted to move quickly in his questions, but his sensitivity to Eleanor's vulnerabilities made him send some love and kindness in her direction. Homicide Detective Lyle Odell was many things, but the one trait he had that he honed over years and years of dealing with people, both evil and good, was being in touch with their emotions. To see within their minds and their souls.

"I gotcha, Eleanor. C'mon over here. Ya shaking. Trembling."

She dove into his arms. Odell could feel her tears on his neck. In between struggles of tears, Eleanor Burgess managed to spit out some words.

"You are right. Something awful happened here. Please help me. Solve this. Protect me."

"I will. I have this now. Just a few more questions. But first, ya also must know that you might own fifty-five percent of the shares, but the other majority owners of your company are a conglomerate of the Livingston family. I did my homework on these clowns. Vance, Reid, and Art Livingston bought up about thirty-eight percent of Standard Insurance Company shares from other private shareholders in side deals. They wanted this company, and they had something on Randolph Burgess that he was not going to give up or give in quite yet. They want to take over, get their hands on that pile of cash, and you are in their way."

"I did not know that, nor would I pay attention to that bullshit. I have zero interest. The Livingston family. Rich and powerful. I am not surprised they are buying up shares of stock. Even less surprised when your flowchart of the cast of characters explained their involvements. My plan was to leave it to Herbert to handle. Now, everything points to a behind-the-scenes conspiracy."

"Old Herbie, huh?" Odell set his feet. He mussed with his hair and out of the side of his mouth he asked. "He keeps popping up more and more in this case. Ya gotta remember in these corporate settings, the general counsel sees the upper management team as clients, but the duty to the shareholders is the primary mission. It is a weird and powerful duality of loyalties. I think the Bible warns 'bout serving too many masters. It is in the Gospel of Matthew. Somewhere around verse six or so."

"Odell, your knowledge never ceases to amaze me. It is boundless across the chasm."

Odell said, "Well, I am old now, but I keep on chugging. Since you are an S-corporation, you have a board of directors, I guess? Are their terms up? Have you picked new members for the board? How does that work?"

"Honestly, I have to get into that. I know that there is a small board. Most of the board members were business connections of Randy's. From what I know, the terms of the members all expired, or they resigned when Randy passed. That was another thing I was going to leave for Herbert and the legal team to handle."

Detective Lyle Odell processed that information for a few seconds. He ran his hand over the tactical notepad and his chart as if he was absorbing the information systemically. After closing his eyes for a few seconds, he then opened them and looked over to Doctor Burgess.

Odell said, "Gotcha. I understand it is a lot to understand and handle. Especially since it has zero interest for ya. I am gonna need some kind of letter from ya, Eleanor. Giving me permission to investigate corporate emails, have access to records, everything, internal matters, poke around in dark corners . . . carte blanche . . . without search warrants or subpoenas, and without old Herbie or your head of corporate security interfering in my investigation. Please. Can you do that? Have it written up and notarized and signed, and blessed by an attorney. Ya gonna have to find an independent attorney guy and make that happen."

"Of course, Odell. I will make those arrangements and have that drafted and signed and witnessed and all legal and sent to you as soon as possible."

Odell seemed very pleased. He shifted his feet, closed his eyes, and was deep in thought for a few seconds before opening his eyes wide and speaking once more.

"Thank you. Yuppers. The Livingstons. All weasels and snakes hiding in the low and the high grass. Lily Livingston. The common denominator in this entire mess. She was on the cruise with your half-brother when he died. Lily. Beautiful. Alluring. Brilliant intelligence. Did ya know that Reid and Vance Livingston were also on that same cruise?"

Eleanor shook her head to signal that she did not know about their attendance on the cruise.

"Yuppers. They were there too. No reason that you should know that fact. Most likely, they hid in the shadows. You can only kick the can down the road for so long until you come to an intersection, run out of road, or wear the can out. Doc, sorry, I must ask."

Doctor Eleanor Burgess broke away just a little with the embrace of Odell, and she leaned back in his arms while his strong arms supported her balance. She wanted to focus her gaze on him while she spoke. Odell gently reached to her cheekbones, and he flicked away her tears.

Thereafter, Eleanor took control of the conversation.

"No need. I will ask and answer the question for us both. Do I think that Lily Livingston and my half-brother were having an affair? The answer is perhaps. Do I think that he possibly tied one on one night, had too much Scotch, and slept with her? The answer is yes. I think that is a possibility. And maybe some dates and ongoing hookups after that first time. Yes. That would be precarious because he was not overly trusting of women in relationships. Leery of their intentions with his wealth. Yet, Lily might have been the ultimate allure for him. He seldom had steady girlfriends or even gal pals. Randy drank way too much top-shelf, very expensive, single-malt Scotch. In fact, I only ever saw him drink Scotch, water, and tea. He loved tea. All kinds of tea. But he greatly enjoyed fine-single-malt Scotches. Too much. Bad mixture with his many medications. His weak heart and other medical issues made physical activity a chore for him. I would think that having an ongoing affair with a young woman less than half his age might be too much for him. Scandalous to certain persons for an old executive like him to be loving on a young woman. I would have no trouble with that—good for Randy! He was a very handsome man. He had a very weak heart . . . in fact, his last checkup was awful. His cardiologist reported that his heart did not really pump much, as it was more of a spilling motion now. The pacemaker was not effective any longer."

Eleanor Burgess finished her long diatribe and looked to Police Inspector Lyle Odell for his reaction.

Odell continued to hold her tightly in his arms; he nodded and mumbled, "Thank you. Teas. Coffees from around the world. The best of the best. Fine selection of various expensive whiskies. I noticed and made careful note of the glorious wet-bar in the executive conference room on the night when we toured the corporate facility. Very impressive. As is the wet-bar here in this penthouse apartment. I know what to do. Let's go have a shot of Irish. Do you drink Irish?"

"I do now."

"Okay. Then we will go back to sleep. Tomorrow, the

plan elevates to a higher level. Odell moves into action. Please forgive me for being bossy here. It is for the best. For safety. You will need to go along with my plan. Without questions. We are having breakfast with George and his wife Marjorie at Grundy's Bar and Grille in the morning. It is a Saturday tradition for us. We discuss the business, and we share our lives together. I want you to meet them. They are very special to me. Then we move into phase two."

"Sounds like I need to be ready. I will be, Odell."

Odell seemed pleased with her reaction and willingness to accept the crime at hand. He had one more request.

"Good. For now, please no more smoking and morning coffee routine on the balcony."

When she heard his request, Eleanor's eyes narrowed, and she went into deep thought. It was obvious that she was replaying the questions and conversation with Odell. His flowchart. The cast of characters. Then, when she made the connection, her eyes widened, and she pulled Detective Lyle Odell into her even tighter.

She mumbled into his shoulder, "Jack McDermott. Retired. United States Army Rangers. A sniper. I guess that I am in danger."

"Yuppers. Sorry. We are all always in danger, Eleanor. Just some days more than others."

Chapter Five

Intent and Danger

It was now just barely daybreak. Contractors generally start work early in the day and end work early in the day. They were behind schedule on this project, so Saturday became a regular workday.

A cellphone in the jacket of Mr. Art Livingston rang just as he was about to meet the concrete contractor's foreman and his crew to check on the newly poured concrete footings on the project's excavation site.

It was his burner phone. Trouble.

"I must take this call. Sorry. Excuse me," Art Livingston said to the foreman, and he stepped away from the group. He pushed the answer button.

"Yeah, what's up?"

The voice on the other side of the call was firm and concise.

"I received the order. Make the call. Make the move. Now. Odell is sniffing around. He made some connections, and he might be on the trail. We need control now. Before he gets into this any deeper. Odell is speaking to and hanging around now with Doctor Eleanor Burgess. The good doctor knows too much now. Besides, she is in the way. The old guy is in the way now, too. He knows too much. He outlived his usefulness."

Mr. Art Livingston took a deep breath. This was not the call he ever wanted to take, nor the words that he ever wanted to hear.

"Damn. Really? Are you sure? Won't this set off Odell even more?"

There was a slight pause on the other end of the call. As if the person speaking on the other end of the line was pondering the question.

"Odell! Harrumph! He is old, confused, washed up and trying hard to stay sober. He will go back to drinking, and we are in the clear. That is why they gave him that inspector rank. He said it himself that it is bullshit. Not worried about his detective protégé, either. Detective Bradford. He is just an Odell-wanna-be. And the mountain of muscle known as Grundy is retired. C-S-I guru, Lieutenant Crump, is busy staring in microscopes. Odell's little Latino civilian sidekick with the crime-solving mind is busy having babies. His elite team of police experts is history. Nope. Not concerned about Police Inspector Lyle Odell."

"Understood. I hope you are right and sure of this. Odell is a legend. Even without his team."

"Odell was a legend. Now, he is old and cooked. I am sure. Do it. And this guy of yours better be as good as what he says and you say he is. I want one shot. One clean kill. On each of them. Then, two dead bodies."

"My guy is great."

"Okay then. You had better hope that he is great. Because if he screws this up, then his ass is grass anyway. Drunk at the grand opening party celebration for the building. Lewd comments to the good doctor. Sexual advances spurned by the gorgeous professor of plants. He is nuts from combat action . . . PTSD. The crazy combat veteran. Drinks too much. Does drugs, too. His daughter is loose as a goose with her body and with the drinking and drugs, too. They are both nuts. She goes down if her old man goes down. Despite her serving a specific purpose. She is hot and always willing, but she ain't that hot. Anyway, the crazy vet comes back for revenge at the rejection of his love. Has a vendetta against Standard Insurance. We have a back-door setup for him if he proves to be a chump."

"Understood. It will not come to that point. He will succeed."

"Okay then. Do it. No worries. Invoke the plan as we discussed. Upon clean, confirmed kills, and a successful escape by him, we pay him. He then disappears without a trace. Toss this burner phone. I will send you a new one."

"Click."

The connection went dead.

He received the call. Now, he had each of the target's location mapped for this morning. His escape route was perfect. His plan was perfect. No flaws. No mix-ups. His vehicle, his weapons, and his footsteps were untraceable. At first, he was a little leery of using the construction truck for this mission, but after thinking about it, he thought it would blend. Not stand out. Lots of contractors around these days. Especially in downtown Mohawk City, with the attempted revival of the urban areas. That is one good thing about working for these rich clowns; they have deep pockets and can provide you with the best of everything to succeed. This was the big payday. Finally. After rubbing elbows with this group of corrupt and conniving blue-bloods, and having to kiss their collective asses, all the while, working like a dog for years; doing their dirty work. Work, as in actual construction work, but also being the strong-arm man. Beating up punks and threatening cheating contractors. Finally, this was his chance at retirement. A new life, a new identity, on an island in the Caribbean. Goodbye, snow and ice and cold and miserable Mohawk City. Millions of dollars. No more work. No more taking orders from billionaire rich dopes. No more kissing ass. His daughter can handle her own situation. She had one of them in her pocket and in her bed, too. They will, and do, pay her handsomely. Fair trade. She gives him what he wants and needs. He takes good care of her. Not a proud life for his daughter, but lucrative. Better than he could ever provide for her as a terrible father.

One is an easy shot. Just about fifty yards. The other shot would be trickier, but it was nothing that he could not handle. The military taught him very well.

Retired Master Sergeant Jack McDermott studied his watch. Time to go.

Those who knew him, said of Homicide Detective Lyle Odell, that he took snapshots of the world and everything around him with his eyes. Constantly. His mind never stopped processing what his eyes captured. It was more than just his penchant for his famous statement of exact details and facts are very important in investigations. It was his keen sense of how the normal world operates versus how the underworld operates. Any slight thing that was out of place triggered an Odell reaction.

As he usually did, Lyle Odell parked his car a few blocks away from Grundy's Bar and Grille. Kept those premium parking spots in the parking lot behind the establishment open for the paying customers. It was only a short walk to the corner of Fifth Street and Main Street from where he parked on the side street at the corner of Fourth Street and Main Street. Besides, it was a pleasant Saturday morning. Just a little chilly, but Doctor Eleanor Burgess did not mind. She wore a light jacket and a headscarf wrapped around her head while hanging on the arm of Lyle Odell. She was right where she wanted to be. It had only been a few days since they met, but there was a growing magic behind their companionship. She found him ruggedly handsome and sexy, eccentric, but fascinating and brilliant, and he found her warm, intelligent and, of course, beautiful. It went beyond some flirting and attempts at seduction. Beyond the attractions and the new friendship, along with the deep conversations and his probing in what he felt was a homicide case; it was a deep connection. They bridged the chasm together. Yes, his hair was messy; he looped his necktie in a haphazard faux knot; the necktie hung all over and flopped in the breeze while they walked. He looked like he had slept in his suit, but she knew that was not the case. He did to have the looks of a Hollywood movie star; he was something much better. A real man. She felt safe with Odell around despite the unknown situation and the rather ominous feelings surrounding her.

This morning, Eleanor was looking forward to meeting two of Odell's best friends. Lyle Odell had told her some stories of police lore with his police companion of so many years. Detective Lyle Odell added the tantalizing tidbit of how it would take years to tell of their adventures together. She believed that was a fact for sure. If you could even tell them all. The legend known as the now retired Police Lieutenant George Grundy was more than just an immense mountain of a man, full of power and immeasurable strength, but he was according to Lyle, a man of character, and courage and supreme dedication to his family and to justice. He also was a well-known storyteller and a man who loved food. Lots of food. And drink, too. Doctor Burgess knew little about Odell, but she did know that he had little or no family left. But George and his wife were his family. As well as a woman that he mentioned only once or twice, a certain Mrs. Christina Fuentes Columbo, who Odell told her was his third best friend.

Odell said, "I hope that you can meet her someday soon. She is beautiful, and special, and brilliantly intelligent, too. Helped me in many cases with her keen crime-solving input. She is a very dear friend."

Of Mrs. Grundy, Odell said, "Of course, Marjorie Grundy is one of my business partners, but she is the perfect companion to George Grundy. Dedicated and loving, as well as a tower of strength. Special. We became extremely close the last few years. Especially after George was shot in the line of duty. It was an emotional time for all of us, and we leaned on each other for support during a critical turning point in our lives."

She was looking forward to being part of the Saturday morning tradition of breakfast at Grundy's Bar and Grille, with Marjorie and George. Odell labeled it as a weekly business meeting of the partners, but Eleanor could tell that it was much more that a business gathering. They all sat together, ate breakfast, and shared their lives together. All before they opened for the day to the customers. Sharing memories and making some new ones, too. Eleanor hoped that she could be part of the tradition for a long, long time.

Early this same morning, Doctor Burgess had reluctantly risen from bed and found Odell in the living room; dressed and ready to go for the day. He no longer wore his tee shirt and his sweatpants. Odell's attire and his actions fascinated Doctor Burgess. It all seemed like a well-orchestrated routine for him. She was fascinated by his purposely baggy suit and pants. The oversized suit jacket stuffed with various gizmos and gadgets of which he did not even identify to her as she watched; despite her fascination. A foldable magnifying glass, a pair of tweezers, various rolls of tape—small widths, wide widths, and clear and dark tapes. He had a small flashlight, a metal probe of some sort; a telescoping steel piece with a magnet on the end of it. His tactical pad went in his shirt pocket, and of course, his already crushed packs of cigarettes and a few lighters. While he assembled his gear and attire, he mumbled the locations of the items aloud to her and the walls and his own brain. Eleanor surmised that was the method he used to try to recall where they were.

"Left suit jacket pocket, right pants pocket. . .."

There was an awful lot of information processing in that brain, and finding the location of the various gizmos and gadgets that he stowed within that complexity was not an easy task.

Eleanor was particularly observant when she watched Odell clip his police badge to his belt, and he added two shoulder holsters and, after a careful check of the weapons, and loaded ammunition, and extra ammo that gathered in a pack stuck to his belt, Odell stuck the weapons into the holsters. Underneath his pants, at his ankles just above his twelve-inch-high tactical boots, he strapped a knife in an ankle holster. Eleanor sensed that this was what Odell meant by moving into phase two of the investigation.

She asked Odell, "I guess it is time for me to get moving? Phase two. Correct?"

"It is. Correct. Breakfast, some business, and friendship first, and then I hit this case hard. You can hang out with George and Marjorie if you want. I will be back to pick you up after I check out a few things."

"Okay, Odell. I will get going but first, coffee," Eleanor said.

As she turned and was ready to totter off to the kitchen, she was well aware that all she wore over her naked body was a thin robe. The sunlight streaming in the windows gloriously and unabashedly revealed her nakedness and beauty to Lyle Odell. She made no effort to cover herself more or to hide her beauty from Odell, and instead she studied Odell's eyes and his reaction to the scene.

When she sensed his intensity and his eyes remained glued to her face, and not her underlying nakedness, Eleanor commented, "You seem serious. Teasing and seduction still do not work. I know. Friends. For now. I guess that I'd better get a move on. Are you sensing something that I should know about?"

"I am, but that is all part of it. Part of the reason that I feel better if you hang with George today. At least for a little while. Sorry, Eleanor. Gotta get on this case now. It has nothing to do with you, or your incredible beauty, or the potentials. Friends. Yuppers. Time to roll. After coffee."

She reluctantly understood. Homicide Detective Lyle Odell stuck to his word and the mission.

Now, as they walked down the city sidewalk, she glanced over at Odell. His hair was long and messy, and the unlit cigarette hung from his lower lip as if Odell glued it there. The stubble on his face from the lack of shaving was prominent, and she never felt safer or happier than she did right now. And she thought Detective Lyle Odell was the sexist man alive.

The happiness was short-lived.

Odell pointed at the front of Grundy's Bar and Grille and he said, "There it is. A few more steps. . .."

Odell suddenly stopped short in place. He clenched Eleanor's arm, and his eyes darted all around. Odell's senses were on full alert. His eyes landed on a truck rounding the corner onto Main Street.

Within mere seconds, Odell studied the truck, and he pushed at Eleanor and yelled, "Contractor truck with no ladder on the ladder rack. Down! Flat! Here! Behind this car. Don't move. Stay as flat as you can!" Odell then pushed Doctor Burgess onto the sidewalk as she screamed a horrific scream. Once Odell knew she was flat and safe, he drew both of his service weapons and assumed a kneeling shooter's position. The first shot rang out from the driver's side of the now-stopped truck. It sailed high and wide of Odell and struck into the storefront window of Grundy's Bar and Grille. Glass shattered and rained down upon them. Doctor Burgess continued to scream, but she kept low and tight as she could. She covered her ears and screamed. Terrifying! Mayhem!

Odell kneeled next to her, while protecting and shielding her as best as he could do so. Odell used the parked car as a shield. He returned fire simultaneously and rapidly from both of his weapons. Another rifle shot rang out, and this one struck the parked car in the driver's window and exploded it into millions of pieces. More rifle shots fired rapidly and powerfully rang out in the morning air. Odell ducked down lower behind the parked car and then he crawled to find an opening to return fire. It was obvious that the shooter outgunned Detective Odell; the shooter in the truck had a high-powered rifle, and it was obliterating the parked car and raining gunfire upon them. The few pedestrians on the street yelled and ran and ducked for cover. It was a one-on-one gunfight. Odell versus the rifleman. Yet, Detective Lyle recognized the weapon the shooter was using, and he was counting the shots.

"Eight! Reload time, George!" Odell yelled aloud.

Hoping that Grundy was nearby and would recognize an upcoming pause.

Odell was correct.

Twice.

There was a pause in the rifle fire. Obviously a reload . . . and suddenly, the front door to Grundy's Bar and Grille burst open, and Eleanor watched as one of the most massive men she had ever seen in her life appeared in the door. He was holding a large, long-barreled rifle equipped with a scope.

'George Grundy,' Doctor Burgess thought.

As large as he was, he moved like a cat. It was obvious that Grundy was there watching and listening for an opening in the action, and the predicted reload gave him a few seconds to make his move.

"Odell! Here!" With one flick of his massive arms, Grundy tossed the rifle to Odell. Detective Odell plucked it out of the air, and in return, Odell tossed one of his service weapons to Grundy. George Grundy grabbed it out of the air, and he ducked down and covered Eleanor Burgess with his massive body while assuming a shooter pose. Years of working together provided systemic teamwork and motion. Intuitive. That allowed them to toss weapons in the air to each other as if they were a military drill team.

Odell did not hesitate. Within seconds, he had the rifle aimed, and he quickly and heavily returned fire. Outgunned no more.

Odell fired off multiple rounds, and the truck shattered into pieces. Glass, mirrors, steel. Bullets flying! Lyle Odell was now standing and firing relentlessly with the powerful ammo, and the driver could not find a chance to return fire. Instead, the driver decided to bail. The driver jammed the truck into gear and punched the gas pedal to speed off and escape. Police sirens wailed in the distance. More help was on the way.

"Get up, Doc. Hurry! I gotcha. Ya'r okay now," Grundy growled.

Grundy lifted Doctor Burgess as if she were a feather and within seconds, he had her safely inside the restaurant. Odell moved out into the street. He stood in the center of the road and took one shot. The left rear tire of the fleeing truck blew out. The next shot—the right rear tire blew out. His marksmanship was remarkable. Then Odell carefully aimed and bang! The rear window of the truck exploded in a horrifying explosion of sound and glass mixed with the pangs of death. The driver slumped over at the wheel, and the truck, with the gas pedal no longer applied, glided to a slower speed. The truck, unguided and unmanned, crashed into parked cars on the opposite side of the street. Mohawk City Police Department cruisers sped in, and police officers jumped out and surrounded the wrecked and now stopped truck.

Lyle Odell yelled out, "Officers! Homicide Detective Lyle Odell here!"

Most of the police officers already knew who he was. . ..

Even the rookies. He actually was Inspector Lyle Odell.

"Move in slowly. Carefully. Create a circle around the truck. Assume firing positions! Watch my every move. Let me lead. Follow my rifle barrel signals. Cover me!"

Detective Lyle Odell crept closer and closer to the wrecked vehicle, keeping his rifle aimed, and ready to fire while assuming a classic rifle-aiming pose until he reached the driver's door. The police officers all remained on alert, watching Odell as he reached the vehicle and closely examined the situation. After a careful check of the driver, Odell lowered his rifle and slung it over his shoulder. He then reached in and felt the driver's neck and shook his head.

Odell yelled out to the team, "Most of his head is gone. He is history. It was a clean headshot. The truck is a manual transmission. The engine stalled when the clutch popped. Weapon dropped, but it is still on his lap. One hand on the trigger." Odell turned to the team of officers and waved them over. "Come on in. Holster those weapons. Who is in command here?"

A middle-aged police officer wearing sergeant stripes raised his hand and began to trot over to Detective Odell.

"I am, Inspector Odell. Sergeant Drummond. Stewart Drummond."

Odell was patting his jacket, looking for a cigarette, and he found the pack, shook one loose and stuck it on his lower lip. Then Odell looked around at the gathering crowd of on-lookers.

"Detective Odell, Sarge Drummond. Detective Odell, please. Or just plain, Odell works, too. That inspector title is bullshit. Ya better push this crowd back. Find a blanket and cover the body. It is pretty gruesome. I will wait for you to control your team. Gotta take a few puffs here. Take the edge off. That was a little stressful."

"Yes, sir," Sergeant Drummond barked and saluted and jumped into action. Odell found his lighter and struck a flame and leaned into a few puffs. He leaned on the side of the truck and waited for Sergeant Drummond to control the situation, give out some orders and return. He did so.

"Nice work, Sarge Drummond. Hold all those sirs and salutes. Thank you for the respect, but no need for that bullshit. Hey, listen up. I have got to book. Another life is in the balance. Take notes. The deceased shooter is going to be Retired Master Sergeant, United States Army, Jack McDermott. You will have to pull his identification from something other than what is in the truck. He was a military sniper in the Army, but this truck was a front. Should've put a ladder on that ladder rack if he was trying to pose as a contractor. No ladder up there. Any wallet or identification that you find on the body will be fake. Going to be a messy cleanup. Lots of shells and bullets and glass all over in front of Grundy's joint. His objective was to kill Doctor Eleanor Burgess. He rounded the corner and opened fire on us as we walked down the street to Grundy's Bar and Grille. I know the reasons why. It is part of an active investigation of mine. Any other stories will be a smokescreen. Do you report to Lieutenant Larry Hicks?"

"Yes, siiii, roger that. Sorry for the almost, sir," Sergeant Drummond caught his words.

Odell said, "Good, get ahold of Hicks and explain, and he will take charge. Tell 'em that Odell requested his presence and that I apologize for the mess and having to leave. I couldn't avoid it. And I am finally taking advantage of this inspector bullshit rank. Ain't gonna be any administrative leave for me because of this incident. Inspector Odell is staying on this case for a few more days. I will write a report when I can do so and submit it to my chain of command. That will ruffle some feathers on your side, but Hicks and the police commissioner will plow the road for me. I will leave the weapon that I used with Grundy. I will not need that heavy fuel firepower anymore. Once I have the bad guys and gals under wraps, the captain and the chief can grill me all they want. Not now. I have a job to do."

Odell continued to puff the cigarette, and he turned to walk in the direction of Grundy's Bar and Grille. Sergeant Drummond called out in the direction of the retreating Detective Odell. He ignored Odell's previous requests, and Odell knew why he did so.

"Yes, sir, Inspector Odell." And he followed it with a proper salute. Odell stopped and turned and looked at the sergeant. "Detective Odell, I must say that was a remarkable piece of shooting. This guy was a military sniper. Incredible shots. Thank you for taking out the shooter and saving lives. He would have outgunned and outclassed us for sure." Then he pointed at Odell and said, "And you are not wearing a vest."

With the cigarette bouncing from his lower lip, and the weapon still slung over his shoulder, Odell answered.

"Don't ever sell yaself or ya men short, Drummond. Under fire, ya rise to the challenges presented. Vest? Nah. Seldom wear a vest. It restricts my aim. If Hicks needs the rifle for his final ballistics check, I will leave it with Lieutenant Grundy." Odell started to turn, but then he stopped and fired off a return salute to the good sergeant. A show of mutual respect.

No one questioned Detective Lyle Odell as to the wherefores and whys, or sticking around for paperwork, or following police protocol. They all knew he was Inspector Lyle Odell. Despite his objections to the title.

Detective Lyle Odell found George Grundy out in front of Grundy's Bar and Grille, assisting one of the kitchen staff in cleaning up the glass and debris gathered on the sidewalk. Grundy was wearing gloves and picking the spent shells and bullets out of the mix and piling them aside. On Main Street in front of them, bedlam ensued. Sirens wailed and lights flashed. Ambulances, fire trucks, more police cars, the media with radio and television vans, people running all over the sidewalks. Bedlam.

He looked up as Odell approached and shook his head a little. "Damn. What a mess, Odell. Ya doing, okay?"

Lyle Odell jumped to his question first.

"Is Eleanor, ok?"

"Oh, yeah. She is okay. Terrified, but okay. Shaking like a leaf and screaming about you. I gave her three shots of Irish and calmed her down. Marjorie has her. She is in good hands."

"I knew you had her. Thank you for protecting her when I moved up the flank to position better. Thanks for the save here, George. Yeah, I am okay. A little tired from all of this. Sorry 'bout the mess, George. I had to duck, so the bullet took out your window."

Grundy turned and pointed at the pile of spent ammo and said, "Our window, Odell. Our window. Glad you ducked. As far as the thank you goes, well, yeah, of course. I might be retired, but we are still a team. How did you know to react in advance? I caught you out of the corner of my eye and saw you study the truck and then push Doc Burgess to the sidewalk just seconds before the driver fired."

"No ladder on the ladder rack. And the fake name painted on the freshly painted truck. And older model, but Lorance Contractors? What kinda bullshit name for a construction company is that? Lorance here in Mohawk City. Should've been Irish contracting or construction."

Grundy nodded and tossed another shell casing onto the pile, along with the others.

He commented, "Gotcha. Odell stuff. Noticing stuff that no one else would ever notice. Saved your life and Doctor Burgess, too." Grundy pointed at the pile and said, "I am making a collection there for the evidence files. That is the last of 'em. Crump coming?"

"Nah, Hicks." Detective Lyle Odell turned and pointed at the bullet-ridden car, which afforded Eleanor and Odell protection. Odell asked, "Do you know whose car this is that got rung up?"

"Not one hundred percent sure, but, but I think it is a guy in the apartment next door. I imagine that he will be down shortly. I think he works nights. But with all this chaos going on, I bet he wakes up shortly. Poor guy. Hope he has good insurance."

"Yuppers. If not, then the city will take care of him. I am sure. Thank goodness that he parked there. Saved our lives. Here," Odell said as he handed off the rifle to Grundy. He then took one last remaining drag on the cigarette, ground it out on the heel of his boot, and then stuffed in one of his suit jacket pockets. "Right side suit jacket pocket," Odell mumbled, then he perked up and said, "thanks for the heavy fuel here. He pinned my ass down quickly. Did not expect that old M1. That thirty-awwt-six was no joke. The rifle that won a war. Should've known he would go old school with an untraceable oldie but goodie. Ex-Army sniper guy."

Grundy nodded in the direction of his helper and put his massive arm around Odell.

"Oh, boy. Yeah, that explains the weapon. I realized that the shooter pinned ya down. Heard the pops and judged the caliper and that it was an old M1. Waited for the reload and the bolt to slide and when I heard you yell eight, I made the move. Figured you needed the heavy fuel and some backup. Marjorie made the call to HQ for the backup. The way it was popping out there, I bet there were a million calls to police hotlines. That was fierce. I have your service weapon behind the bar. You dropped him, huh? Head shot?"

"Yuppers. One shot. One kill."

"You were always a crackerjack with weapons. The best we ever saw in the Mohawk City Police Department. I had this guy behind the bar. It is yours. Issued to you. I kept it here for safekeeping when you were riding those Irish whiskey benders. Thought it would be better here with me.

At least ballistics can trace it to you. If they even ask. Come on inside. Give the doc some attention. Have a few shots of Irish. She needs ya." Grundy draped his massive arm over Odell's shoulders. Odell was not a small man, but in the arms of George Grundy, he seemed miniature.

"Glad ya okay."

"Thanks, George. Retired my foot. You are still the man. I love ya."

"I love ya, too. There, get inside and go check on her."

Detective Lyle Odell nodded, and after the embrace, Odell allowed his best friend to lead him inside. As good as Odell was, the stress and the pain of the gun battle brought him some weariness. Odell walked more slowly than usual.

Doctor Burgess looked up; she spotted Odell; she ran and practically jumped in his arms. Between the tears and the embraces, Odell assured her that he was okay, she was okay, and that everything was going to be okay.

"I have a plan, Eleanor. I will explain in a few. Right now, I must make a phone call. A life is at stake. Please sit with Marjorie and have another shot or try to eat something. I will be right there."

Doctor Burgess nodded and headed back to join Marjorie Grundy. She would wait. Her trust in Odell and his plan was immeasurable.

Odell walked over to the bar and asked, "Can I use your cellphone, George? I don't know where my cellphone is."

"Nothing changes. It is most likely that the battery is dead anyway," Grundy mumbled as he handed Odell his phone. The good detective sat on a barstool, and he watched as Grundy poured him a shot of Odell's favorite Irish whiskey. As George poured, Odell took his tactical pad out of his shirt pocket. He thumbed through it and settled on a page. His eyes darted along while he dialed the number. The receiver on the other side of the call answered on the second ring.

"Officer Ben Crane."

"Crane. Odell. I need ya help. Right now. As hard and as fast as you can. I have no time to call your commanding officer and request this. Trust me. I will do that, just not right now. I need ya to move."

"You got it, Odell. Ready. Give me the orders."

"Josie McDermott. Ya need to find her and protect her. It is Saturday. She should be at home. Hopefully. Get to her apartment, find her. Get her into protective custody just as soon as ya can do it."

"Roger that, Odell. I am on it. Can I ask what is up?"

"Sure. I just killed her father in a gun battle. The bad guys hired her father, who was an ex-Army sniper, to kill Doctor Eleanor Burgess and, perhaps, someone else here in Mohawk City. He failed to kill Doctor Burgess. The other person I do not know yet. Josie is now expendable. Her father failed. She knows too much. You have her info and license plate from our adventure. Pull the info. Shake ya ass and get to the address. Bring back up. Please, Crane, be safe. These are very bad guys. Go, Crane. Keep me posted. Thank you."

"Roger."

The line went dead. Grundy pointed at the shot. Odell nodded and handed the cellphone back to George.

"Holy Moses, Odell. Sumthin' tells me we ain't watching the hockey game at your place tonight. And having pizza from Frank's and sum beers. All this from reading a damn newspaper article. I saw ya dig up sum bones over the years, but this might take the cake."

Odell downed the shot and nodded to George for a refill.

"No hockey, my old friend. Raincheck. Give me a few days. We will catch the Bears versus the Rovers for that game next Wednesday. I will have this wrapped up by then."

"Gotcha. What are ya dealing with here, Odell?"

Odell toyed with the shot, and then as it hovered near

his lips, Odell explained, "Oh, let's see. Where do I begin? First, we have the murder of Mr. Randolph Burgess, the CEO, owner, and president of Standard Insurance Company. Next, we have the attempted murder of Doctor Eleanor Burgess. Then a wonderfully evil-laced list of corporate conspiracy, fraud, embezzlement, blackmail, plotting the illegal takeover of a company in order to steal seven-hundred-million dollars. A little illegal drug dealing or two or three or more, payoffs and shakedown of construction contractors and some local officials, and to top it all off, with a red bow of nefarious intentions, possibly, unless Officer Ben Crane of the Boston Police Department can get there first, two more homicides."

Odell downed the shot and placed the empty glass on the bar counter.

He added, "Yuppers, George. All from me reading a damn newspaper article."

Grundy did not react to the statement, but he walked behind the bar, plucked Odell's service weapon from the confines, and handed it to Detective Lyle Odell, who holstered the weapon.

Grundy pointed towards the holster and commented, "They both need cleanin' and dressin.' I can smell 'em from here."

The front door opened, and Sergeant Drummond looked around, and when he spotted Odell and Grundy at the bar, he made his way there.

He stopped in front of where Grundy and Odell were and saluted.

Drumond spoke, "Inspector Odell. Lieutenant Grundy. Sorry to interrupt. The worker out front opened the door for me. Detective Miles Bradford has been trying to contact you, sir. He says your cellphone goes straight to voicemail. It is urgent."

Odell pointed to Grundy and then to the shot glass and said, "Please, George. Another one. One more homicide confirmed. Pray for Officer Crane. That young officer is racing to save another life. Please, Drummond, it is Detective Odell, or better yet, just plain old Odell. Let me guess, Sarge. Detective Bradford has a homicide on his hands. A Mr. Herbert O'Leary, the General Counsel for the Standard Insurance Company, was found dead in his driveway or somewhere in his house or near his house this morning. His head exploded from the impact of a high-powered piece of ammo. Say, a thirty-awwt-six piece of ammo."

Doctor Eleanor Burgess was sitting with Marjorie Grundy, and they were within earshot of the conversation. Everyone could hear Doctor Burgess gasp at the harsh reality predicted by Detective Odell.

Odell looked over at Doctor Burgess and mouthed that it was going to be okay, and he waved with his hands to try to project some comfort that he had this under control. Burgess covered her mouth with her hand and nodded in the direction of Odell.

Mrs. Marjorie Grundy stayed close to Doctor Burgess and calmly reassured her that Lyle Odell was going to make sure that everything was okay. She had ridden these waves of crime and turmoil for years. Marjorie Grundy was a seasoned veteran of Homicide Detective Lyle Odell's cases.

Sergeant Drummond seemed shocked and then he caught his emotions.

"Why yes, Detective Odell, that is correct."

"Thank you, Sarge. The streak continues. I never have any damn luck with attorneys. You will find that the weapon used by the now deceased Mr. Jack McDermott is a ballistics match to the bullet that killed Mr. O'Leary and the spent shells that Lieutenant Grundy collected and left in a pile on the sidewalk out front of here. Jack McDermott's first assignment on his lethal mission was a success. His second—a failure. He was a hired hitman based on his skills as a former military sniper. According to his military records, he was a very good one, too. Please relay that information to Bradford and tell him that I will call him shortly. In the meantime, please tell him to use our usual investigation methods. We worked together for years. Detective Miles Bradford is a great detective, and he knows what to do. And please, no salutes."

"Roger, sir."

Odell downed the shot; he turned to look over at the table where Marjorie and Eleanor sat. They looked back. Waiting patiently for the plan. Of the news of what is going on.

Odell slid the empty glass over to George, and he shook his head to indicate that was the last shot.

"George, what was it that you told me that since you retired, you still specialize in?"

Despite the stress and pain of the situation, Grundy smiled. Odell knew that look. For over thirty years.

In contrast to his usual booming voice, the immense man leaned in and said, almost in a whisper, "Dicey bullshit."

"Good. I am going to need ya, George. Because this is exactly that. Dicey bullshit."

Chapter Six

Grundy Time

"I will have the guys grab some plywood and board up that front window. Can have it replaced next week. We still have about forty-five minutes before we open. Let Lieutenant Hicks handle all that mess out there. He knows where we are. I am hungry. Let's eat. It will do everyone good. I am having the kitchen whip us up a great big breakfast feast. Scrambled eggs, toast, sausage, some fruit. The works."

George Grundy relayed his plans to Odell as George rubbed his belly. They both made their way over to the table with Odell. They were set to join Marjorie and Doctor Burgess. Detective Lyle Odell slipped in at the table and sat next to Doctor Burgess, who clung to him like flypaper.

"It's okay, Eleanor. I am sorry but I had a feeling about O'Leary. As I mentioned, I have very little luck with attorneys. Honestly, there was no way to prevent his death. I only had my gut feelings to go on, but obviously, he knew too much, or was in the way, or a combination of all of those things. And we are dealing with a kingpin above O'Leary. For sure, we now know he was not the Kingpin. Someone ordered the hit on O'Leary and on you, too. Anyway, leave all that to me now. You are safe now, and you have my word that everything is going to be okay. Food will do you good. You need to eat something. I see you've had a few shots and are having tea now. That is good. It is going to be a long day for you."

George had settled in now at the table, and he glanced

first at his wife and then to Odell and finally to Doctor Burgess.

Grundy asked, "I second the motion that the food will do you good. I am starving. A long day, Odell? Ya mean, even longer than it already has been? Geez, it is still early in the morning, and it has been a mess. What 'cha got in mind?"

"You are always starving, George. Yuppers, George. Gonna, need ya help."

Odell turned to Marjorie, and she swallowed hard. She knew that Odell look. It was not high on her favorite-looks list.

"George is retired, Lyle. Must I remind you of that fact?"

Doctor Burgess made careful of the fact that Mrs. Grundy called Odell by his first name. And Detective Odell did not correct her. Eleanor realized the special connection. The respect. The love. She tried to imagine what the three of them had been through for all of these years. George, his wife, and Homicide Detective Lyle Odell. The commitment. The honor. The pursuit of justice. She could not fathom it or understand it, but she could respect it.

Odell replied.

"No need to do so. But I can only trust George with this mission. Please. Forgive me. Can you, and Annie, and Meredith run the bar and grille for a few days?"

Mrs. Grundy nodded and said, "Sure. Annie is ancient but efficient. The college gal needs extra money. She always needs extra money. Spends it all on frivolous stuff. No trouble with running the place. We have plenty of help."

Marjorie Grundy finished speaking. She reached across the table and motioned for Odell to clasp her hands. Odell did so, and Marjorie studied his eyes for a few seconds. Both George and Eleanor sat silently and studied the heartfelt interaction between these two special friends. Friendships can be more valuable than precious gold. They shape us and define us and comfort us. They are precious parts of our lives.

Marjorie said, "Oh, my dear, dear Lyle. I do love you so, but my George. All we have been through. Together. My goodness. I thought retired meant retired. We are all so happy running this place. Together. All three of us. It is our dream. You should retire too. You have nothing left to prove to anyone, Lyle. Now we have this mess today. Bullets and horrific situations. And dead men and blood and broken glass. Terrifying for Eleanor and for us. Why not call in help with Miles and Larry and Oliver Crump? Let them handle it from here. You just coach them along."

Odell hesitated for only a few brief seconds. While he still held Marjorie's hand, Odell's words arrived.

"Because a little snow on the roof does not mean there is no longer a fire in the furnace. That new chain of command. They all wanted to put me out to pasture. Give me this inspector bullshit rank and set me on display like a museum piece. Dust me off and put me in the game when no one else could figure things out. After all, I did. All those years. All those cases. The so-called legend of Homicide Detective Lyle Odell becomes some figurehead of a police detective. Nope. Ain't gonna happen. I just wanted to remain as Homicide Detective Lyle Odell. For a few more years. Then go out on my terms." Odell swallowed hard. You could see the swallow travel down his throat. His emotions were powerful.

"And those guys. Our guys. Our team. I still love them all. They are my brothers in arms forever, but they did not go to bat for me either. I get it . . . they have to work with the new captain every day and the new chief and deal with all the politics. I am at the end of the line. Only George went to bat for me, and he caused a giant ruckus defending me to stay as a homicide detective. The new police chain of command does not like ruckuses. They knew George was at the end of his road, too. So, they offered the juicy retirement package, and they retired the powerful and courageous, Lieutenant George Grundy. Nope. Now it is Odell on his own. On a mission. It is what my soul needed right now. Yuppers. Gonna ride solo on this one."

Odell paused in his diatribe. He clenched his fists a little and then opened them. You could see and absorb and feel the passion in his voice on this subject. The hurt of how it all occurred was still fresh and painful.

Odell continued to explain, "I answer to the police commissioner and his board, not to them, and they have no issues with me doing my thing because they respect experience and my record. That is the trouble with these younger generations. They don't respect experience and think they know everything. And what they don't know, they can search for the answer on the internet and plug it into their lives. Well, I have news for them. Certain things ain't on the internet, and the bad guys and gals have the internet, too. Sometimes, it takes blood and guts, and courage, and getting ya ass out of a chair in a cozy office, and puttin' that same ass on the line. Just as Officer Crane in Boston is doing right now, and we did here. It ain't easy, romantic, or fun. We call it justice, and it is what George and Odell, and you, and the team, fought to uphold for all our careers and lives."

Detective Lyle Odell glanced over at Doctor Burgess and he motioned with his head for her to join in their clasp. Doctor Burgess, despite the stress of the day, almost smiled, and she eagerly joined the grip. Then Odell did the same with Grundy, who also joined in, so that all four of them locked their hands together.

"As you can tell, Marjorie, this one is now very personal."

There were rims of tears in her eyes, but Marjorie Grundy knew what she had to do.

First a deep breath and then an exhale. They broke their handholds, and all sat and watched and waited.

George Grundy carefully studied his wife for her reaction and reply.

She nodded and asked, "I understand, Lyle. You have my blessings. As, I said, I love you. What is the mission?"

"Thank you for understanding. I love you, too. George will escort Eleanor to her penthouse apartment at the corporate headquarters. There, she will pack up a few things." Odell leaned forward and went on a frantic search of his pockets. He tried his suit jackets, then he stood up and went through his pants pockets. He looked over at Grundy, who watched him carefully.

Odell asked, "Wallet?"

A few of the kitchen staff arrived and began to drop plates of mountainous food on the table. Suddenly, everyone was ravenous. The breakfast food broke the tension and stress. The shots of Irish whiskey might have helped, too.

Grundy plucked a strip of bacon from a pile of strips and popped it in his mouth as the rest of the food went around the table.

While still chewing, Grundy pointed at Detective Odell and said, "Usually in your inside suit jacket left side pocket. Inside. Not the outside. Ya are patting the outside. Wrong pocket."

Odell nodded, and sure enough, he plucked the wayward wallet from the Grundy-recommended pocket. Odell continued to explain as he settled back into his chair, opened his wallet, and handed a credit card to Doctor Burgess.

"Yuppers. Thanks, George. Inside, not outside. Mixed that one up. So. Today proves the case. The danger. I cannot risk this any longer. We need to get Eleanor out of here. Ordering local police protection does not work for me in this situation. I would need to jump over to the other side of the fence in the department, and I do not have the time or patience to deal with that right now. The new chain of command over there will make me fill out requisition forms and budget allocations and bullshit paperwork and then ponder it for days and days. No time for that nonsense. Lives are at stake. This new inspector rank comes with some perks. I can void protocol and procedures and have the big brass backing me up. Please, right now, on that credit card, you will buy two first-class tickets to San Francisco, and Doctor Burgess will return to her home in Berkeley, with Grundy as her bodyguard. There, you will wait and be safe until I wrap this all up. Should only be a few more days. I will be in touch and provide updates as my time allows. My promise."

George Grundy was already digging into forkfuls of scrambled eggs, and just watching him eat made a good case for the rest of the table to eat. Doctor Burgess spooned out some helpings, as did Marjorie. Odell did not. He did, however, start to sip a cup of black coffee.

He continued to explain his plan. Eating in the world of Detective Lyle Odell was optional. He generally subsisted on pizza, whiskey, coffee, and cigarettes.

"Do you still have your service weapon, and are your licenses to carry in order?"

Grundy was doing a deep dive into some toast and jam.

"I do, and yes, but doubt that I will need it. What do you always say 'bout me?"

"That you are a weapon, George."

"Exactly. I gotcha, Odell. No one will get near Doctor Burgess. If they try to or do, then I will crush them like bugs. Weapons are good to go. I keep a duffel bag packed. Just in case. I can move out in fifteen minutes. As soon as I finish eating."

"Thank you, George," Odell said with a nod of his head. He studied Doctor Burgess for a few seconds. He smiled at her, reached over, and put his arm around her shoulders.

"Are you doing, okay? You need to eat. It will help settle you down."

"Yes. I am doing okay. Now. I am going to eat. It smells fabulous. Those shots of Irish whiskey really helped. It was all so terrifying. And it happened so fast. I was not even sure of what you saw or what was happening until the bullets flew. Your bravery is remarkable, Odell. Thank you for saving my life. I do like your plan. I will be safe there. With George." Doctor Burgess looked around, and she smiled and said in a low, gentle voice, "Thank you all. For everything. I must say, George. My goodness, you are the largest man that I have ever seen. They grow them big here in Mohawk City. Thank you for scooping me up off the sidewalk and carrying me in here to safety. Your strength is immeasurable."

"Ah, no trouble. Odell and I have been through some tough ones. That one was a tough one. You are safe, and you are welcome. By the way, I like Odell's plan, too. Get ya the hell outta here."

Doctor Burgess commented as she began to eat her breakfast, "At least you will not have to eat on the airplane."

George waved his fork in the direction of Doctor Burgess as Marjorie scoffed a little. His wife knew what was coming.

"Ah, no, Doc. This will hold me over until the flight. I can eat on the plane. First class, ya know!"

"You will still be hungry after eating all of that food?"

Odell answered for Grundy as George made his way into mountains of hash browns.

"He is always hungry, Eleanor. Always. Warning. He gets grumpy when he is hungry."

"Oh, I see. I will make note of that fact. By the way, Odell. I can buy the tickets for the flight for George and me."

"Nope. Use only that credit card for all expenses. It is not trackable. Not sure how deep these thugs can reach. Use your credit card, and they might see the charges for the plane tickets and be able to track you to the final destination."

Odell plucked a slice of toast off the pile and dropped it on his plate. It appeared as if he was going to take a bite when Grundy's cellphone rang. George grabbed it, took a look, and a wave of concern flowed across his face.

"Boston number. That must'b that Crane kid."

Odell nodded as George set his fork down and answered the call. "Retired Police Lieutenant George Grundy here. Ya want to speak to Odell? Yup. Hang on."

Without another word, Grundy handed the phone off to Odell, who took it, mumbled, "Excuse me," to his friends, and stood and began to walk away from the table. All eyes and ears leaned his way. Even Grundy paused in his breakfast consumption.

"Crane, what 'cha got? Hoping for good news."

Officer Ben Crane was on the other side of the line, and he spoke excitedly.

"Well, it is not great, but you were right on, Odell. Josie McDermott is still alive. She is comatose and rushed off to Boston Medical, but she is alive. She overdosed on something and everything. Needles and drugs are all around. We broke the door down, and there she was on the floor in the living room. It looked as if she had crawled there from the bedroom. Trying to get to her cellphone, which was on the sofa in the living room. I don't believe for a second that she took those drugs willingly. Some signs of a struggle in that apartment. In my opinion, whoever did this are amateurs. Poor job of staging a scene."

Odell listened intently. He took a deep breath and mussed his hair and then searched with his one free hand for his cigarettes.

"Great work, Crane! I knew you were a good one. Right on. They juiced her up. Made it look like an overdose. She would have died without your getting there in time. . .."

Officer Ben Crane interrupted Detective Lyle Odell.

"Without your phone call to get me there. You were right on, Odell. Let's hope she makes it. The paramedics did all they could. They said it was iffy. Another five minutes and she was gonzo. What is the next move, Odell?"

"Crane, I appreciate this more than I can ever say here on the phone. Ya okay, Crane? Ya team, ok?"

"I am, okay. The team is too. I am a little shook up, but okay."

"Good. I will speak to your commanding officers as soon as I can. Please, the best detectives and crime scene guys you have need to comb that apartment. Guard it twenty-four seven. No one gets in without your blessing. We need Josie to stay alive, for her own wellbeing, but also, she can nail 'em. Let's pray for her and the doctors and nurses. Got to be clues there. DNA, fingerprints, evidence—you must comb the joint. You guys are very good up there. Be great. Keep me posted. I have three stops here in Mohawk City, one stop in New York City, one in Westchester, and then I will head your way. Hopefully, by Monday morning."

"My command is all in. Patrol Sergeant is a huge fan of yours. And get this, he roots for the Rovers, too."

"I knew that you guys would come to their senses up there. Talk to ya soon. Thanks again."

Odell hung up the call. He wandered back to the table and handed the cellphone off to Grundy.

He announced to his friends, "Big break. Josie McDermott is still alive. That is the assassin's daughter. They tried to wipe her when they heard that her father failed on part two of the mission. I figured they would and made the call to my contact there. He reached her in time. Now, we have to hope she makes it. She knows all the bad guys. And gals. She can spill the beans and fill in all the parts and pieces, too."

Doctor Burgess gently grasped Odell's arm and said, "That is good news. I will pray for her to live. Please. Odell. Sit and eat something."

"I did eat. Had some of that toast."

They all turned and looked at his plate. The toast was untouched.

Odell watched their eyes, and he added, "And I had coffee. And Irish. Lookie here. I have to go. Now. Much to do, and time is ticking. A few things I have to do right away and then hit the road for a downstate mission. George has this. I will be in touch." Detective Lyle Odell sat down next to Doctor Burgess, whose eyes now welled up with tears. He embraced her for a minute or two and gently kissed her forehead. "You will be safe. It will only take me a few days now. I promise. Please listen carefully. Eleanor, not a word to anyone of where you are going. Only send one email from your penthouse computer to one person, who you will put in charge of the company while you go dark. Then no logins from emails, no texts, no phone calls. I will work through George, and he will make and assist in any of the calls and communications that you need."

Odell turned to Grundy and explained.

"Buy a burner phone when you land, George. Send me the number. Please."

"Gotcha, Odell. Roger that."

Doctor Burgess seemed puzzled for a second, and her brilliance then shone through.

"Lawrence Rinehardt," Doctor Burgess said. "You want me to leave this company in the hands of our facility manager? Not Gerald Palmer? The CFO?"

"Yuppers. For sure. Not Palmer. I am digging into him next. I have about as much luck with numbers guys as I do with attorneys. Rinehardt is smart, resourceful, and knows a lot of behind-the-scenes bullshit. All facility managers do. He is loyal to you. A company man. Proved that he respects you when he defended you from our now deceased hitman. I will speak with him too. Put him in charge. One quick and brief email. No details. Just tell 'em that you have some business to handle. He runs the show.

Nothing else needed in the message. On the heels of old Herbie losing his head to a heavy metal bullet, that decision will cause speculation and blowup the office chatter. I am anxious to see Palmer's reaction to that news."

Doctor Burgess still seemed very upset and uncomfortable.

With some noticeable shakiness in her voice, she replied, "Will do, Odell. I understand. Yes. Thank you."

"You need to get me that letter, and I also need access to your half-brother's medical records. Specifically, what medications he took and his last heart exam and the blood work. I need his expense reports, Old Herbie's expense reports, Palmer's reports, and Lily Livingston's expense reports."

Doctor Burgess tried hard to pull herself together. She took her napkin and wiped her eyes. She nodded and stuttered a bit, but managed the words. All the while still intensely holding onto Lyle Odell.

"Okay. I will work on that as soon as we get home to Berkely."

Grundy stopped chewing for a few seconds while loading his plate with some bacon and sausages, and he added, "We got this, Odell. No sweat. No worries. Roger on the plan and the information."

Homicide Detective Lyle Odell seemed pleased. He leaned over and into Eleanor Burgess and they whispered some words to each other. Lyle stood up to get ready to leave.

Odell said to his friends, "I am out of here. Marjorie. George. Eleanor. Thank you. I love ya guys."

Marjorie Grundy said, "We love you, too. Be safe, Lyle."

She stood up, and she walked over to Lyle Odell and hugged him, as did George, too. Grundy motioned for Doctor Burgess to join them, and she did so. The group hug lasted for a minute or two, and without another word, Odell broke the embrace, spun on his heels, and headed out the front door.

Out onto Main Street. To the mission at hand.

They all watched him together as he disappeared into the daylight.

Then retired Police Lieutenant George Grundy looked at his food, rubbed his belly, and said, "One more helping of eggs and a few strips of bacon and then we need to get this show on the road. Grundy runs on heavy fuel. It's Grundy time. Also known as dicey bullshit time."

Homicide Police Detective Lyle Odell did not have to wait too long in the waiting chairs of the barbershop. In fact, one gentleman who was ahead of Odell recognized him and graciously allowed Odell to take his turn before him. Lyle Odell was polite and quiet, kept his discussion to a minimum, even when the television in the barber shop played the news and mayhem of what had happened earlier that same morning on the screen over the barber chairs. The barber sensed the mood and flipped the channel over to a sports channel.

The barber was Odell's regular barber. Odell had been getting his haircut at this same shop for countless years. The barber did not even question Detective Odell, when Lyle gave him instructions on how he wanted his haircut. It was not the usual Odell haircut.

Everyone knew this new style. It was part of the mission.

The barber set the hair trimmer to the zero setting. As per Homicide Detective Lyle Odell's request. High and tight and beyond zip. Just some stubble on his skull. Then the barber, razor shaved Odell. A hot shave. Not a single extra whisker remained.

After the visit to the barber, while now at home, Detective Lyle Odell, dressed in his Mohawk City police inspector's tactical shirt. His special inspector's badge logo emblazoned on the left chest area of the shirt. An American flag patch sat on the right shoulder of the shirt with the stars facing forward. The back of the shirt, stenciled in large block gold letters; POLICE. Odell reached for the small black metal device. It had a razor edge on one side, a small nook like a bent fishhook on the other. It had male-configured sticky tape on the back edge. While peeling away the V-neck of his tactical uniform shirt, Odell carefully applied the sticky edge of the device to the female mating sticky material sewn on the inside edge of the shirt. He patted the device down to make sure it was secure. It was very tight and secure. Next, Odell climbed into black police-issued tactical pants, his badge clipped to his belt, and he added two shoulder holsters with his service weapons stuck in each to his body. Extra ammo and a few Odell crime-fighting gizmos and gadgets stuck in the pouches and holders on his M.I.K.E belt. Odell packed a small tactical sling pack with some more items, his tactical notepad with his notes, a small telescoping spotting scope, some hand tools, and a small length of thin razor wire. The final piece of the puzzle was his rescue and survival knife from his Coast Guard days, tucked in an ankle-strapped holder. Long ago, Odell inscribed his initials on the cold steel of the blade. The initials were still there. The knife now sat on his right ankle above the polished tactical boots. Twelve-inch-high boots with a side zipper and a sticky strap.

Odell was sober. Odell was on a mission. Odell tuned in and dialed in. Tactical Homicide Detective Lyle Odell. A criminal's worst nightmare. With George Grundy escorting and guarding Doctor Eleanor Burgess back to her home in California, Odell was now truly riding solo on this mission, and he was ready for the task.

Mr. Warren Colbert was the Mohawk City Police Commissioner. Mr. Colbert grew up in Mohawk City as the son of a New York State Trooper. Police work ran in the family, as it does with so many police officers, military service persons, firefighters, and first responders. He joined the United States Army Reserves as a young man, attended college part-time and eventually moved on to being an officer in the reserves while marrying and settling in a medium—size city in New Jersey. There, he joined the local police force and worked his way up the ranks until he was the chief of police there. Then . . . retirement from both the military and the police force.

He relocated back to his roots to be closer to family, and now he owned a home and lived on the outskirts of Mohawk City. In what George Grundy would label as "The High-Rent District." The new mayor of Mohawk City lured Warren out of retirement to serve as the Police Commissioner, and Warren told him that he would give him two years. Warren and the mayor were old boyhood buddies from the same neighborhood near downtown Mohawk City. When the city was nicer and the downtown was not teeming with, as Odell would say, "People with nefarious intentions."

Two years. No more and no less. Then it was permanent retirement.

Police Commissioner Colbert sat in the guest chair in Lyle Odell's office at Mohawk Police Headquarters. It was now just after noon. Detective Lyle Odell called the commissioner and requested they meet. He needed to fill in his chain of command on the details of this case. Especially after the morning's events. Odell sat behind his office desk, which had piles of papers and stacks of books mixed in with general mayhem. There were pens and pencils and a computer that, most likely, Detective Odell seldom used or turned on. The ashtray on his desk, filled to the brim with twisted, unsmoked cigarettes. His office was rather Odell-like. Odell did sip a cup of black coffee that looked more like mud than coffee. He pointed to the coffeemaker perched on the top of a file cabinet to offer Commissioner Colbert a cup; but he declined.

That was probably a very good choice to decline the Odell-brewed mud.

Commissioner Colbert asked, "Are you okay, Inspector Odell? That was one hell-u-va mess downtown there. Incredible." Commissioner Colbert waved in the direction of Odell, and he used his hand to capture all of him while he sat behind the desk.

After doing so, he commented.

"I must say, I like the new look here. Almost did not recognize you, except I saw this look a few years back at that medal ceremony and your promotion to the inspector rank. You look badass. You scare the hell outta me and intimidate me. And I am your boss."

"The mission needs a certain look and a certain approach and feel. It is highly personal now. I am feeling fine, sir. Yuppers and with all due respect, as I might have mentioned before, I prefer Detective Odell or just plain Odell."

"Nope. Disagree. Not today, Lyle. Today, you need to be Inspector Lyle Odell. The highest-ranking, most highly decorated, and most respected police officer in Mohawk City Police Department history. Answering to the Police Commissioner and the Board of Commissioners."

"Understood, Warren. Sorry 'bout the incredible mess. It was an ambush. High-powered ammo. My mistake. I did not expect it. Saw the truck out of the corner of my eye, and it seemed out of place. I only had two seconds to react to get Doc Burgess to safety. Good thing that Grundy had my old rifle stashed or the outcome might have been different."

Odell finished his statement; he plucked a twisted

cigarette out of the ashtray and stuck it on his lower lip. He sipped the coffee even with the cigarette stuck there. He simply sipped around it.

"So, I heard. Great job on saving the life of Doctor Burgess. Courageous to stand in there and battle it out with a trained assassin. Of course, the chief went crazy wanting you to go on leave, a full report, sit with him for an interview and the psychological and stress exams and such. I refused that madness for you and told him that you had a mission to take care of and you were going to do it. Now, when Miles Bradford and Lieutenant Oliver Crump confirmed that this McDermott nut job was the killer of O'Leary, well, that helped shut them all up. At least for now. The media are going nuts, too. All the usual misinformation and siding with the bad guys."

Odell took a long sip of the coffee and then set it on the desk.

"I appreciate that, Warren. The last thing I need is a shrink in my head. That poor doctor will never recover. Ya sure that ya don't want a cup of this, Joe?"

Commissioner Colbert looked at the cup and said, "Positive. I would rather drink glue. Odell, how is Doctor Burgess? Rumors are that you two grew close in only a few days. Is she okay?"

"She is okay. Sent her away for a few days. She is safe. Grundy is on a civilian mission escorting her home to California. He will stay with her until I wrap this up in a few days. After this mess, I cannot risk it. Yes, she is a world-renowned professor of botany, but she is a great woman, too. We are close. We are just friends. Nothing more. At least until all this madness is over. We really hit it off. Nothing inappropriate here. She is not a suspect. A civilian. Just an innocent victim of this madness that she did not want or need. I am not working any romance angles to get to the bad guys and gals like some hard-boiled gumshoe. This crazy world should allow me to have a life and feelings. Guess I earned it."

Commissioner Colbert nodded, and he leaned forward a little in his chair.

"Good call on George. The best of the best. I did not mean to imply you were doing something inappropriate. You sure did earn it. Glad you met someone that you care for. You need that in your life, Odell. Only a few days to wrap this all up, huh? Do you have suspects? What are you dealing with here? I don't need all the inside-Odell stuff. Just give it to me from a high-altitude."

The unlit cigarette continued to bounce as Odell answered.

"Sure thing. I will give it to ya, as I told Grundy. First, we have the murder of Mr. Randolph Burgess, the CEO, owner, and president of Standard Insurance Company. Next, we have the attempted murder of Doctor Eleanor Burgess. Eleanor took over the biz for her half-brother upon his murder. Then we have a wonderfully evil-laced list of corporate conspiracy, fraud, embezzlement, blackmail, plotting the illegal takeover of a company in order to steal seven-hundred-million dollars, a little illegal drug dealing or two or three or more, payoffs and shakedown of construction contractors and some local officials, and to top it all off, with a red bow of nefarious intentions, due to the joint efforts of a young police officer, Officer Benjamin Crane of the Boston, Massachucsetts Police Department and Inspector Odell of the Mohawk City, New York Police Department, we have the hopefully, attempted murder and not the murder of Ms. Josie McDermott. Currently, she is in a coma. Time will tell. Otherwise, we will have three homicides in total. To date."

Police Commissioner Colbert sat back in his chair, and he groaned and exhaled. After the groan and exhale, he looked over at the coffeepot and the stack of paper cups sitting next to it. He almost rose to pour a cup and then shook his head and returned to his chair.

Commissioner Colbert asked, "McDermott? Is she related to the now-deceased killer from this morning?"

"Sure is. His daughter. She knows too much. Tried to wipe her out before any yapping could happen."

"Understood. How did you come upon all of this criminal activity, Odell?"

Lyle Odell answered without hesitation.

"I read an article in the newspaper about the Standard Insurance Company and the building of that palatial new corporate building and campus over in the old factory district here in Sin City. I mean, it makes no sense, and it is the key to the case. There are obvious layers of corruption and blackmail involved. No offense to our beloved city and employer, but successful and affluent companies don't build fantastic corporate headquarters here. 'Cept for where you live, Mohawk City is mostly a dump."

That statement invoked another groan and an exhale from Commissioner Colbert. He looked over once more at the coffeepot. It was as if it were calling and pleading with him to sink into the mud of a cup. Something to divert his thoughts from this Odell experience.

Once more, he resisted.

Colbert repeated Odell's answer aloud as a slowly phrased question.

"You . . . read . . . an . . . article . . . in the . . . newspaper?"

"Yuppers."

"Okay. Got it. That is typical Odell-stuff. How is the sobriety going, Odell? I see you have the cigarettes going," Colbert said as he pointed at the unlit cigarette still glued to Odell's lower lip.

"It's going okay, mostly drinking the beer-flavored water. Light beer stuff. I did have three shots of Irish after the incident this morning. Yuppers. Had some shots with George at Grundy's Bar and Grille. Had to steady myself after that incident, but I have not gotten close to the edge of drunken madness or rolled off the cliff in two years now. I mostly taste the cigarettes. No more chain-smoking. For the most part."

Commissioner Colbert stood up. He smiled at Odell, and Odell also stood up. The two men shook hands. The commissioner spoke first.

"Thank you, Odell. In the interest of full exposure here. I called an emergency conference call meeting of the board of police commissioners after we heard of the incident today. There were some grave concerns. We called your old commanding officer. Captain Tucker. He gave us great advice. He said, 'Just let Odell do his thing. He will wrap it all up in a few days. There is a very good reason that he conducted a wild shootout with heavy ammo in downtown Mohawk City. The man is a genius and never does anything without a reason or a specific purpose.' Then Detective Miles Bradford matched the shooter to the earlier homicide, and the details came out about how you saved Doctor Burgess and now all of this that you are working on. Amazing. All from a newspaper article."

Police Commissioner Colbert shifted his feet uneasily. He was a stately and handsome man; and he projected the professionalism of a lifetime of police work in high-ranking positions.

Commissioner Colbert gauged Odell's appearance and narrowed his eyes when he asked, "One question, Odell. Although I think I know the answer already. I sense how personal this case is for you at this point in your illustrious career. I hope that it is not contempt that you feel for the new chain of command in the Mohawk City Police Department and some other members of the police department. Do you want any assistance? From us? From the Mohawk City Police Department? From anyone?"

Odell sipped the last of the muddy coffee; he looked inside the cup to confirm it was empty and tossed the cup in the trashcan next to his desk. Odell then rubbed his high and tight haircut, and then plucked the unlit cigarette from his lip and replaced it in the ashtray.

"Nope. Appreciate the offer, Warren. I am riding solo on this one. But when we wrap this all up and have all the evidence, then I will need your help with finding an independent accountant to study some ledgers and corporate expense reports and books. Gonna be many skeletons living in those books and numbers. An accountant that we can pay properly but who is not compromised towards the police department or any corporations. Also, will need your help in obtaining some documents via electronic means. I am not too swift with those computers."

"Not a problem, Odell. Just let me know, and I will arrange it all."

"Thank you. Other than those items, I will ride solo on this case. I have been waiting for this one. Contempt is a very strong word. Contempt is the one emotion that never goes away. I only feel contempt for the evil bastards of this world who decide to kill innocent persons, ruin lives and families, and break hearts. Those evil bastards that steal and destroy and commit crimes and break the law. As far as that new chain goes, well, let's just go with that just because there is snow on the roof does not mean there is not a fire in the furnace. And with all due respect, Warren. That was not one question. It was four questions. In that aforementioned illustrious career, of which it is still going, I found that exact details and facts are very important in investigations."

Commissioner Colbert smiled again. He reran the conversation through his mind while counting the total questions.

"So, it was, Odell. Four questions. Please be safe, Odell. Carry on. I will handle the press conferences and the media madness and continue to plow the road for you. Do what you need to do and keep us informed as you can. You have both mine and the board and the mayor's full support. As usual, try to keep the expenses down. Budgets, you know."

"Roger the budgets. Thank you, sir. The support means a lot to me. Just a few days and I will wrap this all up. Then I will write all the reports you and they need. Sit with any doctors that I need to sit with and interview and fill out all the forms they need. See ya."

"Odell, warning, the press is outside. You might get accosted. Best to go out a side door."

"Okay. Good. I will do that. I have to pick up some information here and will leave in a few minutes."

The side door proved to be poor advice. Detective Lyle Odell exited the side door of the Mohawk City Police Department, only to find Police Commissioner Warren Colbert holding off hordes of the media. An ambush. Local and some national and some downstate New York media outlets grouped in masses in the parking lot outside the side door; radio stations, television stations, newspapers, and internet news companies. Cameras, lights, action, and shouting. Especially when Odell appeared.

Lyle put his head down and made a beeline for his unmarked police cruiser.

"Inspector Odell! Did you really have to kill a man in cold blood on Main Street in downtown Mohawk City? In broad daylight! On a Saturday morning! What does Doctor Eleanor Burgess have to do with this? Gunfire with innocent women and children and elderly persons all around! Commissioner Colbert, what is going on in the city? Inspector Odell! Inspector Odell! How is the case going?"

Commissioner Colbert waved and empathized, as he had apparently done so many times previously that Inspector Odell would not have any comment.

Commissioner Colbert said, "Now, now, now. Stop! I already told you that Inspector Odell has no comment. I am holding a press conference at three this afternoon. In the

City Hall auditorium. There, I will answer your questions. Not now! Please disperse, or I will have to call officers to clear this area!"

Detective Lyle Odell almost made it to his patrol car when one aggressive reporter broke the line and ran up to Odell while waving his microphone, with his cameraman running after him to video record the moment. Once the young reporter broke the line, then a mad rush of other reporters followed him.

Commissioner Colbert waved his arms in the air frantically, pulled a two-way radio off his hip and made the call for police officer reinforcements.

The young reporter yelled out in the direction of Detective Lyle Odell over the gathering media crowd.

"Inspector Odell! Inspector Odell! Is it true that you were recently in Boston questioning and harassing top executives at the Back Bay Real Estate Group? The same developers who brokered such a wonderful deal for urban revitalization for Mohawk City and contributed so much to the building of the gorgeous corporate complex for the Standard Insurance Company? On a property that once was a desolate, abandoned factory falling down into ruins?"

Odell twirled the unlit cigarette stuck to his lip and narrowed his eyes. He spoke with disdain to the reporter.

"First off, it is Detective Odell. The inspector's title is bullshit. Like what just came out of your mouth is. Ya sound like Charles Dickens writing a story. Tugging at heartstrings. Where did you hear that I was harassing executives?"

The young reporter became a little uneasy. Odell was old now, but still rather intimidating. Especially this tactical version of Detective Lyle Odell. He really looked as if he were ready for battle.

"Those are the facts that I received from a fellow reporter in Boston."

"Facts? Since when do you media clowns deal in facts? You twist and turn and pick and choose and print and report anything nowadays to suit your own agendas. You wouldn't know a fact if you wiped your ass with it. I am a homicide detective. Been one for close to forty years. How old are you, kid? Twenty-five? I investigate crimes and search for clues and bring justice to the evil bastards that choose to break the law. That is what I do. I signed up for this career to do what is right and just, and to serve and protect the citizens of this city. A city full of crime and grit and horribleness. But it is my home. In some crazy way, I love it. Don't break the law and kill people, and you will never deal with me. You spew agenda bullshit and side with criminals to sell stories that work for your agendas. You a detective?"

"No."

"Are you a trained and experienced investigative reporter who works positively with police and digs for clues?"

"No."

"Well, let's try this one. Have you ever seen the naked body of a young and innocent, beautiful woman with her throat slit, and the fresh, red, blood running out of her body on the floor below where her body lay? The dead body with the bloody initials of some lunatic serial killer's obsession carved into her dead body by a knife yielded by that same insane serial killer? And then had to face her unconsolable loved ones and tell them the facts and details about her death?"

The young reporter's eyes welled up with tears. He dropped his microphone and shook his head. The cameraman shut the camera off.

The young reporter's voice was barely audible.

Yet, to his credit. The words arrived.

"No."

"Did ya ever see an old man, a hero . . . a war veteran

who survived combat and fought for our freedoms, and now, his dead and horribly mutilated body floats in a dirty, old river, because he innocently witnessed something that fate allowed him to see?"

"No."

"I didn't think so. I have. Those visions and incidents haunt me constantly. Phantoms of death and horror. Every freakin' day of my life. Okay. Those are facts. Get lost, kid."

Odell opened the door of the patrol car and slipped inside. The engine started. Odell put the car in gear and disappeared out of the parking lot. Off on the mission.

Homicide Detective Lyle Odell was exceptional at his job.

Snow on the roof; fire in the furnace. And this fire was burning as if it were a bonfire.

Chapter Seven

Odell Time

It appeared as if the construction site's mission was to build a medical office complex. At least that is what the "Coming Soon" sign out on the main street announced.

"Art Livingston. You look like ya brother does. Except that you are leaner and ya have worn-out bags under ya eyes. Construction project running late, huh? Not gonna deliver the project on-time and make the contractual agreements, huh?"

Art Livingston stood in the wavy soil of the construction site, a few feet away from a building that was a shell on the outside, but other than some pipes sticking up out of the concrete slab, and some temporary electrical lights, it was empty on the inside. Art Livingston stood next to a contractor, and the two of them were studying a blueprint. Livingston and the contractor looked up and at Homicide Detective Lyle Odell, who approached them and was making his way from about fifteen feet away before Odell began speaking. The contractor carefully observed Odell; his shaved head, with his two shoulder holsters equipped with service weapons, the tactical uniform, the badge, the works, and he looked at Art, nodded, took the blueprints, and scurried away.

Odell continued his slow walk.

"I have that effect on folks. They see me and want to run away. I am Detective. . .."

Art Livingston held his hand up in the air and then waved it in the direction of Odell.

As he did so, Art said, "I know who you are. Everyone knows who you are. You are all over the television news and the radio news. I am very busy. Have to run this project now." He stopped speaking and put his hands on his hips and asked, "How do you figure that this project is running late? What the hell business of that is yours?"

Odell now stood only a few feet away from Art Livingston. Livingston was a man of about medium height, but very stocky. He wore a hard hat on his head, but you could see that underneath, his hair was short. Mud covered the edges of the soles of his work boots; it was apparent that he had been walking around the construction site all day. He had a contractor's work vest on and he wore a pair of contractor's pants with various tools stuck in the pockets and a tape measure clipped to his belt. Art Livingston was the typical construction foreman. Or was he?

Odell removed a cigarette from a crumbled pack that he plucked out of his right leg pocket, shook a cigarette loose, replaced the pack, and stuck the cigarette on his lower lip. There it hung, the typical Odell smoke. Bouncing with the words, he spoke.

"I am a detective. I detect things. That is my job. Here it is on a Saturday. Just about four in the afternoon and here you are still working. Maybe the fact that you lost your foreman today, when he tried to kill Doctor Eleanor Burgess and tried to wipe me out and successfully killed Herbert O'Leary, might have something to do with you still being here. But the sign out there says, opening in November of this year. It is almost October and you still don't even have HVAC units on the roof there. Ya still have construction electrical lights inside and no ductwork. Just some rough plumbing. All those factors, tell me that ya screwed. Construction ain't fun in upstate New York winters."

Art Livingston wanted nothing to do with this conversation. His eyes darted all around and he was showing so many obvious signs of discomfort that you did not need to be Detective Odell to realize and observe them all.

"You can't smoke here and you need a hard hat," Art spouted out.

"It ain't lit. I am just tasting it. Trying to quit. A hard hat. For what? Looking at the crew here, it looks as if most of them are quitting for the day. It's five minutes after four now. About Mr. Jack McDermott, let me ask ya some questions."

Art began to play by the script.

He waved his hands in the air and shook his head violently and he shouted.

"No, no, no! That guy was a loose cannon. Drank too much. Fighting all the time. Mean, bad attitude. If he wasn't drunk, then he was doing drugs. He had severe PTSD from combat. I don't know anything about him. Told the owners to can him years ago. He got into it with Doctor Burgess at the grand opening for the building party. All drunk and stumbling and made all kinds of sexual comments. She rejected him. He got drunk and went nuts for revenge. It's over. Good riddance to that loser. I gotta go. That's all I have, Odell. I don't know anything else. You must leave, now."

Detective Odell stood there and his eyes burned holes in Art Livingston. Then Odell scanned the construction site.

Odell said, "You looking mighty pale, Arty. I have a feeling that it is more than just angst over this construction project schedule. Shady Jack was your construction foreman. Drunk all the time. I guess safety is not much of a factor for Emerald Construction, huh? Drunk and stoned foreman walking around construction sites. Maybe that is why the project is so behind its time. By the way, I will leave when I want to leave. Don't give me orders, Livingston. That might work in this line of work, but I will drag ya ass down to police headquarters so quick and whip up something to hold ya overnight that it will make your eyeballs spin. Even more than they are spinning right now. I have a few questions. I can ask them here or there. Your choice. You can refuse to answer them and lawyer up and drag this all out, but you just said that ya don't know much. Which is it? Ya know a lot? Or not much?"

Livingston did not speak; he just rolled his hands over in the air as an indication for Odell to ask the questions.

"So, did Old Herbie O'Leary reject Jackie-poo's advances, too? So, Jackie blew his head off this morning before he came gunning for Doctor Burgess and Odell."

Art explained, "O'Leary was tough on Jack during the Standard Insurance building construction project. Always playing up to the exact letter of the contract. Constantly beating him up over contractual items. There was lots of animosity between them. Construction meetings were brutal. The guy was a tough attorney. Jack must have finally flipped his cork and sought revenge."

Odell removed the hanging cigarette from his lower lip. He studied it and twirled it around in his fingers and then stuck it back on his lip.

"Sounds like Old Herbie was just doing his job. Business. He was a super-chief there at Standard Insurance. Remind me never to hire Emerald Construction for any project. You guys are a bunch 'a bums. Very hostile. Question. Do you use a Lorance Contractors on any projects?"

Art Livingston answered immediately. He did not think about it for even a half-second.

"Never heard of them."

"I didn't ask you that. Ya very upset and nervous. Lack of focus. What is that all about? I asked if you use Lorance Contractors on any project. Exact details and facts are very important in investigations."

"No. We do not use a Lorance Contractors on any projects."

"Do you know Mr. Gerald Palmer?"

"Yes, of course. He is the money guy at Standard Insurance. He wrote all the checks. I better know him."

Odell stared Art down for a few seconds. He took the bent cigarette out of his mouth and stuck it in that same pocket that he removed it from. But he did not try to place it back in the pack.

Odell mumbled, "Right leg, lower tactical pocket," as he sealed the flap to the pocket. "I guess he paid on time. As far as I know, he is still alive. Here is the drill, Arty. This is just me spouting off here. Nothing official. Let's just say that I am writing a crime novel and I am throwing ideas out for a storyline. Yuppers. Conjecture! Ya a mess because I believe Jack McDermott was hired to kill Old Herbie and Doctor Burgess by whoever the mucky-mucks are that are running this evil sideshow. If things don't come together quickly for me on this case, then old and washed up, Odell will be back to turn this construction site upside down. I am going to interview all these contractors. And some of the contractors who worked on the Standard Insurance building project. I bet Jackie-Poo shook them down for dough. Threatened them, dealt drugs from here. Pushed them around. With all that power and money backing him, it was easy for Jackie-Poo to be a money bully. Make some side jingle for his wallet and for ya guys, too. He sure ain't a money bully any more. And he was the muscle man for Emerald Construction when they needed someone roughed up a bit. I think this is all corrupt. This entire operation is a sham. It reeks of evil."

Odell dramatically waved his arms in the air to include the entire construction site and everything associated with it.

Detective Lyle Odell spoke once more.

"Ya guys are nothing but thugs posing as a construction company and real estate developers. A building like this does not take too long to build. It has been months and months and it still is not done. Yuppers, this novel has it all. Blackmail of Randolph Burgess. Most likely because he fell in the arms of a beautiful black widow. Then he turns up croaked and blue with death on a cruise ship. Sure, he had a heart attack. His health and his ticker were a mess. Old Herbie was a crook. Corporate takeover plans. The construction of that fancy corporate building and campus is a farce, and the key is well, Lily. Dear, sweet, beautiful Lily. Your daughter."

Art Livingston grew angry and his voice reflected the emotion.

"Leave my daughter out of this! All she did was work there at Standard! Lily did nothing wrong. She has left now. Going back to school. I wish she had left a long time ago!"

Odell studied Art Livingston for a few seconds, absorbing his emotions and making careful note of his words and actions. Despite it all failing down around him, Art loved his daughter.

"Well, now. If she did nothing wrong, then there is nothing to worry about, huh? Time will tell on that. I have a feeling that I will come to agree with you on the fact that Lily should have left Standard's employ a long time ago. Speaking of daughters and such . . . I almost forgot. Jackie-Poo's daughter survived the drugs injected in her today. I anticipated that evil move and sent the Boston Police on a rescue mission. She is barely alive, but she is alive, and in a coma. Can't wait for her to wake up and I am praying that she does. She has the best doctors and nurses looking after her. And God on her side. I am sure that a nice guy like ya are, Arty, believes in God and prayer and the survival of a beautiful young woman. Yuppers. This did not go as planned. Oh well. Jackie-Poo was not exactly the crack shot that he was supposed to be. Ya guys are up the old screwed creek, now. No paddles available. That's my conjecture. Potential storyline. My novel's preliminary outline. Just have to sit down and write it now. Make it a reality. Anyway, ya have a nice evening, Arty. I am just starting. On my novel. See ya now."

Odell turned around and slowly walked away.

Art Livingston watched until Detective Odell got into his police cruiser and drove away. Then he ran behind the building and got down on his knees and vomited. Violently.

Art Livingston dialed the number. His hands and fingers were shaking so badly that he fat-fingered the numbers twice. He also realized too late that he was using his own personal cellphone and not a burner phone. Mistake after mistake after mistake.

Odell's visit had him doing somersaults of fear.

The receiver of the call answered on the third ring. "Why are you calling me on your own phone? Damn! Focus! Focus! Too many mistakes! The big guy is fuming! Your crack shot was a bum. You are turning out to be the weak link in this chain. You already dialed me. Damage done. Go ahead and make it quick."

"Oh yeah, well, he can fume all he wants. Odell did not just visit you, or him, and shake you down. I used our cover plan with McDermott being a drunken, ex-military combat nut, and Odell did not buy it one bit. My mistakes? What about yours? Let me recall your words. Oh yeah. Odell is a drunk. Washed up. He will revert to drinking and fade away. Sulking. Too old, no elite team of sidekicks left. I am not worried about Inspector Lyle Odell! Blah, blah, blah. Hell, that supposedly old washed-up drunk, well, he took out an ex-military sniper with one headshot while our sniper guy was driving a moving truck. And Odell took the shot from over fifty feet away. He showed up here looking like some badass World War 2 commando ready to slit throats and storm beachheads. Shaved head, armed with all kinds of weapons. Dressed in tactical clothing for a uniform. Scared the shit out of me by just standing there. This guy is no joke. You miss-judged him. So, let's not talk about my mistakes."

There was silence on the other end of the phone. After a few seconds, the receiver spoke.

"We are wasting time. What does Odell know?"

"Pretty much everything. The guy is a freakin' genius. He basically laid it all out play-by-play, and now he is going after my daughter. Our family. Lily did not do anything wrong. Not in the big picture of this mess."

"Oh yeah, other than having an intimate sexual relationship with an older man and playing him like a fine violin in a symphony."

"That is not against the law. She fell in love with him. It happens."

"I guess. And getting that fancy sports car handed to her by her lover, with money he dipped out of a charity account, did not seem to faze her, too. Don't forget the jewelry, the fancy dinners, the wine, the car, cruises, and vacations . . . all the luxuries of life bestowed upon her in exchange for some great sex. I mean . . . love."

"She told me she loved him. I believe her. And speaking of mistakes and convenient side pieces . . . Josie is still alive. Odell anticipated it, and the local cops made it in time to rush her off to the hospital. In a coma, but alive. I did not sign up for this, brother."

There was another round of silence.

"I heard. Hopefully, she never wakes up. If she does, our strategy will be to discredit her. Her past behavior is not stellar. You did not sign up for this. True. But you did not flinch or complain at all with that money rolling in. That was fine. Right now, I have to tell you that it gets worse. Doctor Burgess flew the coop. No sign of her anywhere, although I suspect that she returned to California. We do not have time to try to find her. Too late for that. Word on the street is that George Grundy is not manning the bar at his downtown place. Chances are Odell had Grundy take the good doctor off somewhere, and Grundy is her bodyguard. Even if we had the time, and the connections and the manpower, we are not messing with George Grundy. That is like trying to blow up a mountain with a firecracker. He would stomp the life out of an entire football team at once. Get this . . . she put the facility manager at Standard Insurance, that big guy, that always played it straight and true, and got into it with McDermott, Lawrence Rinehardt, in charge."

"Shit. What a mess. Odell told her to do that on purpose. He is like a master chess player. Brillant sonofabitch he is. This guy. We are deep in the shit now."

"Okay. I did misjudge Odell. He is brilliant, but so are we. Let's think. Call Lily and tell her Odell is on his way. Tell her to stay calm but answer generically. Threaten to lawyer up when he digs in too deep. She is a genius, too. Odell will meet his match. I will check with the big guy for the next step. Art. Stay cool. Use the burner phone next time. Goodbye."

"Click."

The line went dead. Art Livingston did not feel one ounce better. He wanted to vomit again. Instead, he dialed his cellphone to call his daughter. She answered on the second ring.

"Honey. Listen up carefully. We have some troubles. . .."

It was now Saturday evening at 6 PM. Detective Lyle Odell arrived home. Finally, after a monumental day. Odell might have some miles under his belt now, and seen many, many things over his long career, but there were not many people who could outwork him, or even keep up with him.

Not any twenty-somethings, or thirty-somethings, or any-somethings. His energy remained boundless, and his resilience was remarkable.

He realized when he arrived home and sat in his easy chair that he had not even eaten a thing yet. All day. The toast at breakfast was a decoy. And he had smoked only a few cigarettes. He tasted many but smoked few. It was time to light one up; Odell did so, and he puffed away on it as he settled into his home for the night. There were not too many luxuries or furnishings inside Odell's modest home.

Odell's easy chair sat in the corner of the room; an ashtray overflowing with spent cigarette butts sat on the end table; and his ancient table radio sat next to the ashtray on that same end table. The table radio looked as if it were a museum piece. It had a brown wooden cabinet and a light brown speaker grille stained with nicotine smoke. The table and its contents sat rather wobbly next to the chair, and a pile of newspapers scattered about the floor all around the base of the chair. Every wall had an off-white paint on it, off-white from nicotine, or perhaps the paint was simply very old. On the other hand, perhaps it was a combination thereof. Cigarette odor hung in the room as if it were vines of tobacco drying in a shed. The living room had only one other chair in the entire room. A steel folding chair that appeared to have seen much better days. No sofa, no loveseat, just the easy chair and the rather sad, steel folding chair.

The dining room was empty.

To say that the house was sparse in furnishings was an understatement. In fact, it was barren. No ornaments, no pictures on the walls; no decorations of any sort. In the opposite corner from the easy chair was an antique black and white, tube-type television sitting on an upturned cardboard box, with rabbit ear antennas sticking precariously up in the air. Odell still used rabbit ears for television reception. . ..

Soon, he would settle into his easy chair and tune in for the Saturday night classical music concert on that ancient table radio. It was the highlight of Odell's week and one of his only sources of entertainment.

That was later. Now, there was still much work to do.

Since Odell had left his acrimonious meeting with Art Livingston at the construction site, some more developments occurred. Most importantly, he heard from George Grundy. Gundy contacted Odell via his burner phone, and Detective Odell now had that number locked into the memory bank and had a very good reason to keep aware of his own mobile phone's battery charge and status. George reported that Doctor Eleanor Burgess and he were all settled in now and the flight and trip had been, thankfully, uneventful. It turned out that Doctor Burgess had three residences. One was a more remote cottage residence out a few miles from the city of Berkeley, in the Berkeley Hills, another was a smaller townhouse very close to the university campus where she taught, and the other residence was a luxury penthouse unit in an exclusive high rise building near downtown Berkeley. After studying them all, Grundy chose the high-rise building, and the unit owned by Doctor Burgess to bunk down and ride out the madness. George explained that the high-rise building was home to several high rollers and very wealthy and influential residents. The security was top-notch and fully staffed, even in the parking garage, and the security cameras covered every inch of the property. George Grundy met and interviewed the building's security captain and gave him some vague details of his mission, but enough to feel confident that Grundy could trust them. In typical Grundy manners, he exchanged some code words and phrases to use, just in case of the appearance of some, as Odell would categorize them, "Persons with nefarious intentions show up."

And an added plus in Grundy's decision was the

downtown location offered some quality restaurants close by that would deliver food. They would never have to leave the unit and risk being out in public. And George would stay well-fed. Grundy reported that, via some secure connections and communications, they made a connection with an independent attorney and the requested permission paperwork would be on the way to Odell by midday tomorrow. Eleanor also sent the message to the facility manager, Mr. Lawrence Rinehardt. That decision would be sure to rattle some cages at Standard Insurance Company! Odell's plan was evolving.

Now Odell's mission was research. He had picked up some files from the archives when he was at headquarters, and he did actually have a computer at his home and access to the internet. Mostly, Odell would rely on his library and his connections. And Odell, being Odell, he even had a collection of old telephone books from all over New York, New Jersey, Connecticut, and Massachusetts. With the yellow and the white pages.

Before diving into the research, Odell had four more phone calls to make tonight. He checked in with Officer Ben Crane in Boston, who reported no change in Josie McDermott's condition. She was still comatose. No worse. No better.

Then Odell called Crane's chain of command and spoke with his captain. First, he praised Officer Crane's outstanding efforts and advocated for his actions. Crane's commanding officer thanked Odell and then he went on and assured Detective Lyle Odell that they fully supported his investigation and that he had his best detectives and Crime Scene Investigators committed to the case. Reports and results of the preliminary investigations of Josie's apartment and the crime scene and evidence were forthcoming. The captain hoped for next Tuesday and said that he would keep Odell posted.

The third call was to Frank's West Pizza Restaurant, and

the other was to an old Coast Guard connection.

The owner of Frank's West Pizza Restaurant, Mr. Anthony Battaglia, often said that Detective Lyle Odell helped pay for both his children to attend college. He was most likely accurate in that statement. Matty, the delivery person, had worked for Anthony forever. He could drive blindfolded to Odell's home and claimed that his down payment on his home came from the tips from Lyle Odell's pizza deliveries. For the most part, Odell got by on black coffee, cigarettes, his Irish whiskey, his beer-flavored water, and pizza. Although compared to his previous years, and months, and weeks, and even days, Odell greatly reduced the intake levels of both the cigarettes and the Irish whiskey levels. Odell also enjoyed the occasional grilled cheese sandwiches from Grundy's Bar and Grille. They were a treat!

Odell dialed the number for Frank's West Pizza Restaurant. He did not use his cellphone; he had an old landline telephone hanging on the kitchen wall. Frank's West had caller identification on their phones. Anthony answered on the first ring.

"Hey, Odell. What is the score in the Rover's game?"

"Nah, not tonight, Anthony. A case came up."

"Ah, man. Sorry. Oh yeah, yeah, yeah . . . saw it on the tube this afternoon. Geez. Heavy metal. Are you, ok?

"Fine. Thanks, Anthony."

"No, Grundy then? Just one cheese pie?"

"Yes. Just one cheese pie. I had to put George back in the game. He is on a mission."

Anthony sighed over the telephone and he recovered.

"I ain't gonna ask cuz I don't want to know even if ya told me, Odell. Just be safe. You and George. I will put the pie in."

"Hey, Ant. Ya got any of that beer-flavored water in the cooler that Matty can bring over to me? I am running low and can't risk getting into the Irish."

"I will check. If not, I will have Matty stop and pick up a twelve-pack. You like that stuff?"

"It's okay. I guess that I grew used to drinking light beer. It is like riding a bicycle from New York to Los Angeles instead of driving a sports car. You eventually get there, and save money on gas costs, but the thrill is just not the same. it. Thanks, Ant. Hey, as you saw on the television, it is a little dicey out there for us right now. Have Matty use the knock. I will unlock for him."

"You got it, Odell. The knock."

"See ya."

"Click."

The conversations were well orchestrated, and the routines replayed over the years.

Odell kept the pizza and beer money in a metal coffee can. A can that he kept in the cupboard in the kitchen. The right side, directly above the coffeemaker and to the left of the stove. George knew where the money was. Christina Fuentes-Columbo knew where it was, too. So did Marlin Santini. Odell missed them all on this lonely Saturday night. But he was on a mission, and he was going to focus on nothing but that mission. He grabbed the money from the coffee can. Odell unlocked the front door and set the coffee can on the window ledge right next to the front door. Matty knew what to do. About thirty minutes later, the knock came. Odell fingered his weapons, just to be sure.

One knock. A three-second pause. Four knocks and then five quick knocks. Odell relaxed. Matty opened the door, set the pizza and beer on the floor, grabbed the money, waved and he was gone.

"Thanks, Odell!"

Matty was working toward another down payment. This time, it was on a new boat.

Odell began munching on pizza slices and sucking down beer-flavored water while he sat in his easy chair and began studying some files. He glanced at the clock and he knew that he'd better make this one last call. The admiral went to bed early these days. Saturday night or not.

Another call that would be short and sweet.

Retired United States Coast Guard Vice Admiral Whitney McCauley answered on the first ring.

"Chief Warrant Officer Lyle Odell. What the hell are you getting into now? It made the news even here in Yonkers. My goodness. Aren't you getting too old for high-powered gunfights in the streets? Please don't answer that question. What is up? How can I help?"

"Vice Admiral McCauley, sir. I hope you and Mrs. McCauley are doing well. I will honor your request and not answer that one question. Because if I answered yes, that might make you feel old, too. I will summarize the first question in one sentence. It is one of those cases that seemed like nothing and blew up into a major situation."

Vice Admiral McCauley chuckled a little on the phone. He knew Odell all too well.

"We are well, Odell. Thank you. Blew up on you, huh? Don't they always?"

"It seems to go that way for me, sir. Vice Admiral McCauley, please, any connections with the Blue Ocean Cruise Lines out of lower Manhattan? I need to check out a lead. A specific cruise where a Mr. Randolph Burgess passed away while onboard. The cruise sailed out of Manhattan on the nineteenth of September of this year, and it sailed out to the Bahamas and then docked back in home port in New York on the twenty-fifth of September. Mr. Burgess died on the twenty-fourth."

Vice Admiral McCauley paused for a few moments and then said, "Got it. Roger, the dates, and information. Yes. You are in luck. As a matter of fact, one of the executives there for Blue Ocean is an ex-Coastie. I can make the call early tomorrow and plow the road for you. Who do you need to meet with so I can make the arrangements? The captain?"

"Negative, sir. The bartenders. The waitstaff. The ship's medical doctor, a maintenance mechanic, and the security chief. Anyone else who might recall Mr. Randolph Burgess, Lily Livingston, and Herbie O'Leary, ESQ from the Standard Insurance Company?"

"Interesting collection of folks. Roger that. When do you want to visit?"

"Tomorrow or Monday at the latest."

"I will make the call. You sailing solo on this one, Odell?"

"Roger that, Vice Admiral McCauley. On the official side, I am solo. On the unofficial side, I did have to put Grundy back in the game for a special mission."

"Roger. You do have a way of dipping into retirees. How is George?"

"Solid, sir. As always."

"Good. Give him my best. For an Army guy, Grundy is all right. We need to meet and catch up soon. Odell, please. Be safe. Seriously. That looked like heavy gunfire out there today. I will be in touch as soon as I can."

"Aye, aye, sir. Thanks again."

"Click."

The line went dead.

It was nearly eleven at night. Odell realized the time. His favorite time of the week.

The pizza box sat at the feet of Odell. There were a few slices left. A few empty bottles of beer-flavored water sat near the pizza box. A few more cigarettes piled in the ashtray on the end table. Stacks of papers and files and books sat on the floor all around Odell's easy chair. His tactical notepad crammed full of new notes.

Odell's body and mind screamed for sleep. For rest. For peace. He leaned over and clicked the old table radio on. The dial lights glowed with a pleasant and relaxing orange glow—a nostalgic classic that provided some light in the old home. Odell clicked off the table lamp on the end table so that the old table radio was the only light available. It cast the same comforting warm glow all around as Odell settled back into his easy chair. He undid his tactical boots and pulled them off his feet and set them aside next to the chair. Odell lifted his weapons out of the shoulder holsters, but he set them on the floor, within arm's reach. The vacuum tubes of the radio finally warmed up, and the magic of the radio came alive. The eleven o'clock Saturday evening concert of classical music.

As soon as the first notes sounded, Odell mumbled, "Rachmaninoff. Variations on a theme by Paganini. Sounds like the symphony out of Philly. Gorgeous melody. Glorious."

His exhausted mind and body would not allow him to enjoy much of this Saturday night concert. Not this Saturday night.

Within a few notes, Odell drifted off to sleep. Peace finally arrived. For a few short hours.

It was now Sunday morning. Six o'clock. Homicide Detective Lyle Odell was cruising his way to lower Manhattan in an unmarked Mohawk City Police Department cruiser.

Sleep when you can.

Eat when you can.

Odell was up at four-thirty in the morning. So was retired United States Coast Guard Vice Admiral Whitney McCauley because he called Lyle Odell at four-thirty-eight that same morning. Admiral McCauley plowed the road for Detective Odell. Lyle was not going to ask how Admiral McCauley had arranged all of this after receiving a call on a Saturday night and having virtually no notice. Odell knew the answer. When a three-star vice admiral, retired or not, calls you, no matter the time of day or night, you tend to answer the call. Vice Admiral McCauley reported that Odell was in luck because the same cruise ship was back in dock after a few days at sea. Most of the requested crew members were available for interviewing; except for the medical doctor.

"Odell," Vice Admiral McCauley asked, "is that a concern for you and the case that the doctor is not available?"

"Vice Admiral McCauley, as long as he is not dead, then, no, I kind of expected it. He is afraid of a misdiagnosis. He is not guilty of a crime, just guilty of being a lousy doctor."

It took Detective Lyle Odell about four and a half hours to reach the cruise ship's port. The security chief arranged for Detective Odell to meet with everyone in an assembly room, first for introductions and then, if Odell needed it, he could interview each crew member individually, in a private area. Everyone was very accommodating and cooperative.

"Please call me Detective Odell or just Odell. I am not actually fond of my official title," Odell announced as a prelude to the meeting.

Initially, Detective Odell asked very broad questions of the group, and then he narrowed it down. He showed them photographs of Vance and Reid Livingston. Then, the photos of Lily Livingston, and of Mr. Burgess and of Herbert O'Leary, and provided a general background on each individual. For the most part, Odell was not making much in the way of progress in his investigation or with the questions. Some of the crew seemed excited to be involved in the criminal investigation process, others seem bored and disinterested, and others had a rudimentary interest in the case, and were polite, but they obviously just showed up because their managers told them they had to do so. Throughout the meeting, Detective Lyle Odell used all his usual investigation methods, his keen observation skills, and his extraordinary insight into human behavior in order to detect the slightest display of guilt, coercion, or nefarious intentions. So far, everyone was in the clear.

The security chief, who had an impressive resume, with some police work and several years as a corporate security chief in a worldwide corporation, was adamant that there was no foul play.

"Sorry to say, Detective Odell, but in my opinion, you are wrong about this one being a homicide. Securely locked door. No forced-entry signs. There was only one door in and one door out. Windows intact and secured. No signs of a struggle. Everything in the cabin room was in order and neat and orderly. The deceased died alone in his bed. Even the bedcovers were neatly arranged around the body."

The maintenance mechanic testified as to how the doors and door locks work. Even though he was not the maintenance person on duty for that incident, he listened carefully to the security officer and agreed with the condition of the lock when they used the master key to open the cabin room. That was a secure lock and not tampered with at all. The maintenance mechanic spoke of how the HVAC vents and ducts on both the supply and return air enter and leave the cabin room and how they are too small for a person to remove the grilles and crawl into the room through them.

"Impossible," was his statement.

Right now, everything pointed to a busted theory. Everything that caused alarm initially to Detective Lyle Odell, with his theory of the death of Mr. Randolph Burgess being a homicide, was not adding up right now. The great Homicide Detective Lyle Odell might be incorrect about this theory. It was bound to happen; but it did not explain everything else that Odell felt was wrong about the case. Nor did it explain the mayhem and reactions of his suspects after Lyle Odell began poking around in the case. For a few fleeting seconds, Odell's mind whirled with possibilities.

Was Art Livingston's testimony incorrect?

"That guy was a loose cannon. Drank too much. Fighting all the time. Mean, bad attitude. If he wasn't drunk, then he was doing drugs. He had severe PTSD from combat. I don't know anything about him. Told the owners to can him years ago. He got into it with Doctor Burgess at the grand opening for the building party. All drunk and stumbling, and made all kinds of sexual comments. She rejected him. He got drunk and went nuts for revenge."

Odell's mind whirled, until one bartender piped up. A middle-aged woman named Michelle Gomez, who was quite pretty, and very well-spoken, and had an eye for detail and a memory to back it all up. She was about to tip the case in Odell's favor with her keen observations.

"I recall them all. Very clearly. I love detective movies. I am a crime buff, and as a bartender, I make a living by studying people. Have to maximize my tips. I can even describe what they wore that night. That sat at a table close by the bar and had their dinners and drinks. I saw those two men, the father and son. The Livingstons were speaking at the corner of the bar with the old guy. The Irish last name guy. Then the beautiful young woman walked over and spoke to the Livingston men. The meeting broke up when she arrived. It was if they were plotting something until, she walked into it. Mr. Burgess was quite an attractive man, and his female companion, business or not, much younger, or not, was very smitten with him. She was young, beautiful, and intelligent. Mr. Burgess drank heavily, but he could hold his liquor quite well. He was obviously a regular heavy drinker. The young woman drank too, but she was under control. She paced her drinks. The very old man was very quiet. He studied the interaction between the young woman and Mr. Burgess quite intensely. He only gently sipped a few glasses of wine over many hours." Ms. Gomez waved her hands in the air and said, "I know a woman in love. I also know a man who is jealous of that woman being in love with another man. The old guy was jealous. The young woman was in love with Mr. Burgess."

She then turned to a tall, lanky young man who stood next to where Ms. Gomez sat, and she put him on the spot.

"Curtis. You waited on their table. Do you agree?"

Curtis shifted his feet nervously. It was obvious that he was uncomfortable with having to be in a situation where he had to testify about anything to do with this experience and the situation. He was a handsome young man with thick wavy black hair. Perhaps Curtis was twenty-five years of age at the most. He wore a traditional black and white server's uniform. His eyes studied Detective Lyle Odell and then they wandered over to Michelle, and they seemed to plead as to why she had to put him in the game. Odell sensed the young man's discomfort at speaking, and he diffused the situation.

Odell pointed at the back pocket of his pants and asked, "What 'cha reading there, Curtis?"

The young man seemed surprised that Detective Odell noticed that he had a book in his back pocket. He smiled a faint smile, reached back to his pocket, and worked the book out of its confines.

Curits spoke with a heavy New York City accent.

"It is a pocketbook. I read them on my breaks. I like the classics. I am working at this job to save for college someday. I want to be an English literature major. Teach English someday." Curtis held the book up so Odell could see the cover, and he added, "Great Expectations. Dickens. I love Dickens."

Odell nodded. "The line about March is a classic. Good choice. Keep after your dreams, Curtis. Ya seem like a young man who is determined and will succeed. Ya from the Bronx, huh?"

"Yes, Detective Odell. The Bronx." Curtis was more comfortable now, and Odell's observation skills impressed the young man. He opened up on his comments now.

"I agree with Michelle. The young woman had the hots for the Burgess guy. She called him Randy. The old guy was an angry dude. Jealous, sure, but man alive, that woman was a knockout. I was very attentive to that table because it was worth it to steal glimpses of her. Totally gorgeous. Mr. Burgess might have died, but I am sure he died happy that night. She was all over him. Even when he said the spicy food he had for dinner was giving him heartburn."

Detective Lyle Odell perked up. The testimony was now proving to be very productive. He stared in at Curtis and waved his hands in the air in front of his body, rolling them over in a wave motion to indicate that he wanted Curtis to continue to elaborate.

"Go on, Curtis. Spicy food? What did he order for dinner?"

"Yeah. At first, he did not want it. Said his stomach was not good with spicy food. The old guy convinced him to have it. The gorgeous chick told him not to have it, but the old guy egged him on. He had the jalapeño-citrus salmon dish. It must have been good because he ate every last bit of it, but it was spicy. The old guy gave him a handful of heartburn pills. He popped them like candies. He had a few more whiskies and then he said he had to go to his cabin. The gorgeous chick helped him up and led hm away."

Detective Lyle Odell threw his arms up in the air, and everyone in the room jumped at his actions.

Odell shouted, "Please. Curtis enough! Thank you very, very much! This is fantastic! Please. I need silence."

Eccentric Odell behavior kicked in.

Odell closed his eyes and stood in the center of the room with every eye on him. It was as if he was in such deep thought that he was falling into a meditative state. Odell did not move a muscle, but his eyelids fluttered as they remained closed. Detective Lyle Odell opened his eyes, and everyone remained fixated on his unusual behavior.

Odell said, "Michelle and Curtis. You both have been invaluable. A thousand fist bumps in the air for your glorious attention to detail and testimonies. Always remember that exact details and facts are very important in investigations. Just a few more questions unless anyone else has any further input."

Odell stopped speaking and scanned the group. No one raised a hand or offered a word, so Odell moved on to ask his final questions.

"Curtis, please, your opinion or your facts, because I have a feeling that you, as apparently any red-blooded young man, would watch and observe Mr. Burgess and Lily Livingston leave the dining hall and go to his room. Especially Ms. Livingston. Tell me about that exit."

Curtis was very adamant and excited now to offer his testimony.

"I sure did watch her leave. The dress she wore would make a man's heart melt and your eyes weep from her beauty. Her rear view was something that needed to be on a painting in a museum somewhere. I offered to help them back to the cabin and call for the doctor if he needed it, but he said he was okay. She went into the cabin with him. The old guy had one more glass of wine, and then he left. He was on his cellphone when he left. I watched them and followed them down the main hallway from the dining hall, to be sure. I can show you if needed."

Odell shook his head to indicate no.

"Thank you. No need for that. This is fantastic. Thank you. And the heartburn pills . . . came from Mr. O'Leary? The old guy, as you call him."

"Sure did. He had them in his suit jacket pocket."

Odell almost smiled. He walked over to Curtis, and the young man stood up, tall and straight. Odell extended his hand, and the two men shook hands.

"Curtis. Keep reading. Keep your dreams alive. I know you want to teach, but honestly, ya would make a hell-u-va detective." Odell turned to Michelle and commented, "As would you, Michelle. Crime buff, huh? Ya a pro! Thank you both."

Lyle Odell also shook hands with Michelle and thanked her for her excellent memory and testimony. He thanked the entire group.

"Two questions for you," Odell said as he pointed to the security chief. "Then I will leave you all alone. I suppose each of these individuals had his or her own assigned cabin rooms?"

"Yes, they did," he answered right away.

Odell followed the first question up with the last inquiry.

"How many used condoms did you find in the trash can?"

The security chief seemed to be surprised at Odell's question. He was going to get to that fact; however, Detective Lyle Odell beat him to the words. He now realized that Odell's detective skills were impressive and otherworldly. He knew that Odell had not yet received a copy of his report, which he held in his hand, and had not offered it to Odell yet. The report contained an inventory of all items in the cabin. But it was still in a sealed envelope.

"Two."

"Excellent. Well, it is obvious that the observations by Curtis and Michelle were accurate. They were lovers. And since a cabin occupant secures the lock from the inside, Ms. Livingston left Mr. Burgess after their love-making sessions, and he passed shortly thereafter. He had a bad tummy and a weak ticker, but other parts of his body worked rather well."

Odell was exuberant! He enthusiastically shook hands with the security chief, who handed off the envelope and explained to Odell that it contained his report. In a flash,

Homicide Detective Lyle Odell left the room with a wave over his head.

Curtis piped up and spoke.

"Wow! Once I finish Great Expectations, then I gotta read some Sherlock Holmes."

Chapter Eight

Ms. Lily Livingston

Homicide Detective Lyle Odell stood next to the sports car, and he puffed on a cigarette. The smoke chased up into the air and all around his head. He studied the car and admired it.

He walked over to the front end of the car and took careful note of the license plate. He jotted the license plate down in his mind.

"38 Magic."

Detective Lyle Odell walked around the car and checked out every aspect of it. Black. Hardtop. Custom wheel rims. Turbo-charged. Fantastic.

Odell thought, 'How the car had to be worth at least three-hundred-fifty-thousand dollars or even more.'

While he puffed on the dangling cigarette, Odell leaned in and cupped his hands around his eyes to peer inside the vehicle. It was a glorious Sunday; warm and sunny and a clear blue sky. New York State weather is very underrated. Especially upstate New York in the spring and fall of the year. It can be gorgeous. The drive to Westchester from lower Manhattan was short and rather pleasant. He was glad that he had chosen to drive on the Saw Mill Parkway. It was gentler and more scenic, too. Odell admired the interior of the vehicle; the manual gearshift alone was a thing of beauty, and the dashboard looked like the car should or could fly to outer space. For that price; maybe it should do so.

Her footsteps were soft upon the pavement. Odell

looked up and saw her making her way to the car. Ms. Lily Livingston made her way down the walkway from the apartment house to where she parked the car in the small driveway next to where she lived. It was an upscale apartment. Dripping in luxury. Not a bad crib for a college gal living off campus to lay her head on a pillow. Lily wore a light white sweater over a yellow chiffon dress; a dress with white lace frills on the sleeves, on the hems, and around her neck. The dress licked at her ankles and the top of her medium-height, open-toed shoes. Shoes that laced a little up her ankle with some alternating wraps of leather laces.

Odell thought as he studied her, 'No wonder the guy's ticker gave out. She could melt a glacier.'

He recalled Eleanor's words describing Lily Livingston.

'Anyway, I had limited dealings with her, but I can tell that she is quite brilliant and is a person who has bridged the chasm. Super-intelligent. Charismatic. Well-spoken and dynamic. And of course, as I mentioned last night, she is very beautiful. Shapely. Perfect figure, perfect breasts, perfect smile. Long blonde hair . . . a stunner who I imagine has her pick of the men.'

Lyle Odell mumbled, "Could pick any man. No question. But she picked Randolph Burgess. . .."

Her voice fit her beauty. It drifted through the air like plucked strings on a harp.

"It is quite the car, Inspector Odell. Isn't it?"

Odell studied her. Her long blond hair hung all around her, as if it were a yellow aura of beautiful light. It framed her perfect facial features like a fine portrait frame. Gold dangle earrings and a gold necklace with some gemstones intertwined with the curls of the metal rope. An expensive purse in her right hand.

"It sure is a fantastic vehicle. Interesting custom license plate, too. 38 Magic."

"It is. Not many take note of that license plate. It is my

breast size. I left a letter off to leave some supposition involved. A lover told me I was magic. We put the two together and . . . wah-lah! A custom New York vehicle license plate."

Odell seemed entertained. He almost smiled at the testimony. Instead, he commented.

"Ha! That is a wonderfully creative touch. That might be too much information for our initial meeting, but what the hell . . . it works for me. Please. Call me Detective Odell or just plain, Odell. I am not fond of the bullshit inspector title."

She smiled. Perfect white teeth. Of course, she had perfect white teeth.

"Okay. Fair enough. Detective Odell, it is. Please, you can call me Lily." She waved her hands in the air in the direction of Detective Odell and said, "I must say. You are not looking how they described you to me. You look like some type of military commando. Muscular and kick-ass and a take no prisoners type of thing. Very fit and capable. Badass. I love the look. Most of the men that I run into nowadays are wimps. Their idea of badass is consuming a bowl of spicy chili."

Odell finished the last drag of the cigarette. He ground the butt end out on the sole of his boot and then stuffed the spent cigarette butt into his tactical pants pocket while mumbling the location.

"Right leg tactical pants pocket. Under the flap."

Odell looked up and said, "Thank you for the fit and capable compliment. I bet they told you that I was an old drunken fool and a mess. Baggy, wrinkled shirt and suit, messy hair. Necktie not tied correctly and looking more like a noose than a tie. Never clean-shaven. Looked like I slept in my clothes. Chain-smoking. Red eyes and worn-out. Smells like stale cigarettes and Irish whiskey and stinky clothes with spent cigarette butts stuck in random pockets."

"Sort of. Not quite that awful, but close. Yes."

"Well, you look exactly as described to me."

"What was that description?"

"Stunningly gorgeous."

Odell's blunt statement instantly melted her heart.

Lily almost blushed. Even in the sun, Odell thought that her cheeks were turning red. At least pink.

"You flatter me. Thank you. Kudos. I find you very handsome. Rugged."

This was not the meeting that Odell wanted, nor anticipated. An instant attraction. Magnetic.

Odell glanced at Lily and then over to the car and then set his eyes on the front entrance to the exclusive apartment house.

Lyle Odell shifted gears in a strategic diversion.

He said, "Say, Lily, I would love to stand here and trade flattering comments about each other's appearances and such, and insight into the size of your breasts, but I need to get to asking ya a few official police-like questions."

Lily also shifted gears. She shook her head no. Right away. No hesitation. Lily was confident. She was forceful.

"I am very sorry, Detective Odell. I will need to refuse to answer anything related to your investigation unless you officially bring me in for questioning and I have a lawyer present. I will take you for a ride in my car if you would like. We could go have a few drinks and brunch, but you cannot ask me any questions about what you were discussing with my father yesterday. He called me and gave me very clear instructions."

Odell seemed to respect her straightforwardness.

"I see. Okay. Straight up and fair. We will take the next steps then. I would love to go for a spin in this fancy rig. Sharing drinks and brunch with a beautiful woman sounds amazing, but asking me not to ask questions is like dropping a steak in front of a dog and telling the doggie that he or she cannot eat it. Ain't gonna happen. No matter what the terms and the agreements are."

"Okay. Fair enough. Then what are the next steps? Are you going to pull me in for official questioning?"

Odell began patting his uniform pockets while searching for a smoke. After a quick search, he found the pack, and after a shake of the pack, Odell put a twisted cigarette on his lower lip.

Lily pointed at it and commented, "My goodness, Detective Odell. What do you do to your cigarettes?"

"Not sure. I think that I sit on 'em. Not gonna smoke this one. Just taste it. I would offer you one, but with those gorgeous white choppers, ain't no way that you smoke. I am trying to quit smoking 'em. So instead, I just use them as a prop now. Gives me the hard-boiled detective look, kinda thingy."

Odell twirled the cigarette around and around as he held it in his mouth and as he stood and thought for a few seconds.

"Nope, not gonna drag ya in for official questions. Not yet."

Odell turned and pointed at the sports car and then turned back to Lily.

"I mean, it is not related to the case, so I will ask ya. Where were you going now? Before I intercepted ya."

"To brunch. My father told me to expect you soon. I thought that you would track me down no matter where I went. They say you are a genius. I really have nowhere to hide. Therefore, I figured I would enjoy a nice relaxing brunch and a few cocktails."

Lily smiled and added, "By-the-way, you do look hard-boiled."

"Oh. Gotcha. Thanks for the honesty and the compliment. Ain't no genius, just a homicide detective that has been at it for a long time. I heard that ya got a ton of smarts, too. Pursuing a master's degree in chemistry. That is no joke. Anyway, after we speak a little here, I am heading back to Mohawk City with what I have now. I have a ton of research to study with some new documents that I will receive today. Earlier this morning, I met with the ship's crew on the cruise ship that you sailed on with Randolph Burgess, your cousin and uncle, and now deceased Old Herbie."

Lily's eyes opened wide, and she bit her lower lip. Suddenly, she was very uncomfortable. Odell carefully studied her reaction. Attraction or not, Odell was going to pounce now. He actually used the attraction and banter to his advantage to corner Lily.

"Yuppers. The server who waited on ya guys that night that Burgess croaked, well, he recalled you very well. I can certainly see why. He thought you were the most gorgeous woman that he had ever seen. But Curtis, that is the server's name, agreed with Michelle, the bartender, on one key point. A point that made me realize that up until this morning, I miss-judged you and your role in this entire, complicated mess. But that judgement was only based upon the scant evidence that I had a chance to compile."

Lily fidgeted nervously. She shifted her feet, pushed her hair back away from her face, and she felt the burn of Odell's eyes studying her.

She spoke in her golden voice.

"I imagine that detective work is a lot like experiments in chemistry. You need to have the proper mixtures and keep probing and checking and rechecking and experimenting until you can draw the final conclusions. Otherwise, you can skew the results, and your reports thereof are incorrect."

"Great analogy," Odell said as the twisted cigarette hung onto to his lower lip for dear life. Odell purposely kept his reply short.

Odell waited. A bit of cat and mouse ensued.

"I will bite. What is the key point, Detective Odell?"

Odell's reply was immediate and forceful. Imposing.

"That you were truly and deeply in love with Mr. Randolph Burgess."

Lily Livingston's gorgeous blue eyes immediately welled up in tears. She staggered a little, and Odell hustled over and grabbed her arm to steady her and prevent her from falling.

"Here, Lily. Hold on now. I gotcha. Please. Steady now. My apologies for hitting you with a broadside shell. Do you want to sit here on the steps?"

Ms. Lily Livingston shifted her feet underneath her stance like an ice skater after recovering from a spill and now testing the ice surface for balance. She steadied herself, and she, in turn, held onto Odell with a firm grip. Her perfume floated in the air and surrounded Detective Lyle Odell as if it were a cloud of joy sent straight from Heaven. She smelled like fresh cut sweet peas emitting from spring blossoms. Glorious.

"I am okay. Now. Thank you, Detective Odell. No, I do not need to sit. I appreciate the assistance of your arm for support. Obviously, I did not expect that. My goodness. That hit me hard. Very hard."

She turned, and her face was only inches from Lyle Odell's face as she still held onto him tightly. She wiped at her eyes to remove the tears, and as she did so, she narrowed her eyes and studied Odell.

"You have remarkable gray eyes. Remarkable. I have never seen eyes like yours. No wonder that you do not miss a trick. God gifted you with the eyes of a genius. Your eyes have pain, but they have purpose."

She gently reached out and took the twisted cigarette out of Odell's mouth, and she handed it to him. Odell took it and stuck it into a random pocket. No mumbling this time.

She let go of Odell and flexed her back a little, and stepped away from the good detective. It was as if she required the separation to recover her thoughts and her soul.

Lily thought, 'My goodness, this man is nothing like I thought he would be.'

She mustered up the strength to speak. She had to do so. She was flubbing this entire encounter up now. The plan she made with her father had just gone to hell in a handbasket.

"And you accept that testimony as the truth? A bartender and server's words?"

"I do. As any quality alcoholic can testify to, bartenders and servers are keen observers of human interactions. As a keen observer of human emotions and actions, myself, as a detective, and as a struggling, but sometimes recovering alcoholic, I appreciate their backgrounds and skills. Tips depend on their observations. The best bartenders that I ever met were psychology majors in college. Great background—it is just that they can earn more dough as bartenders. And life is difficult out here. Money helps. And based upon your reaction, I would say they were spot on, and I was smart to accept their testimony. Do you agree?"

Lily shook her head and mumbled, "No answered questions, Odell. Sorry."

Odell searched for the bent cigarette. After a few pats, he found it. He stuck it back on his lower lip.

Odell was going to lay it all out now. He spoke with firmness in his voice. His strategy was working, despite Lily's intelligence. Odell had a way of cracking people.

"Okay. Here is the drill, from where I see it. You took this job when the Standard Insurance Company was here in Westchester. You worked for Mr. Burgess while flirting with the idea of going back to school. It was a prestigious job. Paid very well. Amazingly well. You connected with Randolph. He was handsome, wealthy, confident. Available."

Lily changed her posture and pushed her hair away from her face again. There was a gentle breeze now. She listened intently.

"You really admired him. Loved the job, so you delayed going back to school for your master's degree and stayed working at Standard Insurance. Maybe on a business trip, Randolph and you had a ton to drink. He did drink way too much, and one thing led to another, and you became intimate. It happens. Not a big deal in this world. Yeah, the age gap, and his health was precarious, and ya have the boss thingy, but that is life. There are worse things. The sex was amazing, and from then on in, you two guys were like bunnies whenever you could do so. He fell for you. You began to fall for him. He did something dumb, though, and I will need to dig for that one. I am thinking that he bought ya lots of stuff. Jewelry. Fine dining. Maybe paid for luxuries and dresses and everything. Maybe even this car. Yes. I am thinking that he bought you this car."

Odell turned and pointed at the car, and then he refocused and dove back into his theory.

"Sure, he had tons of dough, but maybe the money guys were looking at his expense accounts and he wanted to cover up your relationship from others in the company until he could figure it out. His hormones were on fire, and looking at ya, I totally understand. Life was fun for a change. No more humdrum endless business days. You made life fun again, and he was reborn. A beautiful young companion rather than endless toil at work. He had a bad ticker and figured that he needed to enjoy life while he could do so. As things go, and life is a funny and treacherous thing, ultimately, you two fell in love. He wanted to keep you and hold on to you. So, he went to the moon for you. Bought you anything that your heart desired. Maybe he took funds from somewhere he was not supposed to. I dunno. I will be checking the books and accounting when I return. In an innocent conversation, when you show up with this car and all these fancy goods, and livin' this flamboyant lifestyle, you confide in ya family. After all, where did all this stuff come from? Sure, your family is very wealthy, but come on now. People put it together now. Ah! There is the kiss of death."

Lily studied Odell, and she stood stoically. No reaction. Cat and mouse once again. Odell dug in deeper with his words.

"Maybe after too many drinks, you casually mentioned it. To your cousin Vance. Now, sorry to offend ya, cousin, and all, but that punk is evil. We had crossed swords before. A few years back and he lost that battle. Sorry, Lily, but you can't pick your relatives. Your family, the real estate stuff, the construction—it is all corrupt. They dug in and blackmailed Randolph with exposing the love affair and the erroneous use of the dough for the expenses, and most of all, the fancy car. He had to build the new headquarters on Livingston land in Mohawk City. With their sham of a construction company. And that construction was all about payoffs and deals of all sorts. Madness. That was the key! Why leave a gorgeous complex in Westchester for dumpsville in Mohawk City? Now the board of directors thinks that Burgess has lost his mind and is letting his male parts guide him and the business is going to suffer. He is doing all these dopey business and non-business moves. Most of them resign in protest over the circumstances."

Lily did not answer. She held her ground.

Odell continued. He was on a roll now!

"Ya see, Old Herbie was evil, and Gerald Palmer was, and still is, the leader of the pack. The big guy. The money guy. He sniffed in the books, and he caught Randolph with his hand in the wrong cookie jar and led the blackmail charge. Poor Randolph thought that all the dough the evil bastards earned on the deal and the construction would appease them and they all would back off. They made a fortune on the sale of the land and the construction. Nope. It is never enough. Palmer also knows how much cash that

Standard Insurance Company is sitting on, and the Livingstons, Old Herbie, and Palmer want it! Vance and Reid and Palmer and Old Herbie move it for a corporate takeover plan. Buying up stock, going to have Randolph removed for steering the ship down the wrong sea. Randolph loves you madly, but he knows the end is near. Doctor's reports say his ticker is at the end of the line. Shot in the ass. Then we have the magic business cruise. The heartburn incident. Old Herbie produces a magic potion after convincing Burgess to eat some fire spice dish of a dinner. Antacids laced with high-octane something or other. Mixed with Randy's heart medication. I suspect he was on digoxin for his ticker. Antacids and calcium are a no-no, and those suckers were extra juiced."

Lily gasped and covered her mouth with her hand. She could no longer contain her emotions. Her memory kicked in as Odell continued to relate to his theory. He was close now, and he would not relent.

Detective Lyle Odell rambled onward. He had Lily on the ropes now. Gorgeous young woman or not.

"Yuppers. I have his medical records on the way for examination. The medicine combined with a few kickers or two of extra calcium, or maybe even three love-making sessions with you back in the cabin, and old Randy's heart gave out. But Randolph Burgess was no dummy. He was a business genius and other than Lily Livingston and his half-sister, he loved the company like nothing else in his life. A few weeks earlier, in a stroke of last-minute genius, he rewrote his will. Handed it all off to his half-sister. Doctor Eleanor Burgess. The half-sister they forgot about or did not even know existed. Even though she drifted in and out of the business to assist her half-brother when his health faltered. Doctor Burgess has zero interest in the company. She has her own successful life, but she loved her half-brother and was, and still is, determined to do the best that she can. Oh, oh! My goodness, that was a twist and turn. Now, the evil bastards need to step it up. Hire the Emerald Construction kooky-nut ex-military sniper to wipe out Old Herbie first, because he knows too much and actually followed orders to feed Randy the laced antacids. Old Herbie is expendable now and is in the way of the succession for leadership of the company. And then kill the half-sister because Palmer thinks he is now next in line. Enter old, washed-up, recovering drunk, Odell. Evil plan foiled. Vance even tried to wipe out his side piece, Ms. Josie McDermott, because she was Jack's daughter and knew way too much. Despite her beauty and expert skills in the sack. That little punk fed her super-laced drugs, shot her up after a super-love-making session and left her dead of an overdose. Nice guy ya cousin is."

Odell stopped speaking, and he took a few deep breaths. He twirled the cigarette in his fingers and searched for his lighter, and lit the smoke up. After a few puffs, Odell finished his statement.

"Right now, you have done nothing wrong. You loved Randolph Burgess and lived the high life. You suspected that your family were awful people, but Burgess never shared anything with you about what was going on. You were just in love and ignored the warning signs. It was so much fun. Fine life with a handsome, wealthy, older man. Most all of this is news to you, but you are brilliant and can tell that I am closing in on the truth. Your family is evil. Your dad is in trouble because he ordered the hits through Palmer and Vance and Reid and did who knows what on those construction sites. But I might be able to loosen it up for him. Maybe I can talk to the legal bees and convince them to allow your father to plea him down on charges if he wants to cooperate. Josie McDermott survived. So far. She is in a coma in a Boston hospital, and if she makes it, then it will be another nail in the coffin of all of this evil bullshit. I am praying for her life. For her to live. For her to turn the tables on evil. You have a chance. Smart, beautiful, studying for a master's degree. Sure, ya miss Burgess, but you will find a new man. The world is your oyster. I know you only care for your dad, but he needs to face the music that his brother and his nephew wrote. You don't need to answer questions or help me. But I might just be able to help your dad. If he plays nicey-kins and decides to tell the truth about his nephew and his brother and whoever else is involved. Your choice."

Lily still did not react or move a muscle. She stood in place and listened and seemed to be processing all the information. Connecting the dots in her head. Odell finished the cigarette. He snuffed it out on the sole of his boot and once more deposited the spent butt in his pants pocket refuse area. Then Odell added the killer statement.

"And I think that Old Herbie tried a few times at seduction and to lure you into his bed. Even at his old age, he had the lust button turned to the on position. You rejected his advances. Old Herbie was jealous and all too happy to feed Randy those nasty pills. Your beauty is both a blessing and a curse, too. I suggest that this is a turning point for you now. A chance for a choice. Save your dad. Begin your life anew. Do the right thing. Oh, well. Your choice. I will be in touch. See ya."

Odell turned and began to walk to his police cruiser. He had taken about five steps when Lily Livingston called out. "Detective Odell! Odell!"

Odell stopped and spun around to face her.

Lily spewed her words.

"Josie survived. Wow! I met her once at a Christmas party. My married cousin with a beautiful wife and two great kids, wholly and completely corrupted Josie. She is down deep, a little rough around the edges, but a very nice person. Only met her father once at that same party. He was a horrible human being. I saw the news reports from yesterday. That was a wild scene. I bet it made the national news, too. It is no wonder that Josie has all these addictions with a doozy of a father like that creep was. You are praying for her?"

"I sure am. Both for her sake and the endgame for this case. Sure, she made mistakes. We all do. It is not about the mistakes, but what we do when we have a chance to correct them that counts. But she is young, and beautiful, and deserves a second chance at life. A happy life. A new life free from evil. It might be difficult to believe, but I am a praying man. A wayward Catholic, I guess. Hardcore Irishman. Religion. It is not a mystery to me. I am not an atheist, so I know how this all ends."

Lily nodded and once more she bit her lower lip. It seemed to be a habit of hers when she was under stress. She pondered the moment in time. For a few short seconds.

"Odell. I would like to take you for a spin in my car. Let's do drinks and some brunch. I know a quiet and perfect place close to here. It is kind of dark in spots and a little romantic, but it is perfect for our needs. No. I am not suggesting romance. Not yet, at least. Nor am I suggesting the dark spots. Today we need the sunlight. They have a great patio. Vitamin D. We need it. Please. Climb in here."

Odell flashed a smile and Lily caught it. Despite the anguish, she sensed that Odell's smiles were few and far between. Lily smiled back as she waved to the car.

Odell asked, "Are you throwing a steak in front of this old dog?"

"I am. For the record, I don't think you are old at all, Detective Odell. I think you are at the top of your game. Age is just a measuring stick. It means nothing. I am not sure I know all that much that might be relevant or helpful to you, but go ahead and ask any question or questions that you want and I will answer them."

"Okay, fair enough. Lemme get rid of some of these weapons and lock them in the secure lockers in the cruiser here. I also have a zipper jacket to throw on over this shirt. Don't want to chase the civilians into the corners of the restaurant thinking that Odell is on a lockup mission during their Sunday brunch."

The restaurant was only a short drive away from the apartment that Lily called home. Detective Lyle Odell clearly enjoyed the ride over to the restaurant despite the short distance. He commented several times on what a fine high-performance vehicle the car was, and he also complimented Lily on her driving skills and handling of the automobile. Odell even cracked a sort-of-kind-of joke. Or an attempt at a joke—for Lyle Odell.

"Be careful of the speed limits around here. Not sure any of these local police will believe me if I tell them who I am. Or even care."

The restaurant was not some random run-of-the-mill joint to eat. It had valet parking. Of course, Ms. Lily Livingston was not going to eat at a random hole-in-the-wall. The valets jumped to attention when they saw the car pull up in front of the entrance; Odell carefully observed the young men's reactions. Not only did they fancy parking the outstanding sports car, but they would get to flirt and ogle at Lily. Disappointment etched all over their faces when Detective Lyle Odell climbed out of the passenger seat. Even covered up in the zipper jacket that covered his tactical shirt and his badge and insignia, Odell looked like a commando ready to storm the beachhead. . ..

It seemed as if Ms. Lily Livingston was a regular here. Everyone knew her; from the waitstaff to the valets to the bartenders, the hostess, and even the owner.

A smartly attired hostess at the greeting station smiled at Lily.

She carefully checked out Lyle Odell with an up and down and all over, and then asked, "Your usual table, Ms. Livingston? There is no reservation listed, but for you, that does not matter. Your usual table is open."

"No, thank you. I think Detective Odell and I would prefer the patio. It is a lovely day to sit in the sun."

The hostess smiled again, picked up two menus, and waved for them to follow her.

Lily leaned into Odell and asked, "Should I not have called you, Detective Odell? Did you prefer incognito?"

"Believe me, Lily, she knew that I was a police officer. Her eyes and observation skills gave her away. She greets people in her job. She is well-trained in identifying professionals, businessmen, lovers, men, and husbands cheating on their wives, and vice versa, and outright losers. She had me pegged. I take it you are a regular here? With Mr. Burgess, perhaps?"

"Yes, and yes."

Odell scanned his surroundings as they stepped out onto the outside patio area.

He stated, "Interesting. I see that you are a celebrity here. By the way, I am all for the sun worship today, but I need to sit where I can see the entrances and the exits, too."

Ms. Lily Livingston took note of Odell's words, and she rejected the first table that the hostess selected, but the second table afforded a perfect view of the surroundings for Detective Lyle Odell to feel comfortable at. The hostess took the initial drink orders, and she hustled off to obtain them. Lily ordered an espresso martini, and Odell ordered ice water and black coffee.

Once the server introduced herself and dropped the drinks, Lily asked a very poignant question.

"You off-loaded your weapons into the gun safe in the police cruiser. What will you do if the bad guys come and get us, Odell? Sure, you will see them coming, but what is the next step?"

"Lily, exact details, and facts are very important in investigations. I specifically said, lemme get rid of some of these weapons. I did not say all of these weapons."

Lily smiled over the rim of the martini glass as she took a sip while admiring Odell's genius.

Odell admired her actions and her beauty. He thought how as of late all he did was surround himself with stunningly gorgeous women. It was as if the older that he grew; the more appeal with the ladies that he encountered. Not that he was able to act upon any of the appeals. Or was he?

Lily ordered eggs benedict and Odell ordered some fruit with waffles.

Brunch or lunch was underway. Depending on what you wanted to call it.

The second espresso martini hit Lily and took her over just a bit.

She began to state her testimony. Odell did not even ask a question yet.

"I don't know as much as you would think that I do, Odell. But I must say that I think your own testimony has many layers of accuracy within it. I did fall deeply in love with Randy. It began very much as you said. I can see why my father told me to tread carefully around you, because this Odell guy is a walking genius. Randy and I worked together very closely. Staying late in the office. Endless projects and hours. I thoroughly enjoyed the job. Randy was handsome, dynamic, wealthy, smart, and available." Lily took a long sip of the second martini. Her next words had some duality of martini-influence on them.

"Warning. I do much prefer older men."

Odell simply sipped his coffee.

"We had a business trip, and things went really well on the final day of the trip. Randy landed a huge deal, and the clients signed on for a long-term agreement for some commercial business property insurance. That night we went to dinner, and we both had a ton to drink. We celebrated our grand success. Overall, Randy drank way too much. Especially on the road. It seemed as if he did not care too much about his health. His heart was weak. The doctors told him that a long life was not in his cards. I guess that he figured that he would throw caution to the wind and live his life to the fullest. Randy would really cut loose, and I was no slouch either. That night, we both went too close to the edge. I drank way too much, too. One thing led to another, and we were lovers. No question that the attraction had been building for a long time, and it culminated in an all-night lovemaking session in his hotel room. It happens. It was a wonderful evening. Despite his health issues, Randy was very dynamic. The next morning, while crawling through the layers of hangovers, we lamented over breakfast and swore that it would not happen again."

Lily paused to enjoy some of her breakfast while she studied Detective Odell for a reaction. He had none. Instead, he munched on his waffles and his fruit and downed his second cup of coffee. Detective Odell was running on fumes now. It had been a long string of days.

Lily ordered another espresso martini.

When the server left to obtain the drink, she coyly tucked a long wisp of her straw blonde hair behind her ear and said, "You are going to have to drive us back. I hope you drive a five-speed stick-shift manual transmission.

"Not a problem, Lily. Baby, I can drive many things," Odell in duality said with a wave of his fork. "I imagine spilling some of this might just be a lot easier with some of those martinis in ya. I would join you in a three fingers pour of Irish whiskey, but it is a long drive back to Mohawk City."

Lily pounced on that statement.

"You could enjoy some whiskey and hang out with me at my place. I do keep a well-stocked wet bar. Top-shelf Irish whiskies included."

Odell hesitated, then sipped his coffee and said, "I have appointments at home. The case. . . Lily. You were saying?"

Lyle Odell steered Lily back on the rails.

The server dropped the espresso martini and picked up the empty glass. She checked on Odell's drink and she hustled off.

"Yes. The case. Well, that wearing off of attraction did not work. Your testimony about the ship's crew was accurate. I did fall deeply in love with Randy. It just steam-rolled me. There were lunches and dinners, and jet-setting and business trips. He bought me expensive jewelry for my birthday, and for Christmas, and on any occasion. It was exciting and wonderful. At work, we tried to keep it low-key, but I suspected a few people knew. We did not care. He owned the company."

Lily paused to finish her breakfast meal, and Odell finished his. Odell pushed his empty plate aside and thought about how it really hit the spot. He was a lot hungrier than he thought he was.

While Lily finished her breakfast and sipped her cocktail, Odell took the opportunity to ask a few questions. Until now, he had remained quite silent.

"Do you think that he loved you? Or was he being the flamboyant big-chief guy flitting around town with a gorgeous young woman on his arm? Getting his last kicks in before old age, or maybe even death, captured him."

Lily was soft now; both the drinks and the emotions and recollections of all that happened greatly affected her now. She took a large sip—almost a gulp—of the martini and then, sensing that might put her over the edge, she set the glass down and stared at it for a bit. This time, Lyle Odell pounced on the moment.

"I know that stare. The Irish got the best of me too many times over the years. I went over the edge a few years back and was lucky to make it back. Now, I sip occasionally, but stick mostly to light beers. Beer-flavored water." Odell pointed at her glass and added, "I assure you that I understand. But there ain't no answers in that glass. Just some sugarcoating."

Lily acknowledged Odell's words with a nod, and she smiled a weak, but knowing smile.

Her voice was softer now, and she said, "Thank you, Odell. But I need it today. Need the numbness. This is a mess, and I am so happy to get this all out and in the open now. I have to do this. To get on with life. Much as you said. To help my dad. If even I am still able to help him. I think it was a little of all that you said. I do think Randy loved me. Yes. For sure. Told me that he did. We had fun, and it was an attraction for him and others when we were out and about. We were always out and about under the guise of business. We did not flaunt our relationship. The rumor mill exploded, of course. But when we wanted to be covert, we were. This place was a favorite haunt. A little off the beaten path. The old corporate headquarters was more toward the interstate, and this restaurant is in a village setting. But he told me that his heart was bad and he would die young, and that if he had to die, he wanted to die in my arms. All he did was work. Never married, or had many women. For not having many women in his life . . . he was a fantastic lover. Yet, the company was his life. I was his second love and fine with being so. His father and grandfather forced the love of the company upon him. He had tons of money, but no life. I became a life for him. For a while."

"Makes perfect sense. His half-sister told me the same thing. He worked himself to death. You said, for a while. When did it turn?"

Lily picked the cocktail back up. She sipped it and then placed it back on the table. She was adamant now about telling the rest of what she knew.

While throwing her head back and thumbing in the direction of the front of the restaurant, Lily said, "It turned with that fancy sports car parked in the valet lot. That is where it turned."

Odell seemed slightly surprised by her statement.

"I am an admirer, but certainly not an expert in those types of fancy foreign sports cars, but that car is what? Three years old? Four at the most? Obviously, you do not drive it too much."

"You are of course right on. Yes. It was a birthday gift from Randy to me for my thirtieth birthday. I will be thirty-four years old next February. The car has fewer than ten-thousand miles. I keep it in the garage most of the time. I have a daily driver. That sports car is my fun weekend car."

Detective Lyle Odell leaned back in his chair. He downed the remainder of his black coffee. He then closed his eyes and sat perfectly still with his hand still wrapped around the handle of the coffee cup. Lily did not say a word. She seemed to sense that this was what Lyle Odell did—part of his crime-solving methods as he deeply concentrated and studied all aspects of what Lily had told him. Odell opened his eyes and looked at her, and their eyes locked.

"You are fascinating, Detective Odell. A true genius. You have great sex appeal, too. I have to say that this next part is going to be very emotional for me. I will order one more cocktail. By then, I will be quite sloshed, and we will gladly rely on you to drive my car and get me safely home."

"Deal."

Odell turned to wave the server over, but in anticipation, the server spotted him first. She hustled over to the table. The server was rather breathless in her voice.

"Yes, Detective Odell. What can I get for you?"

"Ms. Livingston will have a last call with one more espresso martini. I am driving. I will have another black coffee. And the check."

"Of course. Right away."

She stepped off promptly in the direction of the bar to

obtain the orders.

Lily said, "I will pay my share, Detective Odell. I drank most of the tab." Odell quickly dismissed the offer with a wave of his hand.

"Nah. Official police business. Lookie here! Here comes your drink. I can see that you spend a bundle of dough here. These guys are right on it. Now, you have one for the left hand and one for the right."

The server dropped the cocktail for Lily and the coffee for Odell and the billfold with the check on the table. Odell did not even look at it. He removed a credit card from somewhere on his person, stuck it in the billfold, and nodded to the server.

Lily chuckled, a slightly intoxicated giggle as she realized that she still had some of her other cocktail remaining. While Odell sipped at the coffee, he watched as Lily downed the last sips of the older cocktail and smacked her lips. She was quite the character. Odell remained astounded by her beauty. He thought how these last few minutes would be a wild ride. If there ever was a woman that a man could drop, if he had it, three-hundred-thousand dollars on a sports car for a birthday present, then this woman in front of him was the one.

Lily launched her rockets. She was feeling it now, but still under control.

"It was a birthday date, and at dinner, I mentioned to Randy how I was a secret motorhead and always wanted that sports car. It was my dream ride. He, as usual, had a few Scotches in him and said he would buy me one for my birthday. I thought he was joking. He wasn't. Within two hours, we were in a fancy dealership in Manhattan, and he bought it for me. A three-hundred and sixty-five-thousand-dollar sports car. Right off the sales floor. It was the exact car of my dreams. Even the color. I was in heaven and madly in love."

The server returned and dropped the billfold, with

Odell's credit card inside. Odell filled out the total with the tip and closed it up. He studied Lily and could tell she was struggling now.

Lily suddenly lost her voice. Odell leaned forward. He observed her actions. First, a sip of the new cocktail, then tears licked the rims of her eyes. She found some strengths, and Odell remained patient. Lily continued. Lyle Odell sympathized. He reached across the table and gently grasped Lily's hand. He might be the great detective, but Odell had an immense heart.

"I get it, Lily. You don't have to do this."

Lily shook her head in disagreement.

"No. Odell. I do. Because I loved Randy. I still do. Randy mentioned something about not having all the cash in one account, so he borrowed money from another account and he would move the money into the primary account later, when he could do so. My birthday was on a Saturday, and the banking would not happen until the following Monday. I asked him how I would explain owning such a fantastic car, and he said that I made a six-figure salary as his executive assistant and came from a wealthy family that made a fortune in real estate and construction. Nothing to explain. Tell folks you are spending an inheritance. Well, loose lips sink ships. And mine were really loose."

The drinks caught her remark, and maybe some facts floated into her mind, too. So did the tears in her eyes.

Odell interjected with that comment.

"I was in the Coast Guard. Difficult analogy with the sinking ship thingy, but let me finish it for you. You had a few too many at another birthday party or subsequent gathering. Maybe your family held a party for you, too. You mentioned the new car to your evil Cousin Vance. Then, the eviler, Mr. Palmer got wind. They connected the dots. I bet Mr. Burgess borrowed the dough from the Burgess Foundation. A not-for-profit. He did not move the money in time. Palmer went to Old Herbie, and they threatened him with legal wrangling. Inappropriate stuff. Threats to go public. Have Burgess removed as the CEO, crash, burn! It all went to hell, but could be fixed with buying land in Mohawk City from Reid and Vance and building a new complex with the wizards at Emerald Construction. Of course, that was a bold lie. Once the building deal was done, they still blackmailed Mr. Burgess. They made about fifty million on the land deal and the construction and brokering of the new facility, yet it was still not enough dough. Evil knows no boundaries. But in the end, he outsmarted them all by leaving the lock, stock, and barrel to his half-sister."

Lily's drink was almost gone. Again. She dabbed at her eyes. Took a deep breath.

"You, Odell, are always right on. When you first told me your theory, I knew I had to help. You had it all figured out already. I was Delilah and brought a great man down. I will never forgive myself. I miss Randy so much. Of all the people in the world to blab to! Vance was always a weasel. Even when we were children. I slipped and mentioned it at a family gathering a week after my birthday, how I now had this new fancy sports car. Vance connected the dots. They went probing."

Odell motioned for Lily's hands. He sensed she required some comfort. She reached over the table and grasped them, and Odell held onto her.

"Samson might have been one of the most famous of men and one of the first to succumb to a woman's beauty, but he has a lot of company. And you, dear Lily, your beauty could melt the sun. You did nothing wrong. Not your fault, and only if I have to, will I probe and drag you into this more. I think I can leave you out of it. One last thing. On the cruise ship. On the night of Randolph's passing. You took him to his room. His stomach was churning, and Old Herbie conveniently gave him some antacid pills. You had sex at least twice. When you left, he clearly locked the cabin door behind you. You heard it lock, right? A loud click."

Lily nodded her head and said, "All correct except for one detail. Yes, Randy ate some spicy food, and Herbert gave him the pills. At least five or six of them. Randy also drank a lot. You had mentioned before that Herbert tried to suggest we should have sex, and you were correct. He tried many times. The rejection seemed to hurt him deeply. My goodness, he had a wife, children, and grandchildren and was almost seventy-five years of age. I was not interested in him at all. Herbert was super jealous of Randy and of our relationship. You are saying we had sex twice because the report had two used condoms in the trash. We had sex three times. One time was unprotected. Randy ran out of condoms. It had been quite the trip. His heart was bad, but other things worked quite well. I did not care if I became pregnant. He deserved an heir. Unfortunately, I did not get pregnant and be able to provide Randy with a legacy and an heir. Maybe things would have been different. I do not know. No question that I heard the lock click on the inside. He locked himself inside. I am sure of it."

Odell let go of her hands and seemed satisfied. He leaned back in his chair, ran his hand over his clean-shaven head, and then shook his head.

"Gotcha. Thank you. The extra-calcium juiced antacid pills killed Mr. Randolph Burgess. I believe they interacted adversely with his heart medication. I need to get his medical records to confirm. I am working on that right now. In fact, I should have them waiting for me in my office when I return to Mohawk City."

Even in a drunken haze, Lily understood. She gasped. Covered her mouth in horror for a few seconds, and then nodded at the memories.

"Herbert pushed Randy to have that spicy dish. He did that on purpose. He knew what he was doing. That is why they killed him. He knew the plan. How awful this all is!"

"Yuppers. It sure is. Hold on now. I gotcha now. Have to be honest. The super-active sex did not help his shaky ticker, either. I will do what I can for your father. No promises. It might depend on his own choices. To see if he is willing to spill some of the beans on his nephew and his brother and Palmer, too. I need a smoke. Real quick." Odell's eyes and attention lifted to outside of the patio of the restaurant. he pointed outside the boundaries of the patio. "Out there. Let's go. I will smoke, and then we can call for the car. Do you have any friends that you can visit for a few days? Outside of the New York, New Jersey, Connecticut area. A friend that you are overdue to visit?" Odell stood up and offered his hand to help Lily up. She was a bit wobbly, but once up, she clung to Odell like glue. They made their way to the exit while Odell recovered a wayward cigarette and found his lighter.

Lily's speech was a little halting and slightly slurred, but she was still with Odell.

"I have a friend from my undergrad days in college. She lives in Toronto, Ontario. She keeps inviting me, and I never go. I have my passport all in order."

"Perfect. Book the ticket. Today. Call her. Get there no later than tomorrow. I do not think you are in danger. This is your own family, but who knows with Vance and Palmer? I will give you my number, and you give me yours. I will keep you posted. Ya might miss a few classes, but I bet ya GPA is way up there anyway. You can return no later than Wednesday of this upcoming week. By then, it will all be under wraps."

They were now on the sidewalk outside the patio, and Odell lit the cigarette up while Lily still clung to him for dual purposes. One purpose was to steady herself, and the other purpose was to entice Detective Odell into a little playful seduction. She placed her large and full breasts on the side of Odell's body while he smoked. She knew that she did so and made sure that Odell could feel her breast's reactions to his touch. Lily looked at Odell; she smiled and waited for a reaction.

"Do you mind?" Odell asked.

Lily's beautiful smile was slightly wicked, and her words were a growl.

"I don't mind at all. You feel marvelous. I find you very sexy and attractive, and I have not been with a man since my time with Randy. You will be the perfect man for me now."

Odell took the last drag of the cigarette and blew the smoke into the air. He then snuffed out the cigarette butt on the sole of his boot and stuffed it in the tactical pants pocket.

"Lily, I meant the cigarette smoke."

Lily giggled and held onto Odell as they called for the car. In a few short minutes, they were pulling into the garage at Lily's apartment. Odell drove the car effortlessly. He certainly enjoyed the spin and adventure of driving a high-performance sports car. Even if it was only for a few miles.

"Come on, Lily. Let's get you safely inside and into your bed for a nap. Samson might have succumbed, but Odell is not going to. Despite your beauty and invitations. I want to make sure you're safe, so I will make a few calls and get my notes in order while you nap this brunch fun off."

Lily protested.

"You are such a party pooper, Detective Odell. Mr. Police Rules. All uptight and stuff. We could have such fun together."

The drinks hit Lily hard now, and once inside the apartment, she made her way to the bedroom, wobbling and nearly falling, but Odell kept her upright and on the rails.

"One last chance to change your mind. Take a good look," Lily slurred as she unlaced her shoes and kicked them off with a fling on each foot. In a flash, she stripped her dress off, removed all her undergarments, and they fell in a heap at her feet. Lily stepped out of the heap, and she stood naked and smiling and seductively in front of Odell. The good detective took a deep breath and stole a glimpse or two (more like a stare) at her indescribable naked beauty, but he resisted.

Odell thought, 'Oh yeah. Thirty-eight magic. The missing letter must be a d. For sure.'

He peeled the covers down and waved at the bed.

"I will remain a party-pooper. Rules are rules. Laws are laws. In ya go. Nighty-night, dear Lily. Nap time. I will be in the other room."

She huffed and puffed but climbed into the bed. Lily was asleep in seconds. Her blonde hair flowed all around her pillow and her like layers of sunlight. Her breathing quickly fell into a relaxing rhythm. Odell knew that Lily needed that brunch meeting. All of it. The drinks, to flush all that madness and stress out of her. Her story. The pain washed. The guilt lifted. She was now free.

Odell picked her clothes off the floor, carefully and neatly folded them, and set them on her dresser.

Odell then mumbled, "She might not be a Black Widow, but that is some amazing web she weaves. Randolph went out. But he went out a champion. I picked a hell-u-va bad time to stop drinking. I must be crazy to be sober."

The free time proved to be advantageous to Detective Lyle Odell. He took the time while Lily napped off her overindulgence and the drama of their brunch meeting to catch up on phone calls and make notes in his tactical notepad. A telephone check-in with Grundy proved to be a morale booster. All remained quiet and safe there in California. The requested paperwork was in order and was couriered to Odell's office for immediate delivery. Eleanor was still a little uneasy, but much calmer than she had been. Back home, she had her plants and her garden to tend to, and that kept her busy.

Of course, Grundy had to report on the food situation. He pronounced that the food was very expensive but, "It was not too bad. Doc Burgess eats all that fancy stuff, but I stick with my burgers and grilled cheese sandwiches and a few gallons of beer to wash it all down. The pizza stinks out here, but the other stuff ain't too bad. We found a couple of joints that work for us. I can cover the entrances and exits from where we sit, and the food is pretty good."

A fed George Grundy is a happy George Grundy.

Lyle gave George a quick overview of the case and promised to check-in tomorrow after he performed two more interviews.

"George, I think by Tuesday, I will have this all wrapped up and ready to go for arrests. Wednesday at the latest."

Odell's next call was to Officer Ben Crane, who reported a slight scare for Josie McDermott when she showed some signs of kidney failure and some preludes to organ shutdown, but the doctors and nurses pulled her through. She was still in the intensive care unit and in a coma, and even if she wasn't, the doctors would induce one. Her body required healing after the detox. Officer Crane also reported that the best detectives had combed the apartment along with the Crime Scene Investigators, and they did find some evidence and clues, but they were still about twelve hours away from any official reports posting or any results released. A waiting game.

Detective Odell spoke with Commissioner Colbert and gave him a rundown and synopsis of where he stood now and what his next steps were. Commissioner Colbert reported that much of the requested information, files, and documents were in Odell's office and on his desk at police headquarters.

Colbert told Odell the best news of all.

"There is also a special expedited delivery document package on your desk. It is from retired Lieutenant George Grundy out in California."

Odell thanked the commissioner. He explained that he would be on his way back to Mohawk City shortly and that package was special because it would unlock the rest of the clues that Odell required to wrap the case up and make some arrests. Unless Josie McDermott wakes up first. . ..

On a trip outside to steal a smoke, Odell reacquired his weapons and now, both of his shoulder holsters packed his two service weapons.

Odell was sitting on the sofa, sipping some black coffee, and making more notes in his tactical notepad, when he heard the door to Lily's bedroom open and the padding of her as she made her way barefooted on the hallway floor. Lily appeared, dressed in a fluffy white robe. She looked slightly bleary, but happy to see Lyle Odell.

Odell commented, "Welcome back. Coffee is in the kitchen. I just brewed some in the machine there. I hope you don't mind."

"Mind? No way? I am joyous. Thank you," she said with a smile and wandered off to the kitchens to obtain the coffee. Odell grabbed his coffee; he stood up and followed her. Even wrapped in a heavy robe, Odell could follow the wondrous curves of her body underneath the heavy clothing.

Of course, some special insight provided by a rather inebriated Lily guided that tour. . ..

"How do you feel?" Detective Odell asked.

Lily had grabbed a mug from the cupboard, and she was pouring the coffee. She seemed rather sheepish. "I am fine. My head is fine. No hangover. I actually feel so much better. All that weighed on me so heavily. I needed those drinks to give me the courage to spill the beans and clear the air. I am just so sorry for acting like a drunken fool. I am so embarrassed and ashamed. What I recall of it was that I was a mess. Trying to seduce you. Stripping naked in front of you. It was awful behavior. . .."

Odell cut her off and waved dismissively in the air toward Lily.

"No apologies required. You are speaking with the king of drunken fools. I have been there and wandered around drunk and acting like an idiot for much of my life. My love of the Irish brought me insight and clarity to solve cases, but a drunken fool of incredible magnitude was my reputation. Sometimes, you need the alcohol to get you through. To chase away the phantoms that haunt us. So what? You stripped naked? It is just skin. We all have it. Sometimes you need to be naked to expose your soul. Let the demons out. It is not like I sold tickets to the show or something."

Lily nodded and took a first sip of the coffee. Black worked for her.

"I bet we could have made some side money if you did sell tickets," Lily said with a smile and a wink.

"Yuppers. No doubt. You are absolutely stunning. Took my breath away. But I was not Samson. Thank goodness."

Detective Odell waved his hand in the air at his surroundings. "Who pays for this fancy apartment, Lily? Since ya back in school. I know ya lived here before when Standard Insurance was here, but when ya moved to Mohawk City, ya must have had a place there."

"Emerald Construction pays for this apartment. It is a meager amount for the wealth of that company. A token. Back Bay Real Estate Group owns it. I grew up in Mohawk City. We had a family home over on Shiloh Drive. On the north side."

"Gotcha. Shiloh Drive. Yuppers. Another Back Bay development. It used to be apple orchards when I was a kid. My best friend and I used to go sledding there in the winter. Farms and apple orchards, all owned by the Palmer family. Ah yes, there is a connection. Mr. Gerald Palmer.

Lookie here, glad you are feeling better. I took the downtime to make some phone calls and to capture your phone number. I put mine in your phone, too. Ya ought to use a password to protect it. One number keeps ringing it and blowing your phone up. I bet it is your father. The plan is still the same. Take a shower, pack ya bags. Call ya friend. Book that flight. Get the hell outta here. I will keep ya posted. I do not think you are in danger. The only muscleman they had is pushing up daisies now. Ya uncle and cousin and Palmer are all evil, but they are just corrupt businessmen. Not professional killers, they are amateur criminals."

Ms. Lily Livingston nodded and sipped her coffee. She placed the mug down on the counter and adjusted the waistband of her robe.

"I am on it. The plan. Let me finish this coffee and catch my bearings a bit."

"What will you tell your old man?"

"I will tell him the truth. That Odell was here, he already knew pretty much what went down, and he better lawyer up because you are coming for them all. I will not tell him all the details, and I will not tell him where I am going. Just that I am taking a few days off to visit a friend."

Odell seemed very pleased. He downed the rest of his coffee and spun on the heels of his tactical boots. Lily marveled at his energy and his athleticism, and her mind wandered again to potential romance.

"I am heading back to Mohawk City now. Long drive. Long night ahead. I need to study some files and documents. Some more dots to connect. Keep in touch. Lemme know you are safe and off to ya friend's house. Give me a few days and I will wrap this up."

Lily reached out and gently held Odell by the arm. He turned around and faced her. Her blue eyes were wide open and clear. Her beauty flowed all around her.

"Detective Odell. Thank you for everything. Thank you

for doing what you can for my father. I know you will do your best. And because I must ask, and do not give up easily, you can join me in the shower. . . if you want."

Odell smiled a rare smile.

"Lily, ya a prize. Some man is gonna be a lucky man for sure. Old Randy, he died, but ya made him very happy. Truth is, I am kinda stuck on a gal. Just tiptoeing for now. But a little chance of something or something. I dunno. Maybe. I will stay in touch. Ya flatter me. I am an old man now, and to have a young gal making goo-goo eyes at me gives my old ass a boost. Thank you. Stay safe."

Lily smiled and nodded, and before Odell could even react, she stood on her tippy-toes and gave him a quick kiss on his cheek.

"Oh my, Detective Odell. You are not old. You are a prize and a rare gift to this world. That woman is the lucky one. I hope it works out. But if it does not work out then, you know where to find me. If it does, then I hope that we can be friends when this madness all ends. Maybe we can have brunch again, and this time, I promise to behave."

Odell tilted his head and playfully asked, "Promise?"

"Promise."

"Okay, Lily. I gotcha. A total and honest promise. No stripping, or drinking to excess, or playful ploys of seduction? Must I remind you that I am a police detective? Lies and deceit are my game."

"Promise. But honestly, I might have crossed my fingers behind my back."

Chapter Nine

Odell Moves In

Homicide Detective Lyle Odell arrived back in Mohawk City around seven that night. He picked up everything that he needed from his office and then headed home. It was a rinse and repeat of the previous evening. A phone call to Frank's West. A mission for Matty. The knock and a pizza and some cold beers. Lily made it to her friend's house in Toronto and checked in to provide Odell with some relief. He studied the files and documents. Made furious notes. Connected most of the dots. Ate slices of pizza pie. Sipped his beer-flavored water. When he studied the medical records of Randolph Burgess that Eleanor authorized and sent to him, and he made a note of his primary medication for his heart, Odell was ready to call it a night. Lyle tapped the paper with the list of medications with his finger.

Right on the word naming the key medication.

"Digoxin," Odell said aloud. "Over-the-counter antacids are an enemy. I am sure Old Herbies were extra juiced with calcium. Yuppers. The calcium increases the effects of the medication. Plus, he is full of booze and drunk off his tookus. Then he had wild sex with Lily. Click goes the off switch for the already shaky ticker. Honestly, the sex alone might have done it. I would say, poor Randy, but that ain't true. The guy lived a good life and went out on his own terms and on a high note. The ultimate note. This calls for a glass of Irish."

A few minutes later, Detective Lyle Odell sat in his easy chair, dressed in his Mohawk City Police Department sweatpants and sweatshirt. He sipped a glass of Irish whiskey, poured neat. The Sunday night classical music was not as special as his Saturday night concerts were, but the music was soothing. The old table radio glowed, and the speaker poured out lush strings. Within a few notes, Lyle Odell was fast asleep. It had been quite the day. Monday was going to be another challenge.

Another grueling day for Inspector Lyle Odell. Yet, he was exceptional at his job.

It was 7:47 on Monday morning.

Mr. Lawrence Rinehardt was indeed a big man. He was at least six-feet-three inches or thereabouts. A solid build, powerful arms, and hands. He looked like a man who had done physical work for most of his career. Mr. Rinehardt was not Grundy-like in his size, just physically fit, and he gave the appearance of being very athletic.

Mr. Rinehardt was waiting for Detective Lyle Odell in the lobby of the corporate headquarters. He stood next to the lobby receptionist's desk and alongside the security officer's desk.

Odell walked through the front entrance revolving door, and Rinehardt immediately perked up, strode across the marble lobby floor, and extended his hand to shake hands with Detective Odell and greet him.

"Rinehardt, nice to meet you. I am, Odell. Appreciate your willingness to adjust your schedule with such short notice."

Lawrence shook hands with Odell, quickly studied him, glanced at the dual shoulder holsters and weapons and the tactical rucksack that the good detective carried. Judging from his facial expressions, Mr. Rinehardt appeared to be inpatient and anxious. On the telephone call they shared earlier, Odell had already requested that he preferred not to use the title of inspector. Lawrence Rinehardt was no-nonsense, and he paid careful attention to requests and situations.

"No trouble. Schedules in my business are always precarious. Used to it. All it takes is a fire alarm or an overflowing toilet to mess up my entire day. You are early. I like that. Nice to meet ya, Odell. It has been one wild weekend of bullshit. Not to mention that our general counsel has no head anymore and is dead. And why am I the acting big chief? I sure do want to find out what the hell is going on here."

Odell studied the big man for a few seconds and pointed at his flaming red hair.

After the study and point, Odell said, "Doctor Burgess did not tell me you were a redhead. Red hair. Honest heart."

"Huh?"

"Red hair. Honest heart. It was a saying my Irish grandmother always said. She had strawberry-red hair. No wonder you were the one we could trust. My grandmother was not incorrect in her old sayings. Lookie here, Rinehardt, I appreciate your time. I guess this has been a mess for you. Confusing. My apologies. We are close now to wrapping this all up. Is there somewhere we can talk? Did ya get the technology guy and ya security chief?"

Lawrence Rinehardt pointed to the rear of the lobby. He then waved to lead Detective Odell in that direction.

"I've never heard that saying. I appreciate the trust. C'mon over here, Detective Odell. This conference room here will work for us. I just have to call them both on the radio here, and they will join us. The two continued to walk in the direction of the conference room. Lawrence Rinehardt was the picture-perfect facility manager. He wore a blue suit, white shirt, and a blue necktie. He wore polished black work boots that were about nine inches high on his ankle. Under his suit jacket, you could see that on his belt, he wore a two-way radio, a large key chain with a multitude of keys, and a multi-tool in a leather pouch. Odell immediately liked the man. Odell's sense of whom to trust and who not to trust seldom let him down. He knew why Eleanor testified about Lawrence Rinehardt's behavior as she did. He was a solid, upstanding man. He did his job and did it very well.

"Is Doctor Burgess, okay? Saw all that madness on the news. Geez. That was some mess. I like her. I did not get to know her all too well, but she seems like a great person. She is very beautiful, respectful, and professional. She seems like a real gem. I liked her brother, too. He was all right. Corporate bullshit put him in a tough spot."

"She is fine. Just needed a few days away. I appreciate the insight into Mr. Burgess. Never met the guy. From what I know . . . I agree with your assessment."

"Good. She sure shocked the hell outta me with her message. The legal department, too. But they are in upheaval anyway. And Palmer just grunted at me when I told him and showed him the orders from Doctor Burgess. Here we go, Odell, grab a seat. You want coffee or water?"

Lawrence slipped one of the keys from his collection into the lock of the conference room door, and the two men stepped inside. It was a plush conference room, nicely furnished with quality furniture and an attractive carpet. The room and furniture smelled new. The paint on the walls smelled fresh. The Standard Insurance Company had only occupied the facility for a short time. Bottled water and a coffee dispenser sat on one of the cabinets in the room.

Odell said, "Yuppers. A coffee will work. Ya joining me?"

Odell set his rucksack on the floor next to a chair towards the front of the conference room table, walked over to the dispenser, grabbed a paper cup off the stack, and began to pour a coffee.

"Just water. For now," Lawrence answered.

As Odell worked on his coffee, he asked, "How was Randolph Burgess put in a tough spot, Rinehardt? Other than the corporate bullshit aspect of it?"

"Oh wow. He was a good guy. I worked for them down in Westchester County. That was a great facility. Best of the best. I see the emperor with no clothes. Every inch of these buildings are mine to know and crawl around and maintain. Had to break the lease there with two years left on it. Big companies don't want to own buildings anymore. I am fifty-two years old. Been in this business all my working life. I know the drill. No assets on the books. Especially buildings. Lease 'em. This move made no sense. Building this facility made no business sense. Except if Mr. Burgess was in a tough spot and had to do it. The board of directors was none too happy with Mr. Burgess. I thought they would leverage him out as the CEO, but he made it through that scrutiny. This place is all shiny and nice, but its bones ain't half the building that one downstate was. The chiller plant there kicked ass. These new chillers drive me nuts. Barely get us forty-eight-degree water. New technology, don't mean it is better. In my opinion, there was no reason to move out to here, except that Burgess got in a bad spot somehow and he got nailed and leveraged. He had a super-hot-super-young girlfriend. Who just so happened to be his executive assistant. Who cares? They kept it professional during business. She is gorgeous. She was always very sweet and courteous to me. To everyone. Mr. Burgess was a straight up guy. Never gave me any bullshit. Solid man. Beautiful, young girlfriend. Who cares? I said, good for him. Mind your own damn business. The guy was older and had health issues. Wanted to enjoy what time he had left. Most of the men in here would die for a night with her. Not me. Happily married, although when we moved from downstate to old Mohawk City, my wife was none too happy with me. But they pay me very well. I liked the challenge of a new construction project. Wife went along with me. My two kids adjusted. They are in high school, so it was not easy for us. But ya do what you need to do for your family and to make a living."

Detective Lyle Odell listened carefully to the facility manager's words. He took a sip of the coffee. Odell picked up a water bottle and tossed it in the air to Lawrence Rinehardt.

"Here."

Rinehart easily caught it, unscrewed the cap, and took a sip.

"Thanks, Odell. How is the coffee?"

"Not bad, actually. For cafeteria coffee, it is pretty good. I get it all. Good for you. Taking care of your family. Facility managers and maintenance guys see it all and know everything. I like the analogy 'bout the emperor. Except you seem like the type of guy who would tell the emperor that he was bare-assed."

Rinehardt chuckled a little at Odell's comment.

"I would. Sure would."

"Rinehardt. You used the words, tough spot. Leverage. Nailed. Leveraged out. Had to do it. All to describe what happened to Mr. Burgess. Would you use the word blackmail?"

Lawrence Rinehardt took a sip of the water. He screwed the cap back on and watched as Odell took the chair opposite him at the conference room table.

"Odell. Ya, the police inspector here. I am a corporate facility guy. You would use the word of blackmail. For now, I will use the words that I did. In the end, I think we might be on the same page and arrive at the same place."

Odell set his coffee aside. He picked up his rucksack, unzipped the top and pulled out a manila folder.

"Here is a notarized and confidential legal document from Doctor Eleanor Burgess. It gives me permission to see and examine anything and everything in this building.

Emails, technology, camera footage, files, documents. Everything. I do not require a warrant as long as I stick to this letter's scope."

Lyle Odell handed the letter off to Mr. Rinehardt. He studied it, gingerly felt the notary seal with his fingers, and held it up to the light in the conference room to examine the secure watermark.

After doing so, he slid the letter back over to Odell, who picked it up and slipped it back into the folder.

"I am good with that. Where do we start?"

"Already started last night. Doctor Burgess sent me a ton of documents. I spent most of last night studying them. Connected lots of dots. Yesterday was also pivotal because I was able to obtain some powerful testimony from a key person in this case."

"Okay. Great. Can I ask who that is?"

"You just did. Exact facts and details are very important in investigations and in our lives, too. You can ask. I will choose to answer. Ms. Lily Livingston."

Detective Lyle Odell picked up his coffee and studied Lawrence Rinehardt for a reaction. There was none. He remained stoic.

Finally, he spoke.

"And what did you think of Ms. Lily Livingston?"

"That Randolph Burgess died a happy and a very lucky man."

Lawrence nodded his head as a sign of understanding and agreement.

"Lookie here, Rinehardt. I am gonna call for some uniforms at some point today. Quite sure that today, I will order them to make an arrest. I don't make actual arrests anymore. I guess it is one of the perks of this inspector bullshit. Although there is something satisfying about slappin' handcuffs on some of these goons. I will do my best not to cause any more disruption. Let's call ya guys in here now and we can go through a quick drill, cut some of the bullshit and fluff out, and get to what I think is the root of the matter. I have a feeling that time is not on my side today."

"You got it, Odell," Lawrence Rinehardt said as he reached for his two-way radio, when Odell interrupted his actions.

"Ah, Rinehardt. Ya do trust these two birds, right?"

"I do. If I didn't, I would not be calling them. It would be just Odell and Rinehardt. I don't play at this job, Odell. I've seen a ton of bullshit and pretenders in my time in corporate America. Bunch of clowns. I do my job. Feed my family and look forward very happily to retirement. This is not always fun, but it pays the bills."

Odell nodded and leaned back in his chair. He folded his arms across his chest and then reached for his coffee and took a long sip, while Rinehardt made the radio calls. Odell knew that his instincts were correct. Lawrence Rienhardt was a stand-up man.

"They will be here in a few minutes," Rinehardt announced. Odell mumbled a thank you. He stood up and walked over to the coffee station and refilled his coffee container. "I know right now that everyone reports to you during this period of turmoil, but who do these two guys normally report to in the chain of management?"

"The head of security reports to me. Security and facilities are together. I did report directly to the CEO. The director of information technology—well, he reports up to Palmer in finance."

"Palmer, huh? Interesting." Detective Odell said as he finished pouring his coffee. Then he asked, "You wanna 'nother water?"

Mr. Rinehardt held up his hand to indicate that he was good, and the door to the conference room opened. In walked two men. One was very tall, and the other man was short, stout, and red-faced. Odell scanned them both and within seconds he identified which man had which role.

Odell's thoughts were concise.

'The tall man was security. The short guy is the techie nerd.'

Mr. Daniel McEvoy was a tall, lean, thin-faced man. He might have been in his early forties, but he was balding and looked as if he needed a large meal of steak, potatoes, bread, and a few pints of a hearty stout to wash it all down. The carbohydrates and calories might help him not look so emaciated. Police Inspector Lyle Odell would describe him as a tall drink of water. Mr. McEvoy was the Head of Corporate Security for The Standard Insurance Company, and the polished gold badge clipped to his belt and just visible under his jacket line proudly proclaimed that status. He stood next to the conference room table and introduced himself to Detective Odell and took a seat next to Rinehardt. He seemed very nervous and anxious not only in meeting Odell but in what was going on within the company.

Mr. Dominic Milan was the short, stout, and red-faced man. He looked as if he spent his life in front of a computer screen. He had a permanent hunch at the shoulders and a crooked bend from years of studying and manning the keyboards and screens of the technology world of controlled electrons. Dominic was the epitome of a perfect information technology worker. All that was missing was the pocket protector full of pens and pencils. Mr. Milan had a laptop computer tucked under his arm, and it seemed as if that computer was simply an extension of his body. As if he never left home without it; he slept with it under his pillow and brought it with him to the supermarket. Mr. Milan only put it aside to select a perfect banana.

He introduced himself to Detective Odell, sat down next to Mr. McEvoy, and immediately opened his laptop computer and put on a pair of eyeglasses. While the computer booted up, Mr. Milan sat back in his chair, folded his hands on the table, and looked at Detective Odell as if he was waiting for instructions.

Odell thought, "The man is a veteran of attending many meetings. These guys meet a lot here in the corporate madness. Endless meetings."

Both men wore dark blue suits: blue suit jackets, pressed white business shirts, and crisp business pants, with neckties. They were a sharp-dressed bunch of professional men.

Odell pointed at Mr. McEvoy and noted, "Right shoulder holster. Ya carrying a nine-mike-mike?"

"I am, sir. I am. Only carry here on this property."

"Gotcha. Just call me Detective Odell or just Odell. The sir stuff gives me bad vibes. Rinehardt, here is the same authorization paper again for presentation. Total transparency here. Please allow them to examine it and to be comfortable with it. Kindly show it to these two gentlemen, and we can start. As I mentioned, time is not on our side now."

Lyle opened his rucksack, obtained the paper, and slid it over to Mr. Rinehardt, who did explain and allowed each of them to examine the paper. Both men carefully examined the paper, and each of them acknowledged the validity of it. Rinehardt returned it to Odell, who once more replaced it in the tactical rucksack.

Lyle Odell then took his tactical notepad and his pen, flipped it open, thumbed through some pages, and began to speak.

"Mens, thank you. I appreciate the cooperation. Feel free to grab coffee or water. I need your invaluable assistance and attention. I am going to say a name, and I would like your description and opinion of the person associated with the name. Let's keep it concise. It is in the flow of my investigation methods. Too many words cause my mind to drift off-course and cause errors. Not too many words. Unless you need to expand on your thoughts. Thank you again. Much appreciated."

Odell looked up, and each man nodded his head in understanding.

"Jack McDermott. Now deceased, by the way."

Rinehardt blurted out first.

"First class bully. Mean, evil, sonofabitch. Sorry to speak ill of the dead. He shook down everyone here during the construction. Sold drugs on the side on the construction site. Told everyone about his military service and how rough and tough he was. Horrible man. Drunk and stoned most of the time. Did nothing construction-wise, except walk around shaking down contractors for payoff dough or dealing side drugs. Got drunk at the grand opening party and lipped off at Doctor Burgess. I set his ass straight. He did not scare or bully me. I stood up to him. Sorry for all those words."

Odell took notes, and he looked up with his eyes first at Mr. McEvoy, who said, "Ditto."

Then he checked with Mr. Milan, who said, "I did not know the man. Cannot say anything. Bad or good."

Odell directed a follow-up question to Mr. Rinehardt.

"Did he lock horns with Palmer and or O'Leary? Maybe during construction meetings?"

Rinehardt admitted. "He did. They did. But this Jack guy argued and locked horns with everyone. Like I said. He was evil."

"Gotcha. How about the now deceased O'Leary, Mr. Rinehardt?"

"A first-class weasel. Made like he was a nice old doting Grandpa figure with a loving family, but he was a weasel. Again, sorry to speak ill of the dead."

Odell took notes and pointed his pen in the direction of the other two men for their responses.

Milan said, "Agree. Weasel. Horrible man. Fake front."

McEvoy nodded and said, "Agreed."

Odell made more feverish notes in his notepad and said, "Forgive me. I usually have an assistant take notes. For over thirty years, I had assistants on huge cases. Now, they put me out to pasture. Tell me I am a big-shot inspector and I take my own notes. I am a little slow here. I have a feeling that I know the answer to this one, too. Gerald Palmer. The money man."

"Horrible human being. Cutthroat," was Mr. Rinehardt's description.

The other two men emphatically agreed.

"This last person might only apply to Mr. Rinehardt. What did you think of Mr. Art Livingston? The big chief of Emerald Construction?"

Mr. Rinehardt screwed his mouth up a little at Odell's words and the question. He took a last sip of water and then answered.

"Emerald is an awful construction company. The worst construction company that I ever worked with in the many years of my career. All corruption. Everything they do is wrong and evil, and they cut corners right and left and try to pocket the extra dough. Put in non-spec materials. Cut schedules. Slash the subcontractor's prices and mark it up on their own. You name the game and they do it. I held their feet to the fire and went back to the engineers and architects and got this place built at least almost right. Art tried his best to do a good job. Way above him, I think it is his brother and his nephew who are the connivers. They pulled the strings and made it tough. Deep corruption, but Art was not a bad guy. Just stuck in a damn awful spot."

McEvoy mostly agreed, but he added, "Art tried to follow the security rules. Jack McDermott was a handful to handle, and those two big bosses protected Jack. Art was kind of powerless in his position. I actually think that he is a good guy."

Other than a spot meeting in the cafeteria, Mr. Milan had little knowledge and no opinion of Mr. Art Livingston. Odell finished his notes, mumbled a thank you or two, took a sip of coffee, and then looked straight at Mr. Milan and delivered his request.

"Milan. You read the letter. I need access to emails. Randolph Burgess first. All his computer files. All his emails. Texts, electronic communications, and files of every kind."

Domenic Milan looked up at Odell, pushed his eyeglasses up the bridge of his nose, shook his head, and said, "Sorry. No can-do, Detective Odell. It has nothing to do with the letter. Or with you. Apologies, again. I wiped his files, hard drives, laptops, desktops, cellphones, and emails and everything clean. Special orders of O'Leary and Palmer. They stood there and watched me do it. It was the day after he passed away. McEvoy was there. He watched, too. They even shredded most of the paper files, too. Guarded them from cradle to grave. I thought the entire situation was highly unusual. But I kept my mouth shut and did my job. They are the executive leadership. No new CEO was onboard yet. I am a director. They outranked me."

McEvoy agreed and said, "We really had no choice. Doctor Eleanor Burgess was not here, yet. She was dealing with the funeral and such for Mr. Burgess. We took our marching orders from the executive leadership, and jobs that pay like our jobs do here in Mohawk City are few and far between. You know that, Odell. You're a Mohawk City guy."

Lyle Odell went into pat-down mode, found his bent cigarettes, and glued one on his lower lip.

He apologized for doing so and explained, "Sorry. Have to taste it. I know the rules 'bout smokin'." No one said a word about Odell's cigarette. That was the least of their concerns.

Rinehardt piped in on the subject at hand as Odell twirled the unlit cigarette in his mouth and thought.

"I was not there. Heard about it afterwards. We really were at the mercy of them."

Lyle Odell said, "Gotcha. I understand the situation. To your point, I was surprised at the lack of business files that Doctor Burgess sent me. Now I understand. Is that standard operating practice for the computer IT guys to wipe out equipment like that when someone leaves?"

Milan answered. "Honestly, I am not sure. Never had a CEO die before. When a regular employee leaves, we just shut down their emails and access. We do wipe laptops and desktop's hard drives clean to reassign the asset to other employees. If it is old and dated equipment, we wipe it clean and give it to a reseller or recycler. Please, take a look here at my emails and my texts on my phone, Detective Odell. Come on over here, and I will show you. Gerald Palmer blowing me up right now to come and wipe out O'Leary's information and equipment in the same way. I had to tell him that I was in a meeting with our acting boss. Mr. Lawrence Rinehardt. He is fuming up there. Now, he is threatening my job if I do not show up in five minutes."

Domenic Milan waved Odell and the rest of the men over to where he sat and displayed his phone and laptop for everyone to see. The three men gathered around and studied what Domenic was showing them.

Odell leaned back and commented.

"Aggressive. Panic time. Just ignore him for now. He is not in charge. He knows that. This is just bullshitting intimidation from a guy used to calling the shots. McEvoy, please get on the horn and alert your security team that Palmer cannot leave this facility. If he gets wind that I am here, then he might try to book outta here. I don't want or need a manhunt right now. None of us wants to have to track his old ass down when he is right here now. Have them guard and control all the exits of the building but not be too obvious. Do ya have enough men to cover it?"

McEvoy shook his head and said, "Not enough. But if Lawrence will allow me some of the facilities team, I can deputize them."

Rinehardt waved and said, "Done. Do it."

McEvoy excused himself and made the call on his radio as Odell turned his attention to the information technology issues.

"Milan, please tell me you can restore this information. I mean, you look like ya live and breathe this stuff. I bet there is a backdoor hack or someway to bring it all back."

Domenic Milan pushed his eyeglasses up along the bridge of his nose again and replied.

"Sorry, Odell. If I could, I would. I mean, it is wiped in a way that it is not retrievable. I guarantee it."

"I know this wizard on the Mohawk City CSI team, Matty Dunlop. No offense to your skills, but I can call him in and see. . .."

Milan was shaking his head.

"All due respect, Detective Odell. The best of the best cannot bring it back. I am a super-nerd. I cannot do it. Everything is gone. Except for the L drive and that information is not accessible by anyone without the password. Impenetrable system."

Odell perked up at the mention of the L drive. He spun the cigarette on his lower lip and dug in.

"The L drive? What is that, Domenic?"

"It is an extra-secure remote drive. It is based on a remote server that you upload ultra-sensitive files and documents to. It resides on a server in our remote data center. The insurance business is super-competitive. We are a small but powerful player in the insurance game. Competitors would love to hack us and see what we are working on and see some numbers. We have some valuable customers and clients. The executive leadership uses the L drive. In our case, the CEO uses it to store information securely for future use, but accessible only by Mr. Burgess. Ah, the CEO. Only." Milan shook his head and added, "Before you ask, can I hack it? Is there a backdoor? Is there a way into the server to his old files directly or indirectly? Nope. It is meant to be super secure. Unless there was a keystroke tracker on his keyboard. There was and is, not. I examined it and regularly tracked network security and protocols. Or if the password was phished, or the user was fooled into giving up the password and the hacker trailed in somehow. Then you cannot access the information. Only accessible with the secure password. And the password cannot be the same password used for your other applications. Not being negative, Detective Odell . . . just factual."

Odell interjected, "I dwell on facts. I like you, Milan, please. Go on."

"I checked the L drive status and integrity the day that those two clowns were barking at me. They knew of the drive and made me check. The L drive is secure. I explained that it is hack-proof. Impenetrable without the password. They were satisfied with that."

Odell closed his eyes, and then he slowly nodded. Everyone in the room remained silent.

Milan broke the silence.

"Unless, Doctor Burgess, had it? Mr. Burgess would not write this password on a notepad and leave it in his desk drawer. I assure you of that. He was too smart to make a slipup like that. It would be a personal thing. A private exchange between them."

"Nah, Eleanor never mentioned it. It is not in her notes or the files that she sent me. I guess that I could ask, but it is a waste of precious time that right now, we just don't have. Besides, you would see her access. Correct?"

"Correct," Milan answered.

"Makes sense. She didn't get into this business very much. Not her bag. Can you show me the access page to this drive?"

"Not on my laptop. I block it on the standard Wi-Fi systems and copper systems. Mr. Burgess had his own dedicated and secure system. We have to access the secure network. We need to get to the NOC. Network Operations Control room. It is here on the first floor. Next to the security office."

Odell removed the cigarette from his mouth and stuffed it in his tactical pants pocket while mumbling the location.

Odell said, "Let's go. Time is bearing down on me now. Let's see what we can do. I do not give up easily. Despite the odds."

Within a few minutes, the four men were in a large room that resembled the mission control room for rocket launches. There were no other people in the room, although the security cameras all around indicated that security heavily monitored the activities in the room. Brightly colored monitors bursting with data hung on the walls of the room, and computer terminals and keyboards and other equipment sat on large wrap around console-types of desks. Mr. Milan took a position behind one of the consoles and quickly typed away at the keyboard. Odell and the two other men stood around the chair that Milan sat in and watched him work. Within a few keystrokes, the screen above the console displayed a log-in screen for the L drive. It blinked at them; requiring a username and then a password filled in the appropriate boxes.

Domenic Milan typed and explained.

"The user's name is easy. I know this one. All our usernames use the same format. This one is r-dot-burgess. Now the password. Who knows? Billions of possibilities. I am afraid the access died with Mr. Burgess, unless by chance we find the password written down or hidden somewhere. I am sorry, Detective Odell. I wish that I could help. You are welcome to call your techie CSI guy, and I will work with him and explain, and we can try, but I know this system. And you keep saying that time is of the essence. It is designed to remain ultra-secure and ultra-secure it is."

Everyone turned and looked at Detective Lyle Odell. He remained stoic and silent. He then held his arms straight out from his body with the palms up as if he was allowing himself to accept meditations of his heart and mind. Then he slowly closed his eyes and dropped his arms to his side and kept his eyes closed. By now, his new companions realized that Odell had some rather eccentric tendencies.

Odell suddenly opened his eyes and looked at Domenic Milan.

"I respect you and admire you, Milan. You are exceptional at your job. I appreciate the honesty and your efforts to assist me here with this very complex investigation. No apologies required. Please, in the password box, type this . . . the figure thirty-eight. No spaces and then the word magic. Please use an uppercase letter m. Domenic Milan looked at Odell, and he seemed confused. He then repeated what Odell wanted him to type.

"Figure thirty-eight, no spaces, and the word magic with an uppercase letter m. Got it. I need to tell you that the system locks you out after three unsuccessful log-in attempts, Detective Odell. I am not sure that I could ever unlock it. Even if, by chance, we needed to hire the world's greatest computer geek."

"Milan, I believe that you are the world's greatest computer geek. Even if we had time, if you say we cannot access the drive, then that is it. If we cannot get in, then I will solve this case another way."

"Okay. Let me type it."

Everyone leaned in as Domenic began to type, and the tension ran high.

He got to the end of typing the password and was ready to hit the enter button when he stopped and said, "Wait. No good." Domenic Milan studied the password and did not hit the enter button.

"That password is one character short, Odell. You need

seven characters. The number and letter combination are good, but you need seven characters. No special characters for this one. That is on purpose. Numbers and letters. At least one uppercase letter. This password is only six characters."

Everyone turned to Odell once again. He closed his eyes once more and rocked a little on his heels. He folded his arms across his chest and then, strangely, moved them out from his body and extended his right hand in the air and opened and closed his fingers. The thought was clear in Odell's mind.

First, he replayed Lily Livingston's words in his mind.

'It is. Not many take note of that license plate. It is my breast size. I left a letter off to leave some reader's supposition involved. A lover told me I was magic. We put the two together and . . . wah-lah! A custom New York vehicle license plate.'

Then he recalled the scene and the glorious vision.

'"One last chance to change your mind. Take a good look,"' Lily slurred as she unlaced her shoes and kicked them off with a fling on each foot. In a flash, she stripped her dress off, removed all her undergarments, and they fell in a heap at her feet. Lily stepped out of the heap, and she stood naked and smiling and seductively in front of Odell. The good detective took a deep breath and stole a glimpse or two (more like a stare) at her breathtaking naked beauty, but he resisted.'"

Then he recalled his thought.

'Oh yeah. Thirty-eight magic. The missing letter must be a D. For sure.'

Odell's eyes popped open. He quickly moved to the side of Domenic Milan and pointed at the keyboard and said, "Milan. The letter D. Type the letter D after the figure thirty-eight and use uppercase!"

Domenic Milan nodded and pushed his eyeglasses back up his nose and typed the password as Odell suggested.

Everyone leaned in and held their breath. Milan hesitated for just a second. He looked at Odell, who made a firm motion to push the enter button. Domenic Milan struck the Enter key. The screen blinked, chimes went off, the screen restored and an entire menu of files slowly and magically opened on the screen before their eyes.

Domenic Milan stood up and he pulled a crucifix necklace out of his shirt, kissed it, and held it in his hands and exclaimed, "Sweet Mary, Mother of God! Thank you!" He then crossed his body several times and slowly sank into the chair at the command post. Poor Domenic was aghast. He simply stared at the screen and watched the files populate in seemingly endless rows.

Rinehardt simply yelled, "Wow! You are in! Geez, Odell! Ya did it!"

McEvoy shouted aloud, "Holy bananas! This is unreal. Damn!"

McEvoy then grabbed a chair and sat on it. Domenic Milan recovered.

He spun in his chair and faced Odell and almost screamed his question. "How did you do that, Detective Odell?"

Odell was carefully studying the screen above them and was in pat-down mode in a quest for his bent cigarette.

He found it, stuck it on his lower lip and, with his eyes still glued on the screen, Odell said, "Milan. It is kinda difficult to explain. I think I will leave it under wraps. Might be best for all concerned." Odell walked closer to the screen. He pointed at the items on the screen and asked, "What are these?"

Odell's words diverted Domenic's attention. Odell tweaked his inner geeky chord, and he dove into the files and answered the question.

"Looks like some documents, some PDF files, and this is unusual, but those files there," Milan reached up and used a pen to point at a symbol on the screen. "Those are m-pfour and three files. They are audio files. In fact, these look as if Mr. Burgess downloaded cellphone voicemail messages to the L drive."

Odell twirled the cigarette in his mouth with a renewed intensity. Lawrence Rinehardt remained silent, but he leaned in closer to the screen, as did McEvoy.

Odell spoke, and the cigarette danced on his lower lip. "Damn. Burgess outsmarted them all. He captured the evidence and used this secure server to preserve it. This is the holy grail of evidence. He must have croaked before he could decide how to leave access to it with the password. He should have come to the law sooner. He must have been waiting to turn the tables on them for a certain time. Or he was protecting either Lily or Eleanor. I dunno. Or maybe he buried and hid the password and we have yet to dig deep enough in his files to find it. I see phone numbers, but I am sure these evil clowns were not stupid enough to use their personal or company-issued cellphones. But they were stupid enough to leave voicemails. Bunch of amateurs, or they were cocky in their power over Burgess. I see New York exchanges and a five-zero-eight, which is Massachusetts. That one is of interest."

Odell used his finger and pointed at the files on the monitor and a line with dates on it.

Odell said, "Milan, please. Can you scroll back on these? I mean, the dates. Back a few years. Let me think. About four years ago. In and around February or March."

"I can do that, Odell. Lemme use the mouse here and click and scroll. Tell me when to stop. There are tons of files here. MP4 files use a ton of storage space. Mr. Burgess was not tech savvy, or he would have compressed these audio files to save space. Luckily, the server has terabytes of storage, but this sucker is crying slow, slow, slow, because it is slap full on storage space." Milan continued to scroll until Odell decided on one file.

"Stop! Click on that one. Play that one. The eighteenth of

February."

Domenic clicked on it, then leaned over to a separate control panel and turned up the volume on an audio system. The file played. It was a voicemail. A male voice came over the speakers. Loud and clear.

"Look, Randolph. No more time. No more stalling. No more bullshit. Your ass is cooked. We don't give a rat's ass if you put the money back the next day from the foundation account. I have already adjusted the books to make it look as if you stole it to buy your chickie-poo her fancy wheels. Sign the lease papers and break it now. Sign off on the purchase of the land in Mohawk City from Back Bay. Engage legals for the construction documents to begin, or Herbie goes to the board, and your days as CEO are over. We will destroy your reputation. Call me. Now."

Lawrence Rinehardt whistled as the voicemail ended.

Odell looked at him and asked, "Is that Palmer's voice? I never met the man."

"It sure is. No question. I will use the word now. Blackmail."

"Does everyone agree that is Palmer's voice?" Odell asked. All three answered in unison, in agreement that the voicemail message was Gerald Palmer's voice.

Odell moved quickly. First, the cigarette went back into hiding, then he jumped into action.

"Okay. For now, this is all we need. These files are treasure troves of evidence. Burgess nailed them all from the grave. Good for him. We must guard them at all costs. I will call for uniforms to respond to the front desk at your headquarters building here. I will also ask for a Sergeant Stewart Drummond, and he will notify his commanding officer. A Lieutenant Larry Hicks. Also, we will get the commanding officer of Mohawk City Crime Scene Investigations here. A Lieutenant Oliver Crump and he will bring Matty Dunlap to help Milan download and preserve all these files. I trust all of you here. Rinehardt.

You stay with Milan. We will have Palmer under wraps, so, Rinehardt, you can have one of your boys meet the CSI team and escort them here to the NOC. McEvoy, we will head for the lobby. Wait for the uniforms and then we go and arrest Gerald Palmer. I need to jot down the charges. There is a hell-u-va lot of 'em. Questions?"

No one had any questions.

Odell almost smiled.

"Mens, you guys have been great. I thank you all for your jobs and dedication. I will make a note of your efforts."

It only took a few short minutes for the extra police officers to arrive at the Standard Insurance Company's corporate campus. They flooded into the lobby, led by Sergeant Stewart Drummond. Detective Lyle Odell and Daniel McEvoy were waiting in the lobby to greet them. Employees of Standard Insurance Company stood around with their papers in their hands, and their mouths open, all while holding their coffee cups and water bottles. On the heels of the assassination of the General Counsel, Mr. Herbert O'Leary, over this past weekend, this was anything but an ordinary Monday at work for the multitudes at Standard Insurance Company.

"Hey there, Drummond. Glad ya were on duty today. I don't like working with new guys." Odell thumbed a thumb in the direction of McEvoy. "Drummond, meet McEvoy. Vice versus. McEvoy heads up corporate security here. He carries a nine-mike-mike. Private security on corporate property. We are gonna arrest Mr. Gerald Palmer. Common spellings. He is currently the chief financial officer for Standard Insurance Company. McEvoy, here, will escort us up to his office in the executive suite. Here are the charges."

Lyle Odell tore a sheet off his now nearly full tactical notepad and handed it to Sergeant Drummond.

Sergeant Drumond nodded.

He took the sheet from Odell, while saying, "Hey, Odell. Hey there, McEvoy. I gotcha. Glad to work again with you, too, Detective Odell. It is my honor."

His eyes went down to the sheet and almost popped out of his head. "Holy Moly! There are about ten charges here! This guy! Do I need to read all of these? I admit, Odell, that I have never had an arrest like this one before! Do you know the penal codes for all of these charges?"

Odell replied, "Most likely, I do. Don't worry. Just one will do it. So, just do the best you can. The legal boys will slap a few more on him by the time this is all done. It is rather messy. After we get this banana into custody, you will head to a construction site on Bennington Street. Near the corner of Emerald Construction Company is the company there. Ya can't miss it. Find Mr. Art Livingston. Arrest him and take him into custody. Here are his charges."

Odell tore off another page from the notepad and handed it to Sergeant Drummond.

"Any questions?"

"Negative on the questions. Roger on all of it."

"Good. Hicks and Crump on the way?"

"Yes, Odell. About one half-hour away."

"Okay, McEvoy, lead us on."

Drummond waved to his two uniformed officers to follow him as McEvoy led them to the elevators.

Sergeant Drummond commented to Detective Odell as they walked, "It sure has been messy. Saturday was a bit much."

They all stood in the elevator as it launched them to the upper floor, where the executives all had their offices in the lofty clouds of corporate mayhem. Odell had stuck the cigarette on his lower lip, and he took it out and twirled it in his fingers in his customary manner.

"Yeah. That was a super-mess. Sorry 'bout that," Odell said between twirls. "I bet the wife was not too happy. What did she say?"

"That I should quit police work and get a job at the home improvement store."

"Well, she is not wrong. Sounds as if you married a very smart woman."

The elevator landed on the sixth floor of the facility. The bell dinged, and the door opened. Daniel McEvoy waved and led the way and waved the team on.

"This way. Just down the hallway after these doors."

The executive suite was luxurious; today, it dripped with some sorrow, though.

As employees looked on at the scene in shock, McEvoy directed, "Second office on the left."

The administrative assistant for Mr. Gerald Palmer sat outside his office door. She sat in a large, open cubicle lined with modular furniture and a few file cabinets. Daniel McEvoy stopped in front of the opening to the cubicle.

He pointed at the team and said, "Carrie. Good morning. We have some business to conduct with Mr. Palmer. I appreciate confidentiality and cooperation."

Carrie did not say a single word. She gave a nod, folded her hands, and remained in her chair. It was almost as if she had expected this to happen someday.

The nameplate on the door of the office stated: "Gerald Palmer. Chief Financial Officer."

Odell made the call.

"Drummond. Keep the two uniforms at the office door. What are their names?"

"Patrolman Julian Higgins and Patrolman Bernie Kinney."

"Gotcha. You and McEvoy come into the office with me."

Odell took the lead. He did not knock.

The sudden and unannounced barge-in and the entry by the team of police officers and Mr. McEvoy startled Mr. Gerald Palmer. He was short, and a thin-faced man, with a round belly and just a wisp of black hair left on the top of his head. Palmer jumped up from his office chair when Odell led the entry into the room.

"What is the meaning of this? Out of my office. Now! I am, Gerald Palmer. Chief Financial Officer here. Out of my office!"

Detective Lyle Odell stood in front of his large oak desk as he carefully studied Gerald Palmer.

Odell turned to Daniel McEvoy and said, "Geez. Ya didn't tell me he was a little, short, weasel-faced guy."

"Ya didn't ask, Odell," McEvoy replied.

"McEvoy!" Gerald Palmer shouted. "I will have your job. Get out of my office! Now!"

"I doubt that, Mr. Palmer. Negative on leaving the office. Official Mohawk City Police business."

Odell spoke, and the unlit cigarette bounced on his lower lip.

"We know who you are. That is why we are here, Mr. Gerald Palmer. Don't care too much about your job title, either. Knew that, too. It is on the nameplate on your office door. Since ya a money man, then I guess you can put two and two together here. I am Police Inspector Lyle Odell of the Mohawk City Police Department. This is Sergeant Stewart Drummond of the Mohawk City Police Department. The two of us are here on official police business. There are two uniformed Mohawk City police officers in the hallway outside. Patrolman Julian Higgins and Patrolman Bernie Kinney. You already know the head of corporate security for the Standard Insurance Company, Mr. Daniel McEvoy. He is here representing the company and ensuring the security and protection of company assets and the safety of the employees."

Palmer's face dropped. His eyes darted back and forth in

his head. They locked onto the center of the desk, and Palmer leaned a little towards it. That is all it took. In a flash, Odell drew both his weapons. Followed by Drummond and McEvoy. Four weapons pointed at Gerald Palmer.

"Bad, bad, bad idea, Palmer. Now, let's put your hands on top of your head. You move ya little round ass and big belly and take three steps to the side and keep those hands on your head and get close to the wall. What are you really thinking here? That you will shoot your way out of this? C'mon, now. Ya really are an amateur here. A joke. Ya just added another charge to a long list of charges. Stupid move. McEvoy. Please. Check that desk drawer. The center one."

Daniel McEvoy moved in while keeping his weapon aimed, and he opened the desk drawer.

"Well, well, well. Look at this. An unauthorized firearm on corporate property. Tsk, tsk. Grounds for immediate termination. But something tells me you were not going to work here any longer, anyway." McEvoy holstered his weapon and carefully took a pencil from the drawer, slipped it through the trigger loop of the handgun, lifted it, and dropped it on the desk.

"Your evidence, Sarge. I don't want it. Chances are it is unregistered, and Mr. Palmer does not have the proper credentials to possess it anyway."

Gerald Palmer cried out, "That is not mine! I don't know how that got in there!"

Odell's cellphone began to ring. He shouldered his weapons and glanced at the number calling.

"I have to take this phone call. Drummond. Do your thing. Do it well. I will check in later."

"Roger," Sergeant Drummond said as he saluted Odell. Odell waved a half-salute in Drummond's direction as he walked out of the office. Sergeant Drummond holstered his weapon. He turned and faced Palmer as he held the notes in his hands and reached for his handcuffs.

"Mr. Gerald Palmer, I am Sergeant Stewart Drummond of the Mohawk City Police Department. I must inform you that you are under arrest on the charges of suspicion of. . .."

Odell stepped out into the hallway. He ducked into a nook next to a cubicle and answered the call.

"Crane. What 'cha got for me?"

"Detective Odell." Officer Ben Crane was a little breathless. "I have lots. Josie McDermott is awake. Looks like she made it. She is talking a little, but the doctors say we need to back off for a bit until she fully recovers. The detectives and the chain of command agree. Otherwise, the evidence and her testimony are tainted by drug influence."

Lyle Odell shifted his feet, and he held the cellphone tight to his ear. This case was evolving rapidly.

"Gotcha, Crane. Josie is a fighter and survivor! This is great news. Good call on your side on backing off a bit. What else?"

"The little she said so far is that Vance Livingston shot her up. The official police and CSI reports are in now. Our CSI teams and the detectives lifted tons of prints from the apartment. Vance Livingston. Security cameras at the apartment have Livingston coming and going on the footage at all the correct times. Neighbors testified to hearing screams and struggles emanating from Josie's apartment. One neighbor saw Vance Livingston in the hallway. All times match. The neighbor is willing to testify to his presence. Josie had skin under her fingernails. Our guys want to get a search warrant for DNA from Vance Livingston. He should have some scratches on his body. Somewhere. Maybe the arms, neck, or his back. Somewhere. Josie sure is a feisty one."

"Yuppers. She sure is. These bums are a bunch of smug amateurs. Mistake after mistake. It all fell apart for them once we dug in. Lookie here, Crane. I am making two arrests here in Mohawk City. Those Livingston clowns are as corrupt as they come. Their money has bought a ton of connections. As soon as they get word that Josie is coming around, and that you guys are getting a judge for a DNA warrant and their big boss and cohort and brother slash uncle are under arrest here. They will flee. Ya got to APB this. All neighboring states involved. Ya got to cover the highways and the trains and the airports and find those bums. They own property all over. My guess is that they will try to get to Logan Airport for an international flight, but we can't rule out Manchester in New Hampshire for a connection to Atlanta. If they get to some obscure Caribbean island, and we don't have extradition agreements for them, it could get dicey. I am leaving now. Heading your way. Can you arrange for the plowing of the road? This needs to be a high-speed roll. Maybe some staties to meet me at the Massachusetts and New York border? I am coming down through Albany on Interstate Ninety."

"Roger. I will notify my chain of command right now."

"Great work, Crane. Great work. See ya, soon."

Odell hung up the call and he sprinted to the elevator. He was on the way.

Just as Detective Lyle Odell crossed over from New York State into the Commonwealth of Massachusetts on Interstate Ninety, there were four Massachusetts State Trooper vehicles pulled over in a turnaround area of the highway. They were waiting for Odell's arrival. The police lights on the tops of the vehicles were all flashing. Odell spotted the gathering, slowed his marked Mohawk City Police Department cruiser, and flipped his overhead police lights on. Odell steered to the turnaround area and braked the vehicle to a slow stop to where the state troopers gathered.

A state trooper jumped out of a cruiser and made his way over to where Odell parked, and Detective Odell rolled down the window as he approached.

"Police Inspector Lyle Odell. Trooper Sergeant Allen, Massachusetts State Police, here. It is my pleasure and my fellow trooper's pleasure to assist you, sir."

The trooper smartly saluted Odell, who returned the salute from the seat of his cruiser. Odell did not try to correct the trooper on the title nor in the use of the sir address.

After the salute, the trooper added, "You are a legend, sir. We are here to escort you to Boston. Local police intel feels the perps are heading for Logan Airport. They secured a search warrant. As per your request, we are covering all the potential escape routes. All of it. Federals sniffing around now, too. They really want you there and present at the apprehension to cover all the charges. Are you ready to roll, Inspector Odell?"

"Roger that, Trooper Sergeant Allen. We gonna be on the universal tactical radio frequency? Channel thirty-eight."

"Roger. Thirty-eight, sir."

Odell reached over to his radio and dialed up the correct frequency.

"Okay, Trooper Sergeant Allen. Roger, the info. Thank you. Lights on. My siren is on. I will stay in the center lane with your cruiser in the front and the other two cruisers on each lane side of me and one behind. Let's get it over ninety but just under one-hundred."

Trooper Sergeant Allen stood back; he saluted Odell and added, "Roger, sir. Please, Inspector Odell. Get 'em. For all of us."

Odell performed a half-wave and half-salute and said, "Hell, yeah. No question. You can count on it."

Within twenty seconds or so, the huge police interceptor engines of the cruisers had achieved high speeds on the turnpike.

Odell mumbled aloud as he gripped the steering wheel and glued his eyes on the road and fell in line with the escort.

"It is just never enough money for these wealthy bastards. Never enough money, or power, or greed. Damn shame. Poor Josie. I hope she fully recovers without long-term trouble. Once more, when ya hang with iffy people, iffy things tend to happen."

The cruisers rolled at high speed. The radio crackled with activity. It seemed as if both Vance and Reid Livingston knew what was coming, and they indeed, as Odell predicted, were fleeing. The Boston Police Department, because of the advance notice, was just a step or two ahead of them.

And it was showdown time in a parking garage at Logan Airport. Airport police, Office Crane, Captain Mike Rutherford (Crane's captain in his chain of command) Boston detectives, some federal officers, and other local police had the Livingstons surrounded and were in the process of enacting the search warrant for DNA and making the arrests, when the state trooper escort of Detective Lyle Odell arrived on the scene and screamed to a halt in the parking garage. It was a dramatic and fitting entry onto the climactic scene. A fitting end to his case. Perhaps, the end of a remarkable career for Lyle Odell. Perhaps.

Odell popped out of his cruiser, and all eyes turned to him as he approached the scene, along with Trooper Sergeant Allen and the rest of the Massachusetts State Police Troopers.

The unlit cigarette hung from his lip as Odell walked slowly to where the team of police officers had Reid and

Vance Livingston standing next to their vehicle. Guns drawn; tension high. Rights and charges being read. They just needed a cheek swab from a CSI technician.

Arrests enacted.

"Hey there, Crane. Cap. All the rest of you guys. Thank you for the assistance here. I am glad I could make it to the party. Lately, several folks have accused my old ass of being a party pooper. That is not always true. I just carefully select the parties that I choose to attend. For those that I never met, I am Police Inspector Lyle Odell. Mohawk City, New York, Police Department. A proud public servant. For a long, long time. Too long. I have my own charges for these two bananas, but it looks as if I might need to stand in line."

Vance Livingston fumed and screamed in Lyle Odell's direction.

"Odell! You washed up, old sonofabitch! I swear that someday, someday, I will make sure you bleed out in front of me and die!"

Reid admonished his son.

"Vance! Enough! Quiet! Don't say another word!"

Odell twirled the unlit cigarette with his fingers while keeping it on his lower lip. He slowly walked over to Vance Lingviston.

"My goodness. Tsk, tsk, and here I thought I was a little late to the party. All that high-speed rolling down the Mass Pike turned out to be worth it. The cornered criminal spewing vengeance. I have to say that I have been on the receiving end of quite a few of those threats in my day. And you are an attorney. And are soon to be an ex-attorney. Another charge of threatening a police officer. I am gonna need a larger notepad. Lookie here, Vance. Ya father's advice is sound. Ya know, it is never enough with you guys. Money, power, greed. Ya had a thriving business making money hand over fist. The world was ya oyster. Real estate deals everywhere. Now, I am sure once we dig deeper, some of those deals were slick moves, too, but ya had it all. Now ya have an empire of dust. The trouble with the world these days is that we don't recall or respect history. All the great empires fell into dust. They eventually get greedy, power-hungry, and rot from within. Ya rotted from within. Ya guys are no different. Should've stuck to real estate because ya sure stink at being criminals. See ya. Wouldn't want to be ya. I haven't read charges in a long time. I guess it is my turn. Well, here we go. Mohawk City, New York, Police Inspector Lyle Odell here. Mr. Reid Livingston you are first. I have to inform you that you are under arrest. . .."

A team of Boston police officers led the now handcuffed Livingstons away to bring them into detention. Odell stood and watched as they were stuck in the back seats of individual police cruisers that sped them away. Detective Lyle Odell felt a rush of contentment at the close of this case. The rest will be up to the legal divisions of the various states and authorities now involved.

Maybe this case was Odell's last hurrah, and what a hurrah it was!

Odell made a point of individually thanking each law enforcement officer and person there on site. When he finished doing so, Odell walked over and greeted Officer Crane. The two police officers embraced and shook hands. Odell then spoke to Officer Ben Crane's captain.

Captain Mike Rutherford shook hands with Odell, took his notepad paper with the charges on it, and said to Odell, "Please, to meet you in person, Odell. The legend. What a case you handled here. Amazing. Thank you for everything. Great call on them fleeing. They were heading for an island, for sure. We have all our charges. I am sure the DNA is a match for Vance Livingston. He is cooked. You can see the healing scratches on his throat. The victim is awake now, and we can obtain a certified, untainted testimony. The doctor cleared her to testify with clarity.

The Feds have some things popping up on these characters, and then New York and Mohawk City can layer in with your charges."

Odell twirled the cigarette on his lips and mumbled, "I have to light this thing soon. My head is going to explode. Rutherford, great job. Appreciate working with you and your entire team. I will punt to the legals and the Feds and let them sort it all out. Seems like the charges in Massachusetts alone will lock them up for quite a while. Then what I have with New York and Mohawk City charges will be the icing on the old-die-in-jail cake. Once we weeded through this all, these guys really were a bunch of amateur bums. Predictable. They became so high and mighty that they figured they were untouchable. Typical corporate clowns."

Odell started to pat his body down and begin his search for his cigarette lighter.

"Say, Cap. Ya might want to promote Officer Crane. That young man is a good one. Plus, he is smart. Roots for the New York Rovers and not the Boston Bears."

Captain Rutherford smiled and patted Odell on the shoulder.

"It is in the works, Inspector Odell. He is a good one. I will let you in on a secret. I root for the Rovers, too. Be in touch, Odell. Be safe."

"You too. Hey, Crane!" Odell shouted and waved in the direction of the young officer. "I am gonna light this cancer stick and make two phone calls. Then I've gotta check into a hotel 'round here. Ain't driving back tonight. What time do ya get off shift? I will buy ya dinner and a few beers."

Captain Rutherford overheard the conversation, and he waved at Officer Crane and Odell and said, "You are officially off shift, Crane. As of right now. Enjoy hanging out with Odell."

Crane leaned on his patrol car while Odell lit up the cigarette and wandered over to the wall of the parking garage. His first phone call was to George Grundy.

Grundy answered on the first ring.

"Odell! What is up? Crazy day, huh? I bet it was a whirlwind."

"Hey, George. It sure was. Eleanor all right?"

"Fine. Safe and sound. Just worried about you. I kept telling her the same old line that no news is good news and you will check in when you could. Sitrep?"

"It's all over, George. Case over. All the bad guys are in custody. Vance and Reid Livingston. Art Livingston. Gerald Palmer. You guys can come back to New York now."

George whistled a little over the phone. Even knowing the history of Detective Lyle Odell, he seemed surprised.

"Ok. A day earlier than the Odell's prediction. I like that. How did that happen?"

"Thank you for everything, George. I owe you. These guys are amateurs. Fell like a house of cards. Tons of mistakes when they panicked. We have so much evidence on them now, it is remarkable. I can fill you in when you two get back. When can you get a flight?"

"Okay, Odell. You owe me zero. It is what we do. Grundy time. Right? Sounds great. Look, I am out of here tomorrow. See ya when I get back."

Grundy's voice faltered a little. He searched for proper words.

"But. Okay. Ya better talk to Eleanor. I gotta say to you, and that is all I am gonna say, but it might not be according to plan. Hold on."

Odell took a long drag of the cigarette and blew it into the air. He glanced over at Officer Ben Crane, who seemed to be relaxing and relishing the peacefulness of watching the planes come and go over the airport.

Eleanor's voice was breathless. She sounded teary.

"Odell. I am so glad to hear from you. Are you okay?"

"Fine. It is all over. How are you?"

"Much better now that I am hearing your voice. I am fine. George is amazing. He took great care of me. We certainly ate well. I must have gained five pounds. Goodbye to my perfect figure."

"Well, yes, that is life with George Grundy. One of the world's greatest foodies. I bet your figure is glorious. I can't wait to test my theory."

"Thank you, Odell. Me, too. George says it is over. Who did you arrest?"

"Well, I have to tell you that the kingpin of this incredible mess was Gerald Palmer. Ya gonna need a new money person."

There was a slight gasp at that news, and then Eleanor sighed a little.

"It is not a complete surprise. I did not know him all that well. In my short dealings with him, he seemed as if he was unusual, and he seemed a bit conniving and ruthless. And there were others?"

"Yuppers. Art, Vance, and Reid Livingston. Lily is in the clear."

Now, there was a longer pause on the line.

"Okay. Do you know what happened to Randy? To my dear brother?"

Eleanor left off the half-brother description.

It was understandable.

"I do, Eleanor. Look, we need to speak in person. I am just wrapping up this mess. I am in Boston right now. Can you fly back with George tomorrow? I am looking forward to seeing you. We can talk all night."

"Odell, I must tell you. I do not want to come back to New York. I have nothing there except for you. I am going to sell everything there. Company and everything. Lock, stock, and barrel. I just don't want it after all of this. Too painful. Too horrible. I never wanted it. Never. The only good thing that came out of this was meeting you. I want to teach during the upcoming semester. I told the school that I was available for teaching."

Odell finished the cigarette. He ground the end of the butt out on the concrete wall and he stuffed it in his pants pocket.

"Can you come to California? I mean . . . when you finish all the paperwork and messiness?"

"Eleanor. I understand what ya have been through. Yuppers. Sure do. Let me call you later tonight. I am checking into a hotel here in Boston for tonight. I will call you from there. We can talk some more. Discuss what you are feeling and what our options are. Right now, I need to move out of this arrest scene and to settle in. Get some food and drink and take a shower. It has been brutal."

"Fair enough. I look forward to it. Odell. I care deeply about you. I fell in love with you right away."

"Eleanor, ya a special prize. I care deeply for you, too. The love is mutual. Lookie here. I will call ya."

"Yes. Good

bye."

"Click."

The line went dead.

Odell stared at the cellphone for a few seconds. He looked up and yelled out to Officer Ben Crane.

"One more call. Then we can go!"

Officer Crane turned and waved and said, "I am good, Odell. Enjoying the peace."

Detective Lyle Odell hit the button on his cellphone for Lily Livingston. She answered on the first ring.

"Odell! I am so happy to hear from you! My father called. He explained about the arrest and the charges. Please tell me he can work on a deal. Are you okay?"

"I am fine, Lily. I told you that I will do what I can. The legal guys need to look at everything. His charges are the lessor of them. If he cooperates, it might not be so bad. We will see. Your cousin and uncle – well, they are not in good shape."

"I only care about my father. Those two will reap what they have sown. I am planning on leaving on Thursday. I had my flight booked from the original plan we made. Having a nice visit here, so the original date works for me. You wrapped this up early."

"I did. Sounds good. I will be in touch. Safe travels."

Odell heard Lily take a deep breath.

She then said, "Thank you. I hope we can meet up soon. I would love to see you and hear the details of the case and the potential for my father. And well, see you. I said that twice because I meant it. Goodbye and thank you for everything, Odell."

Odel did not comment on meeting with Lily.

He simply said, "Goodbye."

Odell stuffed the cellphone in his tactical pants pocket and walked to where Officer Crane stood, while leaning on his patrol cruiser and watching the air traffic in front of him.

"Officer Ben Crane. All done for now. I will take your recommendations for a hotel and follow you. Then after checking in, it is finally dinner and some beers and some relaxation. Then sleep. Contrary to popular opinion, I am a normal human being and need some sleep. Occasionally. I think that I have had about six hours of sleep in three days. Tonight is going to feel wonderful."

"I gotcha, Odell. I can only imagine what you have endured. It has been grueling. Now we can relax. I know just the place. We might even be able to catch the hockey game on the television over the bar. Go Rovers! Follow me."

Chapter Ten

Romance and Pitfalls

Monday. Two weeks later.

It was now October. An early chill set in, and the leaves showed their colors. Fall in upstate New York. A magnificent display of God's creation. Painted palettes of glorious colors loomed. Even in the gritty streets of Mohawk City, New York.

Detective Lyle Odell sat at the bar at Grundy's Bar and Grille. It was shortly past noon. Odell nursed a light beer, and he nibbled on a grilled cheese sandwich. George worked at the bar, along with Annie. Marjorie Grundy and Meredith Jameson worked the dining floor. For a Monday, there was a large lunch crowd gathered. Business was very good. Lyle Odell had been sharing a long and in-depth discussion with Grundy about the Livingston-Palmer-Standard Insurance case. Odell was filling George in with the details. He had not had much extra time in the last two weeks or thereabouts. The legality and duties of the case required his attention. It was all part of it!

George Grundy had some extra time to chat with Odell since Annie was working with Grundy on the bar duty today.

Annie was ancient but efficient.

The legal departments and all authorities involved had finalized the charges for all involved. Odell had completed endless interviews and completed countless reports. Even with the assistance of Police Commissioner Warren Colbert and the board, the paperwork was very extensive. Most of that was complete now, and Odell relaxed a bit. The trial dates were set; Art Livingston had already taken plea bargains, and he was singing tunes that the D-A and prosecutors loved. Lily Livingston chimed in with some tidbits, too. Anything to help her father. Over in Massachusetts, Ms. Josie McDermott sang glorious conviction songs, too. All these witnesses turning testimony on Palmer, and Vance and Reid Livingston, made for mounting evidence, plea deals, and easy convictions. The expense reports and accounting records that the special accountant and auditors examined uncovered mountains of financial corruption, too.

The DNA from the skin under Josie's nails matched Vance's DNA. She scratched him up good and deep. All over his throat and his back, too. That easily countered Vance's claims that their drug-fueled-sexual adventure was consensual. All of this evidence and testimony combined with the treasure trove of evidence on the L drive that Mr. Randolph Burgess planted there would make for swift convictions. Odell told Grundy that Palmer surely would die in prison, since his charges were extensive, including a first-degree murder charge for ordering the successful hit on O'Leary and conspiracy to commit murder for the unsuccessful hit on Doctor Eleanor Burgess. Reid Livingston was the oldest of the bunch, so he would never see the light of day again and would most likely die in prison, too. Vance was still young, but his odds were not looking too swift, either. Even if he pleaded guilty and took some deals.

"Glad to see you are not reading the newspaper. Let's keep ya nose of 'em for a little while. Ya need a refresh on that beer, Odell. That beer-flavored water ain't got much of a head to begin with, and that one sat too long. It looks flatter than a board." George Grundy said as he slid a freshly poured beer to Odell and took the stale one to pour it away and down the drain.

"I follow most everything on the case, Lyle, but one or two things confuse me. That is easy to do. Miles and Crump were always the brains. Hicks and Grundy, the brawn. But you were always the super-brain. Drink that beer. Ya got plenty of time to catch your flight, and I am driving ya to Albany, anyway. Ya gotta start eating. Getting skinny and thin-faced. Why did Randolph Burgess not just go to the law when the blackmail from these losers first began? I mean, he made a mistake with the dough by taking it from the Burgess Foundation money, but he transferred the dough the next business day. I get that he was hot and heavy with his young executive assistant, but it seemed that was not a well-kept secret. Seems as it would have been easy to avoid all this bullshit by turning in these bums to the law and explaining it to the board."

Odell took a long sip of the beer and smacked his lips.

"I am getting used to this stuff. Not sure that is a great idea or not. Great questions, George. No question that Mr. Burgess should've gone to the authorities. Dumb move on his part. Poor choice by a very smart man. Yet, I understand his actions. I think he didn't squeal on them, mostly due to his love for Lily Livingston. Tricky situation for him. A balancing act. It was her family who were evil, and while Lily is quite brilliant and knew that were not angels of Heaven, Burgess wanted to protect her from the pain of knowing what horrible crooks they were. He honestly loved her and did not want to upset her or, even worse, chance losing her. His ego got in the way, too. Super-hot young girlfriend, buying her a birthday present of a lifetime, not having the cash in the right spot to make it happen right there in the dealership. Playing the big shot older sugar daddy role. Sure, he put the dough right back, but it displayed poor judgement. The big chief, smitten with the young hottie. Plucking cash out of a not-for-profit to buy the chickie-poo one of the most expensive sports cars that you can buy. Head over heels in love, putting the business last. Just what those bums needed to pounce on to leverage Burgess out with some good old blackmail."

Odell took another sip of his beer as Grundy leaned in with fascination at the insight Odell had into the human mind and common behaviors of humanity.

"Ya gotta remember. Burgess knew he had limited time. The doctors said his ticker was on its last legs. He was not a great candidate for a transplant, so he was going to live life to the fullest. That included Lily. If ya ever meet or see her, then you will understand. He figured he would protect her, do the deal, and it would all go away. Except O'Leary was evil, too. And Palmer knew how much cash the company had. They all made about fifty million dollars on the land sale and facility and property construction, but that was not enough. They wanted that gold mine of cash. Take over the company, pocket the cash, sell the company off. They were ready to invoke the power and the duty of the general counsel to the board and shareholders. They would remove Burgess as CEO. He still would own the company, but exposing his poor judgement and errors would be painful. For the scandal to make it to the public would be very embarrassing and potentially trash the company and influence business. Effectively, he would be guilty of tainting the legacy of his family's company. Other than Lily and Doc Burgess, and some booze bottles, the company was his life."

Grundy stood back and folded his arms across his mighty chest. The immenseness of Grundy was on full display.

"That does make sense, Odell. But what 'bout the drive thing? Burgess took all that time and effort to put those voicemails and files there. When do you think that he was going to turn the tables on them?"

"You see, George. You are incorrect in your self-assessment of your skills. You are not just the muscles. Ya figured out all the holes and asked the correct questions. That is very impressive. To answer your question—very soon. I think right after that ill-fated cruise, he would've spilled the beans. Most likely to Mr. Milan and allowed him to release the contents of the drive. First, Burgess outsmarted them by rewriting the will and leaving it all to Eleanor. He had a plan, and in retrospect, it was a good one, just in case he croaked. Either naturally or if they plugged him with good old sniper Jack. I do believe that password is somewhere. Carefully hidden in the files and in the cobwebs of time. Burgess was too smart not to leave it in a secure location. It is just a matter of time until we uncover it. Burgess wanted to make sure Lily was in a good place and Eleanor, too. Then he would push them on their asses. Sadly, they got to him first. I will never look at heartburn tablets the same way."

"Gotcha. Hold on."

George darted off to take an order from a newly seated customer at the bar. It was a to-go order, and while he waited, the customer wanted to enjoy a beer. Odell took the time to sip his beer and enjoy the rest of his sandwich. His mind wandered while George was busy with the customer. Odell knew it. He reached a crossroads in his life. In his career. Everyone does. Be them a carpenter, or an accountant, or a policeman, or a schoolteacher, or the manager of the local supermarket; the end of the line eventually arrives. This case was a great way to go out. Odell knew it. He solved a case that would have gone unnoticed if not for his reading a newspaper article. The bad guys would have won. But they did not. It was just another case. He treaded amongst the phantoms of evil once more. Death. Murder. Blackmail. Corruption. Evil. It was a long ride, but it was his mission. Now, he had a chance to ride off into the sunset with a wonderful woman that he loved. A special woman. He deserved it, yet in the world of Lyle Odell it had to feel right.

Time would tell. Odell finished the sandwich and the beer.

George Grundy returned.

He asked, "When is that medal ceremony?"

"The middle of November. A Friday. I think it is the sixteenth. I will get the exact date for you and Marjorie." Odell lifted an eye to Grundy and said, "Ya gonna have to go to Boston, George."

"For you, I will. What medals are you receiving?"

"Not exactly sure. It is a multi-jurisdiction ceremony. Boston, Mohawk City, the Feds . . . I think the DEA. The old Back Bay guys sold more than just real estate and property. Drugs and other assorted goodies crossing state lines, too. We found a bunch of dirt on that from Art Livingston and from Josie and from the accountants. The State of New York will be there, and the Commonwealth of Massachusetts. I think that Mohawk City and New York are awarding me the Combat Cross, a Medal of Honor, and something else. Not sure of any others. The Feds are saying that I am up for the Congressional Badge of Bravery, but that is down the road. We might have to go to Washington D.C for that one. Officer Ben Crane is receiving awards and a promotion to sergeant. I am bringing along Rinehardt, Milan, and McEvoy from Standard Insurance, and they will receive some civilian awards. Should be a nice time. I want to honor Crane. He is a special one. Vice Admiral McCauley and his wife are also attending. It will be nice to see them."

"Yeah. McCauley is a good man. It will be nice to see him. Geez, Odell. Ya gonna need a trailer to tow the medals home. You talk like you are picking up a twelve-pack of beer. My goodness. Is Eleanor attending?

"Dunno. After this trip, we will see."

"I know you are heading out to see her. I bet you are excited. Do you speak to Eleanor often?"

"Every night at eight o'clock, our time. We talk for

hours."

Grundy picked up the empty plate and the empty beer mug, and he stared at Odell. The testimony seemed to shock Grundy.

"Hours? 'bout what? I never heard you talk for hours 'bout anything."

Odell almost smiled.

"I know that is hard to believe, George. We speak 'bout anything that comes to mind. I am looking forward to this time. I sure am. Time to decide. For my life. For my future. The crossroads of life. I reached it. With you, my friend."

Unasked, and unrequested, Grundy poured his best friend a fresh beer and dropped it in front of Odell. Without comment, Odell took a long sip of it while he studied Grundy for a reaction.

"How 'bout that gorgeous Lily, chick?"

"Oh yes. She calls me on Saturday nights. Around seven at night. She is pushing for us to have brunch or lunch and whatever."

"It is the whatever that is tough, Odell. Right?"

"No question. Too many Irish whiskeys in me, and that is a full red alert. But I do owe her some time. She was an immense help with this case. I will figure that out. Somewhere down the road. I will make a phone call and explain."

"Good luck with that. I know you will make the best choice. For you. For her. Ya talk to Christina, lately?"

"I have. Just two days ago. She is fine. Baby getting big. She sends her love. You will see her at the awards ceremony. She and her husband and the baby will be there. And better yet, she is planning on coming up between Thanksgiving and Christmas."

"I'd better stock up on the tequilier. Will love to see her. Gonna give her a big kiss and that baby, too. Uncle Georgie will bounce that baby on my knee and give her some love!"

"Geez, George. Your knee? Bounce! Your knee is the size

of Alaska. Don't send the kid to the moon without a rocket ship!"

"Promise. I will be aware of my own strength, Odell. This will be a holiday season to remember. What does she say 'bout all of this with Eleanor?"

"To do what makes me happy. Ya know. Christina has life figured out. Just do what makes ya happy. It ain't 'bout caution, it is 'bout love. She is a hopeless romantic Latina woman. In the end, she is correct. It is always 'bout love. You need to call her. She is angry that ya don't call her. She says she wants to hear ya voice, and she wants ya body, too."

Grundy almost fell over laughing. He held his sides as the words of their mutual best friend, Christina Fuentes-Columbo, reverberated through their souls.

Recovering Grundy said, "Ha! Yes, she does. She is something else. No filter. Ever. She just wants to join me in a food-eating competition. I know her ways. A foodie! just like I am. I will win. Barely. Love that gal. I will call her. For sure. She is the heartbeat of life. Damn." George Grundy paused and became retrospective in his thoughts.

"I think this is the first vacation that I ever recall ya taking, Odell. How many weeks of vacation do you have?"

Odell answered in a nonchalant manner.

"Fifty-seven weeks of accumulated time. I took two extra days beyond the bereavement period after my father passed away. Eighteen years ago. Those are last days that I took off."

Odell's explanation was so matter-of-fact. Too much, in fact.

George lifted his hands and ran them through his hair. Grundy's eyes filled with tears at Odell's proclamation. He shifted from laughter to tears within seconds. Even as his best friend and being his partner on so many cases over the years, Grundy never imagined that this was Odell's life. A life of dedication to justice; with so much personal sacrifice.

George felt as if he should have paid more attention to Lyle Odell's lifestyle.

"Lyle. Whatever you decide. I love ya. You are the brother that I never had."

Grundy extended his massive hand across the bar, and Lyle Odell grasped it and shook his hand warmly and tightly.

"And you are the same. I love you, too, George. You and Christina and Marjorie are my only family left in this world. Truly, my only family. Let me chug this beer. Then drive me to the airport. Please. It is time for me to take a few days off."

It was a picture-perfect California night. Berkeley, California, at sunset. Some of the most glorious weather on Earth.

From the patio of Doctor Eleanor Burgesses' home, with the proper elevation, you could see the Oakland-San Francisco Bay Area. The bridge. The water. The sunset. The clouds. It was a spectacular night.

The day had been warm, and now that night was falling all around, the temperature dropped a bit. Lyle Odell sat at a table on the patio of Eleanor's home. He sipped at his favorite Irish whiskey, and Eleanor nursed a martini. Odell mixed it at Eleanor's well-stocked bar inside her home. He proved to be a rather capable bartender. Doctor Eleanor Burgess sat opposite Odell at the patio table. She looked stunning, as usual. She wore a dress and a string of white pearls around her neck; and Odell knew that there was nothing that she wore underneath the dress and the only other thing that she wore were the pearls. A glorious dress and a string of pearls. The perfect woman.

Lyle Odell had made a personal investigation of the situation. . ..

And Odell was exceptional at his job!

Eleanor leaned in over the patio table and asked, "What are you thinking, Odell? I see that glorious and intricate mind whirling."

Odell did not hesitate much in answering. Only a few short seconds. He answered while sipping his Irish.

"I am thinking that this is the first vacation that I have had in eighteen years, and it is magnificent. This weather is unreal. My sinuses have not been this clear in my entire lifetime. They charge you for the weather out here. That is why it is so expensive. What was that pizza? Thirty-two bucks? Damn. Frank's West is twelve bucks. Delivered. Plus, a tip for Matty."

"Is it just the weather that is unreal? I mean, you have been here for four days, and we have made love eleven times. Flawlessly. We hardly came up for air."

Odell asked, "You kept count?"

Eleanor's comeback was perfectly spectacular.

"Exact details are very important in investigations and in our lives."

Odell smiled a rare smile. He almost even laughed. He temporarily forgot that Doctor Eleanor Burgess bridged the chasm.

"Eleanor, you are unreal. Yes, you are."

Yet, Eleanor Burgess was uncanny in her ability to read people. And now, she could read Lyle Odell as well as she knew every inch of his body. Now she knew his soul. She lifted the martini glass and downed the remainder of the liquid in one shot.

"But I am a Cali gal and you are a New York guy. That is the crossroads of where we are at in our lives. I want to marry you and stay here in California, and you want to marry me, and we will return to New York. Correct?"

"Correct, Eleanor. Lemme mix you a'nudder martini."

Odell stood up and plucked the empty martini glass off the table, and when he did so, Eleanor Burgess grabbed his arm and held it. Forcibly. Eleanor dreaded the words that loomed and that she knew were coming. The rest of this discussion. Yet, they must say the words of pain.

"Please. Odell. Down your drink and pour yourself another. Mix me another and come back. Soon."

Lyle Odell did return soon with the drinks, and he settled into the chair on the patio opposite Doctor Burgess.

She took a sip of the cocktail and asked, "Have you really thought about all of this?"

"I have. Prayed intensely about it."

Odell's statement of praying seemed to take Doctor Burgess by surprise.

She pushed back in her chair and asked, "Prayed? I did not take you for a religious man. You never cease to amaze me in every single way. You have more layers than an onion, except you are such fun to peel. In so many ways."

"Yuppers. I prayed. Because you are so special and so exceptional that I required guidance from Heaven to make the correct choice. I do not wear it on my sleeve, but in theory, I am a wayward Catholic. I guess that does not mix properly with your scientific mind."

Doctor Burgess did not answer right away. She lifted the martini glass to her lips and then, instead of taking a sip, she set the glass down on the table.

"No. I guess on the surface, it doesn't. The creation and all of that. Adam and Eve. God created the Heaven and the Earth. No, I guess that I am a scientist."

Odell downed the remainder of his Irish whiskey in one shot. He smacked his lips.

After the drink, Odell said, "I get it. The Big Bang Theory. There was a blob and some matter spinning around and around and then, bang! The universe. The only trouble is, where did the blob and matter come from and who lit the fuse for the bang?"

This time, Doctor Burgess did take the sip. It was more as if it was a gulp.

Eleanor said, "Surprise! And that, my dear, Odell, is why there is a God. I cannot study plants as I do and not see the glory of God in the beauty and intricacy of the creation. I am a scientist who believes in God. And God sent you to this world as a gift for so many things. To seek justice. To protect this world. To chase down the phantoms that haunt you and this world. To do the right thing. To do what it is that you do. For me to love you. For you to love me. I will be forever grateful for all of this and for meeting you."

She smiled with tears in her eyes and said, "I know you are going home without me, and you will not come here to California. In a roundabout way, I understand. Odell needs New York, and New York needs Odell. Some things are meant to be. Regardless, I will love you forever. You love the ice and snow and cold, and the grit, and the determination, and New York is where you belong. A remote life and relationship just will not work. I love you too much. I need to absorb you daily. I am a Cali gal. We could marry. I would say yes to your proposal in less than a half-of-a-second. We would have millions and millions of dollars. Maybe a billion? That would not matter to you. It really doesn't matter to me, either. Not at this point. You still would have that old table radio. Classical music. The Saturday evening concert. You are a very simple man. Living a very simple life. I understand. After seeing and experiencing the horrors and evil of humankind that you have seen in your life. In your career. Simple is perfect. Exceptional. Material things mean nothing to you and I understand that. I really do. A black and white television sits on an upturned cardboard box. Who in the Hell still has a black and white television? Odell does. A small house on a side street in old Mohawk City. Pizza from Frank's West. Do you even have a car?"

"I do. I seldom drive it. It is kinda old."

"How old?"

"'Bout twenty-five years or so. Runs great. The interior is like it is new. Doesn't burn any oil."

Doctor Eleanor Burgess wiped the tears from her eyes with her fingers while Odell intensely studied her. She then smiled and downed the rest of her drink.

"I bet it does run great. When are you leaving?"

"Tomorrow afternoon. Grundy will pick me up at the Albany airport. I connect through Atlanta."

"Please, Odell. Never forget me. And if anything changes, please let me be the first to know. Are you going to retire? Finally?"

"I would say that I am sorry, but that does not work. I would marry you in an instant, and you would absorb me, and I don't absorb so well. I have too many rough edges, and out here in California, rough edges don't exist. I need New York and those rough edges. You are unforgettable. I will smell the glorious scent of your body and the whisper of your voice within my senses, forever. My love for you is forever. I will, and yes, retirement looms. Unless something pops up, I plan to pack it in soon."

Doctor Burgess winked and asked, "Good. A last hurrah? The last kiss might kill me."

"Of course. It will be amazing. The greatest lovemaking of all time. It won't kill you, but by chance if it does, I promise to resuscitate you. I do have my ways."

Saturday night. The same week. Around eight in the evening.

Retired Police Lieutenant George Grundy picked up Odell at the Albany airport. They drove back to Mohawk City mostly in silence. Only once did Odell really dive into a conversation. It was simply a question and may or may not have qualified as a conversation.

Odell eventually spoke.

"George. I need to ask you. Nowadays, when you think about all that we did together. All those cases. All that horror that we witnessed. All that senselessness. Do you think more about the victims of the cases we worked on and their families, or the evil and ruthless bastards that we locked up?"

Grundy answered without hesitation.

"The victims. The families."

"Me too. Their pain haunts me constantly. I see bad guys and gals everywhere. All the time. I know that you understand, George. Thanks."

After asking, and accepting with satisfaction his long-time partner and friend's answer, Lyle Odell curled up in the passenger seat, twirling a cigarette around with his fingers. His hair was growing back in. Odell had not shaved in many days. He was a little messy. Commando and tactical Odell were now in the rearview mirror. Regular Odell returned. Grundy dropped Lyle Odell off at his house with a promise to see him tomorrow morning for coffee at Grundy's Bar and Grille. George knew not to ask too many questions. He knew Odell well enough to know that it did not work out as planned, but he also knew Lyle Odell well enough to know that it worked out for the best. Odell waved goodbye to Grundy, slipped the key in the lock, and walked slowly into the house. He parked his luggage next to the door in the foyer. He would unpack it later. Odell made his way to the cupboard and picked up his favorite bottle of Irish and his favorite glass. Now was not the time for beer-flavored water. Maybe he would call for a pizza from Frank's West later. He looked at the cellphone. One missed call from Lily Livingston.

"If anything, she sure is persistent," Odell spoke aloud to the walls and ceilings.

Lyle plopped down in his easy chair. If he had to examine his state of mind and his soul, Odell would admit that he was on the verge of exhaustion. He reached over to the old table radio and clicked it on. The dial lights glowed happily. In the darkness. Odell poured the Irish and took a sip.

"I must be careful. Could slip over the edge tonight."

The radio crackled and came to life. Odell reached over and tweaked the dial a little. It drifted off frequency. He tweaked the dial once more. The lush music filled the old speaker and the humble home. Odell shook his head and leaned back in the chair. He spoke aloud once more.

"I kinda think this is all planned. Yes, indeed. God's plan. Of course, tonight's music would feature Pictures at an Exhibition." Odell listened carefully to the music, and he smiled at the recognition of the music and the memories. In a low whisper, Odell said, "Yuppers. Modest Mussorgsky. Catacombae. Sepulcrum romanum. It sounds as if it is the Boston Orchestra or maybe the Evergreen. How ironic."

Odell placed the whiskey glass on the table. He leaned back in his easy chair, and he gently folded his hands together and placed them in his lap. Odell allowed the glory of the music to absorb into his heart, his soul, and his mind. He allowed the beauty of the memories inside of him, too.

There in the darkness, with only the dial light on the old table radio for light in the entire house, Police Inspector Lyle Odell closed his eyes and gently and eventually drifted off to sleep.

THE END

Epilogue

It was early Tuesday in late February of the following year. Detective Lyle Odell sat at the bar of Grundy's Bar and Grille while sipping his morning coffee and eating some whole wheat toast with jelly. He was heading to his office at the Mohawk City Police Department, very shortly.

Grundy asked, "How is the coffee? Annie made it. She beat me in this morning. Oh yeah. Before I forget. You were right. Annie told me the other day that she had changed her mind. She is not retiring at Christmas. And you were right about Meredith. She is staying on as a server."

Odell looked up and answered. "Kinda figured that Annie would stick around. Retirement must'b overrated. The coffee is great. Perfect. Better than yours is. Annie is ancient but very efficient. Meredith is a smart gal. She knows where she can make some dough and maybe meet a man to take care of her forever. Right here. At Grundy's Bar and Grille."

"I agree. Okay! The truth hurts. Annie's coffee is better than mine is! Geez, thanks, Odell. I know, exact facts. . .."

Grundy replaced the coffeepot in the holder of the coffeemaker, and while he did so, he asked the burning question on everyone's mind.

"When are you putting in the retirement papers?"

Odell immediately answered.

"Next month. On Saint Patrick's Day. Luck of the Irish and all of that. George, I figured that would be the perfect day."

"Can't argue with that choice. Perfect."

The landline phone at the bar rang. Grundy glided over

and answered it.

"Grundy's Bar and Grille. Grundy speaking. How may I help ya?" A pause. "What? Miles! Geez! Damn! No, no, no!"

Lyle Odell looked up at his friend's reaction and the mention of Detective Miles Bradford's name.

Grundy continued to speak. "Yeah, Odell is here. He is having breakfast. Of course. I will tell him, and he will be on the way. Be safe out there, Miles."

Grundy hung up from the call and for a few brief seconds, he hung his head on his chest. Odell stood up and leaned on the bar with both hands.

"George?"

Grundy looked over at Odell and said, "Bradford. They just found the dead body of Sergeant James Reilly O'Malley behind Robinson's Cafe. Sixteenth Avenue. Most of his head is gone. Gunshots blew it apart. Bradford is requesting you on this one."

Odell did not hesitate.

He jumped up and said, "On my way."

About one month later.

Odell's eyes scanned the grave markers until he found the one that he wanted. He looked for the American flag and the police badge marker. When Odell approached it, his keen eyes scanned the grave marker while he mouthed the name inscribed upon the elegant marker stone.

"Sergeant James Reilly O'Malley. Mohawk City Police Department. United States Army. Date of Last Tour. . .."

Odell lowered his head and mumbled a prayer. Yes, indeed, Lyle Odell prayed.

Often.

He finished his prayer.

Odell spoke aloud as the wind blew through, he cemetery. The wind drowned out his voice.

"Glad I could help James on this one for ya, Sarge. That is some quality young man ya raised there. Tough as tough can be. Hockey made him rough and tough, but you made him righteous and dedicated him to the mission. He is a great one. We got all the bad guys on this one. I am so sorry. But ya life lives on through James Thomas O'Malley. He will do great things in his life. He really will. I can tell. I will visit often, Sarge. Often."

Odell's longish hair blew all over his head in the wind. He made no attempt to straighten it.

Lyle Odell turned on his heels and as he did so, he tapped his right rear pocket of his pants and muttered, "Right rear pants pocket."

He reached into the pocket and pulled out a small flask. Odell stopped and lifted the flask in the direction of Heaven. He unscrewed the cap and, with the dangling cigarette still holding onto his lower lip, Odell put the flask to his lips and took a swallow of the Irish.

"Just a quick nip as a toast to a great Irishman and an even better police officer. To you, Sarge O'Malley. Got one more stop to make today. I promised, and I don't break promises."

Odell then turned and slowly walked the rest of the way to his waiting police cruiser.

Four hours later, Detective Lyle Odell stood next to a grave in Westchester County, New York. Ms. Lily Livingston stood next to him. They held hands and mourned together. She tossed a bundle of red roses on the grave of Mr. Randolph Burgess. She sobbed. Odell held her hand even tighter.

"I miss him, Odell. I really do. I think of him every day. Maybe someday, I will find that kind of love again. Someday."

"You will, Lily. You will. Until then, keep your eyes wide open and live your life. Because it all goes by in a blur. It really does. He was a great man. I can tell. He left a legacy. He defeated the bad guys. In the end, he took them all down. Smart man. A genius."

Lily looked up at Lyle Odell and smiled. Her tears slowly stopped, and she sniffed a little. It was very cold, and sobbing in the cold is not always the greatest thing to do. It can get rather messy. Odell began a traditional Odell pat-down and from somewhere within the confines of his vast attire, he found a handkerchief and handed it to Lily.

"Here. It is clean. I think."

"Thank you, Odell. I think."

They exchanged smiles.

She cleaned up, and she stuffed the handkerchief in her overcoat pocket.

"Odell, I will keep living my life. Eyes wide open. For sure. But memories are fun, too."

"They are. Just don't let ya memories kill ya, Lily."

She said, "You say the most profound things, Odell. You really do. I hear you loud and clear. Are you ready to go? We can have brunch."

Lily leaned into Odell and slipped her arm into his as they made their way amongst the many graves and walked back to the parked police cruiser.

"Okay. Sure. We can do brunch. Let's go. Now, Lily, you made me a promise a while ago. A total and honest promise. No stripping, or drinking to excess, or playful ploys of seduction? Must I remind you that I am a police detective? Lies and deceit are my game. I am still quite good at what I do. Despite my age. I am, and always will be, a detective."

Lily laughed and tucked into Odell even more.

Very coyly Lily replied, "Promise. But honestly, I might have crossed my fingers. Again."

"Ya better not have. Lemme see ya hands."

"Okay." Lily stopped walking and held her hands up in the air to show them to Lyle Odell.

She had crossed fingers on both hands.

Odell laughed until his sides hurt.

Folks who knew him well said of Homicide Detective Lyle Odell that he seldom laughed or smiled. In the olden days, that was surely the case. Not so much these days. He sure laughed now. He smiled often nowadays, too. Too many smiles and laughs lost over the years. Odell needed to catch up. Time was running out for him. The smiles and the laughter made both his mind and his heart happy. After the unspeakable horrors he had seen over his long and storied career; one might say that Homicide Detective Lyle Odell earned it.

And then some.

"Lily, you really are something else. Let's go. It is very cold here, and I am out of handkerchiefs. No more slobbering allowed."

Lyle Odell had snow on the roof and a fire in the furnace.

The wind blew strong, with just a hint of edginess buried within it.

As Odell's ancient old car drove away and left the cemetery, the wind blew hard and it suddenly blew extremely cold. It is always so cold in cemeteries.

No matter the season.

It is always so cold.

ABOUT THE AUTHOR

If you ask Paul John Hausleben, he will tell you that he is not an author, he is just a storyteller. His mission is to continue to write and tell stories to warm your heart, make you laugh, make you think, and sometimes make you cry, just a little. Most of all, he deals in memories, and helps you to remember the good times of your own life, and the special people who touched you along the way. He displays amazing versatility in his writing by covering a wide variety of genres.

Paul was born and raised in Paterson, and then nearby Haledon, New Jersey, and began writing at an early age. He revisited a writing career later in his life, and he now is the author of several novels, compilations, short stories, music reviews, a podcast host, and the creator of various audio and video works. Most of his work touches upon nostalgic remembrances of simpler times, and tells the stories of heartfelt, humorous, and special human relationships. Mr. Hausleben is the owner, and the driving creative force of God Bless the Keg Publishing LLC. Paul is a skilled and award-winning photographer, and his publishing company features much of his photographic work. Other than writing and photography, among many careers both paid and unpaid, he is a former semiprofessional hockey goaltender, a music fan and music reviewer, and an avid ice hockey, American football, football, and overall sports fan, and a former military radio operator.

He is an avid supporter of the Nottingham Forest Football Club.

Mr. Hausleben is an avid amateur radio operator. He holds an extra class amateur radio license with the call letters WA2ASQ. Paul is a Morse code and digital mode operator and he enjoys on-the-air radio contests and chasing long distance (DX) stations from all over the world while using very low power (QRP) transmissions to do so.

Mr. Paul John Hausleben now resides in Somewhere, U.S.A., but his heart always remains along Belmont Avenue in good old Paterson, and Haledon, New Jersey.

The Cases of Detective Lyle Odell
by
Mr. Paul John Hausleben

O'Malley (The debut of Detective Lyle Odell)

Where Phantoms Tread

In the Hiss of Summer

Nefarious Intentions

In a Gilded Cage

Snow on the Roof

You may write to the author at ctte27@gmail.com

Published by God Bless the Keg Publishing LLC
Henrico, Virginia, U.S.A.
You may write to the publisher at
Godblessthekegpublishing@gmail.com

"Life's simple pleasures are so often the best ones!"

Follow Paul John Hausleben on Facebook and enjoy samples of his photography, receive updates on new releases, and enjoy his general meanderings

www.ingramcontent.com/pod-product-compliance
Lightning Source LLC
LaVergne TN
LVHW090556110826
845146LV00001B/145

* 9 7 9 8 9 8 9 4 4 9 0 6 4 *